RAINA'S CHOICE

WESTERN JUSTICE
– BOOK 3 –

Raina's Choice

GILBERT MORRIS

SHILOH RUN  PRESS

Print ISBN 978-1-61626-760-5

eBook Editions:
Adobe Digital Edition (.epub) 978-1-63058-095-7
Kindle and MobiPocket Edition (.prc) 978-1-63058-096-4

All scripture quotations are taken from the King James Version of the Bible.

This book is a work of fiction. Names, characters, places, and incidents are either products of the author's imagination or used fictitiously. Any similarity to actual people, organizations, and/or events is purely coincidental.

Cover design: Kirk DouPonce, DogEared Design

Published by Shiloh Run Press, an imprint of Barbour Publishing, Inc., P.O. Box 719, Uhrichsville, Ohio 44683, www.shilohrunpress.com

Our mission is to publish and distribute inspirational products offering exceptional value and biblical encouragement to the masses.

Member of the
Evangelical Christian
Publishers Association

Printed in the United States of America.

PART ONE

CHAPTER 1

November 1891

The room was nothing but four walls with no windows. The eight bunks lined up against the edges were filled with six Mexicans and two Americans. It was one of ten small prison cells that were blazing hot under the sun in the summer and freezing when the weather turned bad as it had now.

Ty Kincaid tossed restlessly and came out of a fitful sleep at the sound of the guards, who were playing poker and shouting and cursing each other. They usually got drunk during the night when they were off duty. Ty tried to block the noise out of his mind, but he could not. He had no idea what the time was, for without windows in the prison hut there was no way of telling. There was only one door, made of solid oak, with three bars across a small window.

One of the prisoners began to curse under his breath. Not loudly because none of the prisoners wanted to call attention to themselves.

With an effort Ty rolled over and lay on his side. He was taken with a coughing fit as he did, and pain like ice picks going through his chest struck him. He finally gained control.

His cell mate, Jim Adams, whispered, "Are you okay?"

"I'm all right," Kincaid muttered. This was not true, for he was ill and had been for several days. It had begun with a runny nose and a mild but persistent cough, but each day's toil in the bowels of the earth working in a copper mine in the unseasonably cold weather had taken its toll on him.

"You sound terrible," Jim said. "There ought to be a hospital or a doctor for you to go to."

Kincaid did not answer, for both men were well aware that the Mexican prison system paid little attention to the ailments of convicts. Many of them were allowed to die when a little medicine or a doctor's care might have saved them. When they did die, they were simply thrown into a hole and covered with lime. Ty had seen this happen more than once in the three months he had been in the prison.

"I don't think I'm going to make it, Jim." Kincaid's voice was feeble and scratchy. He rolled over on his back, threw his forearm over his eyes, and tried to control the coughing that was constantly tearing him to pieces.

"You'll be all right. We're going to get out of here."

"No, we never will."

"Don't talk like that. It's pretty grim right now, but we're gonna make it."

"I don't know what makes you say that."

"The Lord will get us out of this."

"I'm glad you believe that, Jim, but I don't." Kincaid again began coughing, and even as he did a whistle split the dawn air.

Then there was a rattling at the door, which opened a crack, and a raucous voice shouted, "Get up! Get up! Get your scrawny rear ends out of those bunks!"

Using all his strength, Ty managed to sit up, then paused, hanging on to the edge of his bunk. The mattress was made of coarse feed sacks. The straw had not been changed in weeks, and the stench of urine and rotting food was enough to make a well man sick. He tried to stand. Suddenly Ty was so weak he couldn't do it.

Adams, who had the bunk next to his, said, "Get up quick, Ty. You don't want the Pig on your case."

Ty again struggled to rise.

The door swung open, and a big man filled the opening. In the growing dawn Bartolo Azner stepped inside. He made a huge, ominous shadow and was called "the Pig" by the convicts. Not to his face, of course. "What are you doing on that bunk?"

"I'm sick," Ty whispered and coughed scratchily.

The Pig laughed. "You're not on a vacation. Get up!" He suddenly swung the short billy club made out of hard oak and caught Ty across the chest.

It knocked him back onto the bed, and he struck the back of his head on the wooden wall. The blow sent a myriad of sparkling colors like fireworks through his head and before his eyes.

"Get up, I told you!"

Ty felt the huge paws of the Pig grab him and drag him out of the bunk. He fell on the floor and received a kick in the back.

Ty was stunned and had no strength as Azner reached down, jerked him up, and held him upright as if he were a child. "You gringo dog! You come to my country and try to destroy my government!

You'll stay here until you rot! Why don't you die?"

Ty was shoved toward the door then fell against Jim Adams, who caught him and held him upright. The two men joined the other convicts who trooped out into the frigid night air. All of them wore simple cotton garments. The biting air of winter was like a knife cutting through Ty's chest.

"Get going, you dogs!" the Pig shouted.

The men joined the prisoners from the other prison huts and headed toward a larger building.

Tyler Kincaid hardly knew whether he was awake or un-conscious. There was a murky light in the east, but as he stumbled into the mess hall—so it was called—he had to be held upright by Adams, who took him firmly by the arm.

Adams was a big man and had lost weight as had all the prisoners, but still he was not sick and he was stronger than Ty. He eased Ty down onto one of the benches, and then he joined him. "Hang on there," he whispered. "Maybe we'll get a hot breakfast this morning."

Ty was too sick to answer. He just sat there trembling. Finally when one of the prisoners who served with the cook came by and put a bowl in front of him, Ty opened his eyes and saw that it was a bowl of thin rice gruel with beans floating around the top. It was the typical breakfast and would have to do them through a hard morning's work. . .until the same dish would be served at noon, and then again, when it got too dark to work, it would provide the evening meal.

"Eat up, Ty," Adams whispered. "It's rotten, but we've got to get as strong as we can. Need to keep your strength up."

"What for, Jim?" Ty took a spoonful of the rank mixture,

chewed, and managed to swallow it. The taste was atrocious, and he had to overcome a sudden urge to throw up. "We're gonna die in this place anyhow. Why don't we go on and do it?"

Adams leaned over. He had piercing, dark black eyes, and his hair was as black as the darkest thing in nature. He was basically an Irishman through his mother and had been strong as a bull before he was captured along with Ty. "We're gonna get out of here."

"I don't know what makes you think that. Nobody ever does."

"God's going to help us."

"I already told you I don't believe that."

"You need to believe it, Ty. God's our only hope in a place like this."

Ty ate slowly, but other men were scraping the bottoms of their bowls when he was only half through. He washed the rest of it down with tepid water that had a terrible taste and then said, "I didn't know you were such a fervent Christian until we got in this mess, Jim."

"Well, I was going with a woman, and she talked me into going to a revival meeting with her in Arkansas. I went and got saved." He reached over and punched Ty lightly on the arm. "Of course, I ain't always lived like I should since then. I let the Lord down several times, but I know I'm saved. That's what you need, Ty."

"Too late for me."

"Don't be foolish."

"It's not foolish. Why would God be interested in a reprobate like me? I've broken every one of the Commandments a hundred times."

Adams had been through this many times with Tyler Kincaid,

and he never seemed to tire of it. "Well, I did, too, but the Bible says God forgives us when we do what He says."

"You mean get baptized?"

"No, I don't mean that. Getting baptized never saved nobody. It's what you do before."

"I don't believe that anymore. I had some faith at one time, but it's gone now," Ty muttered.

The Pig hollered, "All right, on your feet, you dogs!"

As Ty rose, he grew dizzy.

Jim once again had to grab him to keep him from falling. "When we get in the mine you kind of get over behind me. Those guards don't pay no attention to who's doing the work."

"I can't let you do that, Jim."

"You can if I say so. Now come on."

The two walked outside, and it was all that Kincaid could do to walk the quarter of a mile to the mountain and the hole that enclosed a set of miniature tracks. On the tracks ran small carts that the prisoners filled with the rock after they'd broken it with picks.

Ty went in, and as soon as they were put into place, he reached for a pick.

They were in a side tunnel, and Jim whispered, "You just get there and move every once in a while. They don't pay any attention to us."

"I feel bad," Ty whispered, "letting you do all this because I don't do anything for you."

"Well, when we get out of this, you can buy me a good supper to pay for it."

Ty knew Jim was trying to be lighthearted, but the copper

mine had become his version of what hell must be like. True, it was somewhat warmer in there at this time of the year than outside. In the summer it was a welcome coolness. But now the freezing weather that swept over northern Mexico was phenomenal. No one could remember when it had been this cold. There had been snow in strange places, and in some areas it had even piled up to several feet, which was unheard of in this territory.

Ty tried to swing the pickax, but it was all he could do to bring it over his shoulder. It made a pinging noise as it hit the rocks on the side of the wall, but it made no imprint.

"I told you. You just stand there. That guard ain't looking at me. I get enough rock for both of us."

Ty wanted to argue, but he was too sick. The last thing he remembered was getting dizzy. He felt Jim lowering him, and he slumped against the rocky wall as unconsciousness pulled him down.

Time had no meaning for Kincaid, but then he heard Jim whisper, "Come on, Ty. Time to go get something to eat."

Kincaid had to struggle to get up, and in the end it was Jim Adams who pulled him upright.

One of the prisoners stared at him by the light of the flickering lanterns. "He's going to die, Adams."

"You shut your mouth or *you'll* die."

The Mexican, a little man with a weasel face, shrugged. "He'll die no matter what you do to me. I've seen it before."

"Don't pay any attention to him, Ty."

"He's probably right."

13

Ty and Jim staggered out of the mine and went back toward the mess hall. There was somewhat more talking there as the prisoners whispered to each other.

The Pig wandered around ready to crack their heads if they showed any sort of resistance. He was a monster, and Ty Kincaid knew hatred for one of the few times in his life. The man loved to inflict pain, and he had killed more than one prisoner with that stick of his.

"Eat up, Ty," Jim urged.

"I guess I'll have to." Ty began eating the same weak, watery stew, and this time there was a crust of hard bread to go with it. It was almost impossible to bite it, but Ty soaked it in the soup and softened it. Once again he was nauseated, but he knew that Adams was right. If he didn't eat, he would die.

They had only fifteen minutes to eat, and quickly the Pig yelled, "Get out of here! You're not on a vacation!"

The two Americans were the only white-skinned men in the prison. The two of them had been working for a Mexican railroad when they were arrested. Revolutions shook Mexico on a periodic basis. Neither Jim nor Ty had any feelings about Mexican revolutions, but they had been caught in the middle of one. They had been working on the railroad when the revolutionaries suddenly appeared yelling and screaming.

They killed most of the crew members, but they took the white men prisoners. Ty could never figure why. Jim had said they probably thought they could get a ransom for the two white men. But this had seemed unlikely to Ty, for no one had ever attempted such a thing as far as he knew.

They had worked on the train, teaching the revolutionaries

how to fire up the engine, but it was only a short time before the *federales*, the Mexican police, took over with a large troop of well-armed and fairly well-trained soldiers. They made short work of the revolutionaries and had taken Jim and Ty along with a few other prisoners to the copper mine. "You'll work in the mine until you die," the officer said. "This is what you get for interfering in my country's politics."

There was no answer for that, so the two men had been thrown into the brutal routine of working from dawn until dusk on such meager rations that over time they became almost like human skeletons.

The work went on, but Ty could not do it.

Bartolo Azner kicked him and then said, "Throw him in his bunk. Lock him in without food or water. He'll work or he'll die."

Adams and two of the other men picked Ty up, carried him to the hut, and laid him on his bunk. Adams leaned over and whispered, "You just stay here. I'll smuggle you some water back somehow."

Then Ty Kincaid was left alone. His lungs seemed bound with an iron band, and every time he coughed it felt like he was being stabbed. He coughed and gasped for some time before finally falling into a coma-like sleep.

"Wake up, Ty. I've got something for you."

Ty had been asleep for some time. He knew now that it was dark, for the prisoners were locked up in the hut. "I bribed a guard and got some food and a jug of water. Sit up and eat."

Ty struggled up, ignoring his desire to cough as it tore him in two. He ate slowly. "How'd you get this food, Jim?"

"Oh, I had a little money on me that they didn't find, so I bribed a guard. It ain't much, but it's better than nothin'."

"It's good. Thanks, Jim."

As he ate, Adams sat beside him. "You need to see a doctor."

"You know Mexican doctors and how they treat gringo prisoners."

"Yeah, that's right."

The two men were silent until Ty finished the food, which seemed better than the usual fare they received, although Ty realized this was probably just due to his state of hunger. He drank deeply of the tepid water and said, "You could have gotten in big trouble for this if the Pig had caught you."

"Ah, he's too stupid to catch anybody."

"He's caught two or three. You saw what happened to them."

Adams shook his head. There was at this time one feeble light, a candle that burned in the center of the room. The sanitary arrangements were two buckets, one at each end of the hut, and the smell was overpowering. "You feel pretty bad, don't you, Ty?"

"Pretty bad."

"I don't guess you've ever been in a mess like this."

"Not this bad. Have you?"

"No, I never have. What about people? Have you got a family?"

"I ran away from my home when I was just a young man, seventeen years old."

"Why'd you do that?"

"It's not a pretty story."

"I can't think you'd do anything real bad."

"Well, I did. I got a young woman pregnant. She was only

fifteen. When she found out she was going to have a baby, she told me, and I knew her people. The brothers were all mean as snakes. They would have killed me in a minute if they had found out, so I've been moving ever since."

"Well, that's not a very good story."

"No, it's not. I wondered a hundred times if she had that baby and what happened to her. I was nothing but a coward."

"You were just a kid. Don't worry. We'll get out of here. Maybe you and I'll go find him. Wouldn't it be somethin' if you found a young fellow who was your own flesh and blood?"

"I don't believe good things like that happen."

Adams leaned forward and studied Ty's face in the dim light of the flickering yellow candle.

Ty Kincaid knew he was a fairly good-looking man, but disease and ill treatment had stripped the excess flesh off of him so that his face must look almost skull-like.

Adams reached out and laid his hand on Ty's shoulder. "We're going to get out of this."

There was a silence in the room, and Adams looked around carefully before whispering, "I hadn't told you this, but we got some help outside of this prison."

"What kind of help?"

"I got a friend in the Mexican government. You may have seen him. He came when we were working on the road a few times. I did him a favor, and he always was grateful. When he came in to see me, he said he was going to help me get out."

"How is he going to do that?"

"Well, he tried to do it through the court to prove that we weren't the enemies of Mexico, but Mexican courts ain't known for their kindness and generosity to gringo prisoners."

"So that's out."

"That is, but you remember when I was gone for about an hour a couple of weeks ago?"

"Yes, you're the only one that's had a visitor."

"Well, some of the Mexicans have. But anyway this friend of mine came. He told me he hadn't given up. That he was still going to help."

"How can he do that?"

"He's going to get us two guns and some ammunition. Then all we have to do is knock our guard over the head when we get a chance, grab a couple of horses, and then cross the border."

"You think that guard will stay bribed? He could take the money and then tell the Pig what's going on."

"My friend says he can handle it. He won't give the man all the money until we're away."

"So you think we can shoot our way out of this?"

"I think we've got to do something, Ty. We're gonna die here sure enough. Not just you, but me, too." Jim Adams once again put his hand on Ty's thin shoulder. "God's going to get us out of this. He'll help us."

"You keep saying that, but nothing's happened."

"You remember that psalm I read to you that time? The psalm of David?"

"Yes, you read it more than once."

"Well, you may have forgotten. Your mind ain't too clear. But David had everything. He was the king of Israel. He had money. He had a good family. He had everything a king has, but Absalom, the son he loved most, rebelled against him and raised an army.

David had to run out of Jerusalem trying to keep his son from killing him."

"I remember you told me that."

"You may not remember this. David was in the worst shape of his life. He had lost everything. And then he said, 'I cried unto the Lord.' And then he said, 'The Lord comforted me and I lay down and slept.' Ain't that a wonderful thing that when a man has lost everything he can lie down and sleep!"

"You believe that, don't you, Jim?"

"I sure do, and you need to believe it, too."

"I just can't do it, Jim. Things look too bad right now."

"Just hang in there, Ty. We're gonna make it!"

Two days later Ty woke up in the middle of the night. He knew that much because the door had swung open at least a crack. He saw Jim Adams outlined against the door.

Jim reached out and took something, then came back. The door shut, and the key turned in the lock, making a metallic sound. Jim came back down between the cots and whispered, "You awake, Ty?"

"Yes. What was that?"

Jim leaned closer, and his whisper was barely discernible. "We've got guns and ammunition."

"But the minute we use them, they'll shoot us down," Ty argued.

"No, they won't. Here's what we'll do. We'll do the day's work, and you know how it's always dark when we come out of there. The guards don't pay much attention to us. They can't imagine a prisoner staying in that mine, so we'll let everybody else leave, but we'll stay. As soon as the guards march the prisoners to the mess shack for supper, we'll take two horses."

"Where are you going to get horses?"

"I kept my eyes open when they brought us in here. There's a corral about three hundred yards from the mine. We'd have to go quiet, but there's no reason for anybody to be around at that time of night."

"What then?"

"We saddle us two horses, and we mount up and walk them out of here until we're out of hearing distance. Then we drive those horses straight for the American border."

"I don't know if I can make it, Jim. I'm just too sick right now."

"You'll make it if I have to throw you over that horse and tie you down," Jim said. He slapped Ty's shoulder. "Don't give up, buddy. God's going to help us!"

The guards yelled, "Come on. Get out of here! Leave those tools where they are."

"Stay here," Adams whispered to Ty.

Ty, who was almost past going, slumped against the wall. There had been a feeble lantern, but one of the prisoners leading the way took it out as he always did. Utter darkness seemed to fill the mine. Kincaid listened as the steps grew fainter. He and Adams then found their way out.

Adams said, "Come on. Here, take this."

Ty took the gun and held it in his hand. There was no place else to carry it.

"Don't drop it. I've got bullets in a sack tied around my neck. We're getting out of this place."

They crept through the darkness, and finally Ty heard the nickering of horses. "I can't help you, Jim. I'm as weak as a kitten."

"Some of these horses are pretty tame, and there are saddles here. You wait right here. If anybody comes, don't let them see you."

In the velvety blackness of the night, Ty sat down and heard the footsteps of Adams as he left. He had little hope and no faith at all that God would help him. He had listened to Jim's testimony many times, but it meant nothing to him.

Finally Jim came back leading two horses.

"I can't go, Jim," Ty whispered. "I'll just slow you down."

"We're both going. Get on this horse."

Ty got to his feet and with great effort lifted his foot into the stirrup. He swung into the saddle.

Jim said, "That's good. I'll go first. You just hang on to that horn, and I'll lead your horse."

"Go without me, Jim."

"We're both going."

The sound of the horses' hooves seemed very loud to Tyler Kincaid, but he knew that they were at least three hundred yards away from the house where the guards stayed.

Ty said, "Jim, if anything happens, I want you to know I never had a friend like you."

"You'd do it for me, Ty."

"I hope we never have the chance to find out about that."

They had gone no farther than the edge of the camp when suddenly two guards rode out. There was a bright full moon shining, and one of them called out, "*Hola!* Stop where you are!"

"We've got to run for it, Ty!" Jim turned his horse, and as the two guards rode full speed toward him, he aimed and fired.

The guards began firing, too, and although Ty could see little, he lifted his own gun and threw a few shots. The guards halted. One of them fell out of his saddle; the other turned and rode away.

"We've got to get out of here, Ty!"

"Let's go."

The two rode hard for some time, and then Jim said, "Gotta stop, Ty."

"What's the matter?"

"They got me." Jim suddenly swayed in the saddle then fell off. He hit the ground with a thud.

Ty's head was swimming. As weak as he was, he came off his horse at once. He was dizzy and sick, but he knelt beside Adams and said, "Where'd they get you?"

"In the back." The words were feeble.

Ty leaned down, and even in the darkness he could see the blood beginning to stain the prison garments that Adams wore. "We'll have to take you back to a doctor."

"No, I ain't going to make it, but I want you to." The words came slow.

Ty Kincaid leaned forward. "Don't die on me, Jim!"

"It's a good thing I went to that revival meeting and got saved." Adams coughed, and his voice began to fade. "I'll be with God, but you get out of here. Ty, make your life count."

Ty at once held him, but the life went out of the man. Tears ran down Ty's face. Finally he laid the body down gently, took the gun that was beside Adams, and went back, loosed the lines, and mounted his horse. "I'm too weak to bury you, Jim. I wish I could." He turned his horse's head, and his heart grew darker as he rode off into the gloom, knowing he would never forget Jim Adams.

CHAPTER 2

The steamy swamps of the southern coast of Louisiana put out an unseemly heat during the late summer. This pattern had been broken, however, for it was the middle of December, and a cold spell unlike anything the inhabitants had ever experienced had dropped down from the north. The populace of La Tete were fortunate that the worst of the winter storms were north of them, but they found themselves shivering. Men and woman alike put on heavy coats before going out to face the stiff winds and the dropping temperatures. The Cajun people, who were thickly settled in La Tete, fared no better than anyone else but kept fires burning in their huts in the swamp and in the larger towns to the north.

The feeble candle that Raina Vernay had lit barely enabled her to read the book she held. It cast a yellow flickering corona of light over the pages. Raina was so intent on the story that she hardly heard the door swing open, but she suddenly felt hands placed on her. She uttered a small cry of alarm and with a violent start came to her feet.

She saw her sister's husband, Millard Billaud. He was a big, brutal man with coarse features. As usual he was carelessly dressed.

Raina jerked away from him and moved to get away out the door, but he blocked the entrance. "Get out of my room, Millard!" Raina said loudly. "I told you never to come in here."

Millard was not alarmed by her anger. He smiled, and his thick lips had a brutal cast. His hatchet face was dark, and his flat black eyes gleamed. For all his size he was very quick, as Raina had learned to her sorrow, and she retreated until her back was pressed against the wall.

"Don't be so shy, Raina," Billaud said. "You've been up in this cold room long enough. You need to get downstairs where we got some fire."

"Next time you come into my room, knock on the door," Raina said, knowing her words would have no effect at all.

Suddenly his eyes glowed with anger, and ignoring her protests, he advanced and seized her by her shoulders.

Raina cried out as his mighty grip cut into her flesh like steel hooks.

"You never learn, do you, Raina?" Billaud said. He made no attempt to disguise the pleasure that her gasp of pain gave him. "If you had any sense at all, you'd know that I'm never going to let you get away from me."

Raina struggled mightily, but she was not a strong woman, certainly not one to match Billaud. "You're a yellow cur, Billaud," she said. She was unable to avoid the ringing slap that caught her on the cheek. She gasped, and her eyes watered with the pain. "You can hit me, but you can never have me."

"Oh yes, I'll have you. What's the matter with you anyhow? You ought to be happy that a man finds you attractive."

Raina kicked his leg, and he gave a grimace of pain and let out a sudden gasp. "Get out of my room! Or maybe you want me to scream to let Roxie know what's going on with you."

Billaud stared at her, studying her for a moment. His expression was a mixture of anger and admiration. He was accustomed to having his way with the lower class of women that frequented the saloon that his wife had inherited part ownership in, which he now owned. His eyes wandered over her and took obvious pleasure in her appearance.

Raina recoiled in revulsion. She knew she was considered attractive by many with her large eyes, which were her most prominent feature, well shaped and of a peculiar shade between green and blue. Her hair was jet black and fell in lush profusion over her shoulders. She had an olive complexion, which came from her Cajun mother. Although she was barely five feet five inches in height, her carriage was so erect she seemed taller. She wore a faded calico dress of some indeterminate brown color, but it did not conceal the full-bodied figure that was rather common in young Cajun women. Her curving lips and smooth oval face made a striking combination that had brought her the unwelcome attention of many men since she had been a teenager.

Billaud stared at her with a lustful look in his eyes and shook his head. "You didn't learn anything the last few days, did you?" He slapped his hands together and said, "You tried to run away, but you didn't make it and you never will."

Indeed, Raina had tried to run away. The saloon was the only world she knew. Her mother had owned it and willed it to her sister, Roxie, and herself. Roxie, a plain woman unlike Raina, had made a foolish marriage with Billaud. She had quickly learned that he cared nothing for her but was determined to own the Silver Dollar Saloon.

Frantic with fear, Raina had tried desperately to run away. She had risen in the middle of the night and taken what clothes she could carry and what little money she had saved. She had begun to walk north, but Billaud had been too careful for her. He had guessed her route and had sent James Farmer, the county sheriff, after her, promising him a reward if he brought her back. Farmer had indeed caught her, and Raina had pleaded with him. "Let me get away. He's going to have me," she said.

"I'm sorry, Raina," Farmer had said. He was not much of a sheriff but was a creature of Oscar Butler, who owned most of the land in this part of the world.

Standing before the huge form of Billaud, Raina thought of how she had walked through the cold and had a brief thrill as she thought she would get away, but then Farmer had caught her and brought her back. "I've done nothing," she cried. "He can't force me to stay."

Farmer shook his head. He had some of the aspects of a bloodhound. "I got a warrant signed by Oscar Butler. It says you're charged with grand theft."

"I didn't steal anything!"

"I expect you didn't, but that's the charge."

Farmer had brought her back, and now as Billaud stood looking at her, he read her thoughts. "If you run away again, I'll let them put you in a women's prison at El Paso. You'll like that even less than you like it here, and you'd come out an old woman.

Why don't you listen to reason? You don't want to waste all those good looks."

Raina could not think of anything to say. She knew she would never change Billaud's mind. He was a stubborn, willful man and a womanizer. He had ruined several young girls, and now it was her turn. "I'm not such a bad fellow," he said. "Try to like me. I'll make it nice."

"You're my brother-in-law. You're married to my sister. That's reason enough for you to stay away from me."

"That's not your problem. You're going to have to accept it, Raina. And Roxie knows better than to question anything I do," Billaud said carelessly. He took her by the shoulder, pulled her against him, and tried to kiss her, but she turned her face, and he merely touched her cheek.

"Just leave me alone!"

"I'll never do that. I've got to have you." He turned toward her, but she drew back, and he said, "I want you to go downstairs and wait on the customers tonight. Need a good-lookin' woman down there."

"I can't. I've got to cook."

"Roxie can do the cooking. You wear that dress I bought." He pointed to the one hanging on a peg on the wall. "You'll look nice in it. Hurry up now. The crowd's starting to come in."

A wave of relief came to Raina as Billaud left. She expelled her breath and felt so weak that she had to sit down on the side of the bed. Tears came to her eyes, and she helplessly began to weep.

She heard the door open, and her sister, Roxie, came in. Roxie had worn her life out serving, cooking, and making a saloon work. She stopped abruptly, and her dull brown eyes said, "Is he after you again?"

"You've got to help me, Roxie. He's going to get me."

"There's nothing I can do."

"He wants me to go entertain the customers. Last time he told me I had to sleep with one of them."

"You know how he is."

"He says you'll do the cooking, but you don't like it."

"I don't like anything about Billaud. I don't like anything about this place."

After her sister left, the words echoed in Raina's mind. *I don't like anything about this place.* She had grown up in the Silver Dollar Saloon, knowing no other world. Some of the Cajuns who came in were kind, but most were heavy drinkers, just the kind who would find their way into a saloon. When she was only fourteen, men had begun trying to put their hands on her, and Billaud had only laughed. Finally she had persuaded him to let her do the cooking, and for two years she had done that. Now he wanted more than that from her.

Slowly she got to her feet, knowing that there was no way out. Moving across the room, she picked the dress up, staring at it with dislike. She shook her head in disgust. "Just the kind of dress that man would buy." She slipped off her worn dress and put on the new one. It was low-cut and too tight. She stared at herself in the mirror and tried desperately to think of a way out. Perhaps the reading she had done about romances had given Raina a false idea of the world. Her own life was drab and painful, and she spent hours thinking how life could be different if she were somewhere else. But the Silver Dollar was her universe, and Billaud was her curse. Slowly she moved over to the chest with a small mirror on top and put on a trace of makeup. She did not need it, for her coloring was fine as it was. Her eyelashes were long and shaded her eyes. Taking off her old shoes, she put on a pair of patent slippers that Billaud had bought with the dress. They were too tight and hurt, but she had no choice but to wear them.

Leaving her room, she went downstairs and into the kitchen, which was at the back of the large room that served as a bar and a gambling establishment. She could already hear the noise of the men who had come to gamble and drink, and a grimace swept the pleasantness from her features. Going into the kitchen, she saw her sister cooking at the stove. "I want to stay and cook."

"Doesn't matter what you want or what I want. You know what he's like. If you tell him no, he'll just beat both of us."

"Why did you ever marry him, Roxie?"

"Because I was a fool." Roxie's eyes grew bitter, and her mouth twisted into a scowl. She had long ago given up on trying to look presentable. She usually wore a shapeless dress and kept her hair tied behind her back.

Roxie's own father had been a drifter whom their mother had simply taken up with, but she'd discarded him. When their mother married again, it was to an Irishman who was working on a railroad in the vicinity. He had been the man who had fathered Raina. She couldn't even remember him. No one cared about ancient history like that.

"He's going to try to get me to do evil things, Roxie."

"I can't help it. You know I can't."

Raina sighed and looked at the floor. "What was my father like?"

"After all this time you're asking that?"

"I can't remember him."

"No, I guess you can't. He left when you were just beginning to walk."

"What did he look like?"

"Well, he had red hair. But you didn't get that. You got Mother's black hair. He was not a big man, but what I remember most about him was he was crazy for God."

"I don't know what that means."

"It means all he could talk about was what God had done for him. Somehow he had gotten the idea that God had put special favor on him. Of course our mother didn't want to hear that, and she ran him off after a time."

"Do you know where he is?"

"No, I don't. What difference does it make?"

Raina stared at her sister and knew that there was no help to be had from her. *She's worn down. She's not going to be able to fight Billaud off. I wouldn't be surprised but what he'll kill her one of these days.* "We'll try to talk him into letting me cook and then you can rest."

A brief smile touched Roxie's face. "You're a good girl, Raina. I'm sorry I married such trash, but there's no way out of it."

That phrase entered into Raina's thoughts repeatedly. *"There's no way out of it."* As she passed into the saloon, the odor of alcohol, strong tobacco, and sweat struck her. She had always been sensitive to things, loving the scents of flowers and of a bottle of perfume that she had used sparingly.

A small white-haired man was banging away on a piano, and a woman in a scanty dress was trying to sing along with him. Both of them were half drunk, so the music was not exactly beautiful.

Raina made her way across the floor toward the bar.

The bartender, a heavyset man with muddy brown eyes and black hair, said, "Hello, Raina. Billaud tells me you'll be serving tonight."

"I guess so, Juan."

"Here. Take these drinks over there in the corner. Gonna be busy tonight."

Raina took the tray and threaded her way across the crowded floor. There were tables around an open space, and couples were trying to dance. The noise was horrendous, women's shrill laughter and men yelling across the room at each other. She knew that sooner or later a fight would break out, for Cajuns were hot tempered. All she could do was stay away from them.

"Well, thank you, sweetheart." The customer looked up and grinned at her. He was a bronze-skinned man with a shirt that had once been white. It was open to his belt, and he was hairy as an animal it seemed. "Why don't you sit down and help me drink up this stuff?"

"I can't do that. It's against the rules."

"Rules are made to be broken." He reached out and grabbed her hand.

She wrenched it away. "I can't do that. The boss wouldn't like it."

"Why, I'll make it right with the boss."

"Just leave me alone," Raina said sharply.

"Think you're too good for me, do ya?"

At that moment, the bartender, Juan Rolando, suddenly appeared. He was a huge man, running to fat but strong as a bull. He grabbed the arm of the man who was reaching for Raina, squeezed, and said, "Drink your booze, and leave the help alone!"

"I just wanted—"

"I know what you wanted. Now here's what *I* want—get out of here or I'll break your neck!"

Raina watched as the customer staggered out. Then she turned to Juan. "*Gracias*, Juan."

"If you have any trouble, just give me a call."

She moved back toward the bar and got another order. For the next half hour she filled her time with serving the customers. The smells, the odors, and the profanities that rose in shrill voices all were an offense to her.

She had read a book once about a meal in a fancy New York restaurant where everything was quiet except the man with a violin who played beautiful music during the meal of the heroine and her lover. A longing rose in Raina, and she knew she would give all she had to have one meal like that where the men weren't drunk and the women were pure and the music was sweet.

That'll never happen to me, Raina thought, and all the joy of life faded from her as she continued to serve the drunken patrons. She saw that Billaud was scowling at Juan but said nothing.

She passed by a table where a tall, well-dressed man was sitting, and smiled at him. "How are you, Mr. Channing?"

"Fine, Miss Raina." Mason Channing was the one decent man Raina had encountered in the cantina. He was a lawyer and had the respect of everyone in town. He always called her "Miss Raina" and was ever polite. "A little trouble, Miss Raina?"

"Oh, nothing unusual, Mr. Channing."

Channing studied her and said, "A pretty tough life you have here. Did you ever think of trying something else?"

"What else is there?"

"Not much in this town, I know."

"If everyone were as nice as you, life would be a lot easier."

Channing considered her words then said, "I'm sorry it has to be so hard."

"Not your fault."

"No, but I hate to see a fine young lady have to put up with the trash that comes in here."

"I'll be all right."

"Did you ever think of getting married?"

"To who? One like Juan threw out the front door a little while ago? That's about all we get—except for you. And you're already taken. How is your wife, by the way?"

"She's doing just fine. In fact, I should be getting home to her now. Well, if I can ever help you, just let me know."

Raina would have been suspicious if any other man she knew made the remark, but she smiled. "That's like you, Mr. Channing." She walked away, hopelessness filling her completely.

CHAPTER 3

Tyler Kincaid pulled his worn shirt closer around his neck then buttoned up the top button of the heavy mackinaw coat he wore. The sky overhead was a dull lead-colored canopy that pressed down upon the earth. It was late morning now, and the temperature was dropping rapidly.

When Ty had left Houston, the weather had been mild enough, but as he'd traveled toward the northeast, the cold seemed to lower itself upon the earth, chilling him to the bone. Tiny granules of what would turn into snow were already falling, and he blinked his eyes to clear them then stared up ahead. Somewhere he would reach the Louisiana border, and his goal was to make it to Baton Rouge where he could continue his journey on a paddle-wheeler.

His horse had been a poor one to start with. Now he felt the animal tremble with the cold. Ordinarily Ty would not have ridden a horse in this condition, but there had been little choice for him.

Suddenly he was seized by a spasm and began to cough. The

cough from his imprisonment had returned when he had left Houston. He had gone there after his escape and worked at odd jobs to earn barely enough money for this trip. He muttered into the stiff wind, "Getting sick again. Better not be too serious this time."

He rode for another thirty minutes, and when he felt the horse's pace faltering, he knew that he'd have to rest her. He found shelter in a grove of hickory trees and tied the horse up, although there was little danger of her running away in her condition. He studied the animal closely and then shook his head. "Never make it, I reckon."

He turned to the task of fixing some sort of breakfast. He found a fallen tree and was able to break off small fragments of the dead limbs. He made a pile of them, and taking a match from his inside pocket, he struck it, waited until it burned blue, and then pushed it down into the pile of dead wood. "Come on, burn, blast you!" he muttered. His words had little effect, but soon the wood caught and a tiny yellow blaze flared up. Carefully he added larger pieces until he had a respectable fire going. The warmth of the flame would have cheered him, but it was so small and the weather was so bitter that it did little good.

Going back to his horse, he pulled a skillet and several small bags out. One of them carried grain, and he put it on the horse's head. Tired and weary and sick as the horse was, she began to eat. "That's about all we got, girl," he said. "You'll have to make out until we get somewhere to get some more."

Going back to the fire, he broke wood and made a pyramid. He balanced the skillet precariously on top. As soon as the skillet got hot, he dropped in three thick slices of bacon, the last of that store, and dumped a can of beans beside it. There was a small end of a loaf of bread, which he put on top of the frying bacon, letting the grease soak in.

As the meal sizzled and sent a good aroma to Kincaid, he squatted there, trying to estimate how he would be able to make it all the way to Arkansas. That was his master plan, to get from Houston to Fort Smith, Arkansas, which was a difficult thing under any condition. He was a man of silence, but he was planning ahead how he could, perhaps, sell the horse for at least enough to get a ticket partway up the Mississippi. The big river didn't go to Fort Smith, but the Arkansas River cut into the Mississippi, and the smaller paddleboats and sternwheelers made it all the way up to the Indian Territory and Fort Smith.

Ty ate slowly, chewing thoroughly, pulling his coat around his shoulders and his hat down to avoid the tiny fragments that stuck to his face and burned like fire. Finally he straightened up, put the skillet and the pitiful remains of the food into the saddlebag, and studied the horse. "You got to go a little bit farther, girl. Sorry about that." He was a man who cared for horses and had no use for men who mistreated them. He knew that the horse could not last long, but he stepped into the saddle and urged the animal forward. "Come on, girl, you can do it." The mare started forward, and in short steps they headed northeast.

The cold wind was sucking the energy out of both man and horse, and as Ty looked down the road, he shook his head. He had been told at the last stop that the small village of La Tete lay in front of him, and it wasn't far from the river itself. He rode slowly, and finally the horse stumbled and nearly fell. Stepping out of the saddle, Kincaid grasped the bridle and leaned forward. "Come on, now. Without all my weight you ought to be able to make it." As the two plodded along, the wind whistled a dirge like a funeral hymn. It was a depressing moment for Tyler Kincaid, but there was no way he could do anything except continue on his way.

La Tete was indeed small, and as Ty staggered into it at almost noon, he saw a sign that said CECIL'S LIVERY STABLE, halted the horse, and dismounted.

He was greeted by a tall, lanky man who appeared at the livery's door. He was bundled up against the cold, his red hair extending beneath his hat. He had a pair of sharp blue eyes. "Bad weather to be travelin', my friend. My name's Cecil."

"I'm Kincaid." Ty was almost too winded to answer, but he took a deep breath and began coughing again. When it finally stopped, he said, "I need to leave this horse with you until she gets rested and then find me a room."

"It sounds like you need a doctor more than any of that."

Kincaid smiled. "You know one that works for nothing?"

"Well, not really, but you could maybe work it out. Albert Vance is a pretty good fella for a doctor. How far you come?"

"All the way from Mexico."

Cecil whistled and shook his head. "That's a far piece on a horse like that. What were you doing down there?"

"Went to work on a railroad, but I got caught in one of their revolutions. And I was on the wrong side, at that."

"You headed far?"

"Headed for Fort Smith, Arkansas."

"Well, you're going in the wrong direction, you know."

"I know. Fort Smith is northwest of here, but I was hopin' to get to Baton Rouge. I could get on one of those sternwheelers and head up that way."

Cecil shook his head, took a toothpick out of his pocket, and stuck it in his mouth. "I doubt if this hoss will make it." He wiggled his toothpick up and down. "And the Mississippi don't go to Arkansas."

"No, but the Arkansas cuts into it. They got boats go all the way to Fort Smith, I hear."

"I guess that's right, but I doubt if this hoss will make it."

"No, I'll try to sell her."

"She ain't worth much, you know." The toothpick wiggled up and down again. He turned his head to one side and added, "The fare is pretty high on those paddleboats."

Kincaid wanted to get in out of the cutting wind. "I planned to work my way. Where can I get a room and something to eat?"

"Down the street there. The Silver Dollar Saloon. It ain't nothin' but a saloon, but they got some rooms, and they cook some meals. You can sure get some whiskey, maybe warm you up."

"Well, grain this horse, Cecil. Get her out of the cold."

"Sure, but I doubt she gets you very far."

"Well, maybe I can swap with someone."

Cecil shook his head doubtfully. "I'll ask around, but you ain't got much to swap with."

Kincaid paid Cecil then started down the street toward the saloon and did his best to keep from coughing. His chest was already sore from the wrenching it took with each spell. He reached the Silver Dollar, identified by a handmade sign. He walked inside and was struck at once by the heat. A woodstove blazed at one end of the saloon, and several tables were gathered around it, their occupants taking advantage of the heat. He started for the stove and noticed that a pretty girl with long black hair was singing a song, but he was too beat to pay much attention.

A large man with coarse features approached. "Help you, mister?"

"I'm Kincaid. Can I get something to eat and a room?"

"Yeah. This is my place. I'm Millard Billaud. You be stayin' long?"

"No, I'm heading for Baton Rouge then headed up north to Arkansas."

Billaud shook his head. "The weather is gettin' worse. Got a fellow that came in from the north just a little bit ago. He says the snow is fallin' thick and fast up that way. Better stay here until it clears up."

"What I need right now is a room."

"Go up the stairs. First door on the left. Ain't no locks. People carried the keys off a long time ago. Just put a chair under the knob if you want to, but nobody will bother you."

"Thanks." After giving the man the cost of the room, Kincaid climbed the stairs. He felt the weakness of his legs and struggled to restrain the coughing. He felt hot and knew that he had a fever coming on, and that made it worse.

Entering the room he saw that it was about as primitive and ugly as a room could get. It was papered with yellowed sheets of newspaper, some of it peeling off now and hanging by strips. There was a bed with a sorry-looking mattress that appeared as if it had been slept on since the Flood, one chair, and a table with a pitcher and a basin on it. He poured the cold water into the basin, washed his face as well as he could, then moved over, took his boots off, lay down, and pulled the dirty quilt and a blanket, equally dirty, over him. He began coughing and knew that the fever was going up. Finally he went to sleep, but the coughing woke him from time to time.

When he woke up it was dark outside, and the room was freezing. Kincaid felt awful. He summoned what little strength he had, pulled on his boots, and went downstairs. He went up to the bar.

A balding man, who was obviously the barkeep, had a filthy apron on. He turned to Ty. "Something for you?"

"Whiskey." As soon as the man handed him the drink, Ty threw down some coins, took the glass, and swallowed the liquid down in one gulp.

"The woman will cook you something if you're hungry."

"That'd be good. Whatever she's got will do me."

The girl who had been singing was now moving from table to table, carrying drinks on a tray. She stopped in front of him.

He glanced up and saw that she had a beautiful complexion, but he was not at all interested in women at the moment. The smell of cigarettes, stale smoke, unwashed bodies, and alcohol flavored the air, but it was that way in all saloons. He chose a table and sat quietly, paying little attention to what was going on.

Finally the girl came over and said, "Here's your breakfast."

He looked down and saw that it was ham with some eggs and thick-sliced bread. "Can I get coffee?"

"Yes, I'll get it for you."

There was something odd about her speech, and Kincaid wondered what. And then he realized that this was Louisiana country, full of Cajuns who spoke French and English, but French better than the latter. "Thanks," he said and began eating. He ate slowly and managed to withhold his cough.

The table next to him was occupied by three men, all of them wearing lumber jackets, heavy coats, and fur hats. One of them said, "Wanna sit in on the game, mister?"

Kincaid looked over and shook his head. "I don't have much money."

"Ah, it's just penny ante poker to kill the time. I'm Beaudreux. This is Johnny. That's Conroy. Come on, set in while you thaw out and maybe have another drink."

Kincaid did not feel like gambling, but neither did he want to sit alone. He joined in the game and listened to the men talking, figuring out they were lumberjacks and most of them had grown up in swamp country. One of them was telling the story about how he had landed a twelve-foot alligator with his bare hands.

"Oh Conroy, you always tell the best lies," the tall man called Beaudreux said. "What's your name, mister?"

"Tyler Kincaid."

"Well, pretty cold out there to be travelin'. You headed far?"

The young woman came with drinks, and he took his and looked up and nodded at her. "Thank you, miss."

His politeness seemed to shock her. For a moment she stared at him, then said, "You're welcome."

Kincaid turned back to the men and the game. "I'm heading for Indian Territory."

Beaudreux asked, "What for? They say that ain't much of a place."

"Oh, I thought I could trade with the Indians. Do something. Maybe become one of Judge Parker's marshals."

The man called Johnny shook his head mournfully. "I hear that's a rough crowd. Been more than fifty of them marshals kilt chasin' around after bad men and Indians."

"That's right," Conroy said. "Every crook in the world winds up in that territory. Hard on them marshals. I heard about that Judge Parker. Feller said he'll hang 'em half a dozen at a time." Conroy shook his head. "He must be a hangin' judge."

Kincaid noticed that the girl did not get far. She apparently had lingered to listen, but he could not understand why. The talk seemed mundane to him. He continued playing poker, and finally he said, "Well, too rich for my blood. I lost nearly two bits."

At that time an older man with a star on his vest came over and said, "I'll have to take your gun, mister. I'm Sheriff Farmer."

"My gun? Why would you do that?"

"I got a poster with your picture on it. You're a wanted man, even got a reward out on you."

"Who's offering a reward for me?"

"Mexican police put it out. Claims you shot a national big shot down there."

Ty stared at the sheriff. "That was one of their revolutions I got caught in."

"You did some shootin'?"

"I got caught in one of the fights between the nationals and the revolutionists. I defended myself and got out of there."

"Have to hold you, Kincaid. Maybe you can get some help from our government."

Ty saw that argument was useless, so he handed the sheriff his gun, and the two of them left the Silver Dollar.

The sheriff led Ty to the jail, and as he locked him in a cell, he said, "Sorry about this, son, but I've got no choice."

As soon as Farmer left, Ty collapsed on the bunk. A bitterness filled him, and he muttered, "I'll either die of whatever sickness I've got or rot in a Mexican prison."

An old man with bleary eyes came into the room and stopped to peer into Ty's cell. "Guess you could use some grub."

"Not too hungry."

"I'm Gabe Hunter. We got some stew left over, and I'll get you some fresh water."

"I appreciate that."

"Whut you in fur?"

"Got mixed up with a shooting down in Mexico. They put out a reward on me. Guess I'll be in jail for a long time."

"Hope not," Gabe said. "It ain't no place for a young feller like you. Life's too short as it is."

Ty felt miserable, but when the jailer came back with a bowl of stew and a pitcher of fresh water, he took it.

Gabe stood and watched, and when Ty had a coughing fit, he shook his head sadly. "Sounds like you got something bad."

"Hope it's just a bad cold."

"No, hit's down in your chest. You need something to break that up. I've got some medicine that might help." He reached into his hip pocket and brought out a half-pint bottle. "Try a bit of this."

Ty took the bottle, took two swallows, and then went into another coughing spasm. He managed to say, "Thanks, Gabe."

"You want me to get a doctor or maybe a preacher to pray over you?"

Ty stopped coughing long enough to whisper, "No thanks, Gabe." Then he lay back and tried to sleep.

CHAPTER 4

The night had drawn on forever, or so it seemed to Raina. She had tossed and turned and gotten up more than twice to get an extra blanket, for the room was not well sealed. Frigid air blew in from the cracks around the window and through the other passages.

While she had been tossing and turning, suddenly an idea came to her. It was like nothing that had ever happened, but she had been thinking for days now about how to get away from Billaud. The thought startled her. At first she put it aside and tried to go back to sleep, but she did not succeed. The idea kept coming back, and she kept building upon it and found herself growing excited about the possibility that her plan might hold.

Finally dawn broke, and although the sky was a dull gray and the sun was only a feeble light as it came through her window, she got out of bed and quickly dressed, putting on her woolen underwear and her warmest dress. Going downstairs, she stirred up the fire in the stove and quickly cooked a supply of ham and then scrambled eggs. These she put into a basket along with half a loaf of bread that she sliced carefully. No one was stirring yet.

She had taken on the job of feeding prisoners in the jail for the small pittance that it paid. Putting on her heaviest coat and a shawl over her head, she left the Silver Dollar and made her way down to the jail. When she got there the door was locked, but she knocked and soon it opened.

Harry Jackson, the night man at the jail, looked at her out of sleep-filled eyes. "What are you doing here so early, Raina? You're not usually stirring around at this hour, are you?"

"Well, I just woke up early today and decided to go ahead and get breakfast ready for the prisoner and for you, too, Harry."

"Well, that's right nice of you, Raina. Come on in. Get out of the cold."

She stepped inside and put the tray down then suddenly turned. "Oh, I forgot."

"What's that?"

"That beer you like so well. I was going to bring you a bottle of it, and I just walked off and forgot it."

"Well, tell you what. Why don't you go back and get it?"

"It's so cold. Would you mind going for it? If you'll go, you can get two bottles of the beer for having to make the trip."

Harry's eyes lit up. "Well, sure I'll be glad to do that. I'll have to lock you in here though."

"That's all right. The prisoner can't get at me. I'll slip his breakfast under the bars."

"Okay. Where's the beer?" Harry listened as she told him the location of the beer, and he left at once whistling a cheerful tune.

As soon as she heard the door lock, she moved out of the main office back to a row of four cells, two on each side of an aisle. There was no one in there except the one prisoner. She saw that the man was lying on the bed and said quickly, "I brought you some breakfast." She watched as he got up and saw that his face was flushed and that he moved carefully. "You're sick," she said.

"I guess I am a little bit. Nice of you to bring breakfast."

She slipped the tray into the space underneath the bottom row of the horizontal steel bars. "I brought some coffee, too." She put the cup between the bars and he took it. He sat down slowly, and she saw that he had started eating, but he did not act hungry. "How long have you been sick?"

"About a week. I hope it's not pneumonia, but the doc said it probably is."

Raina hesitated and then, knowing her time was short, said, "I heard you tell some of the men in the saloon that you were headed north to Indian Territory."

"Well, that's where I was going. Doesn't look like I'll make it now though. From what everybody says, I'll be in jail for a long stretch."

Raina took a deep breath and stared at him. He did not look at all trustworthy. He had a rough look about his face. There was a scar, she noticed, on the left side pulling down his eye into a partial squint and his mouth open to what looked like a sneer. The scar spoiled his looks. It gave him a sinister appearance, but she knew she had no choice. "If I get you out of this place, would you take me with you to the Indian Territory?"

He looked up. "Why, I never thought of such a thing, but it won't work. You can't get me out of here."

"I can get you out, but you'll have to promise me two things."

"What's that?"

Quickly Raina said, "First, you have to promise to take me with you all the way to Fort Smith."

"Well, if I can get there, I'll get you there."

"You have to promise to—to leave me alone. Not to put your hands on me."

"Sure. I'm not much on forcing myself on women. But I don't think it can be done."

Raina was afraid that Harry Jackson would return. "I can do it."

"I don't see how."

"I'll come by late tonight. The jailer, Ben Hogan, is a real drunk. I'll bring some whiskey by and tell him it's my birthday and I want him to help me celebrate, but the whiskey will be drugged with laudanum. It'll put him out. Whiskey does that to him anyway."

"What then?"

"Then I let you out and we leave."

"You might get me out of here, but they'll be looking for us."

"Remember, you do anything I ask no matter how crazy. Let's just get you out of here tonight; then I'll tell you the rest of my plan."

He smiled briefly. "I'll be here. I won't be going anywhere."

Mason Channing said, "Why, Raina, good to see you. Won't you come in?"

Raina walked into Mr. Channing's office. She had been there before. He was a lawyer and often sent for meals from the saloon, and she had brought them.

47

Channing gave her a warm smile. "What can I do for you, Miss Raina? Most people come to see lawyers because they're either in trouble or about to make trouble for somebody else."

She glanced down at the floor and then she looked Channing straight in the eyes. "I've got to get away, Mr. Channing. If I don't there'll be trouble."

Channing studied her face. He picked up a letter opener, balanced it on one finger, and then said, "Who's going to be in trouble?"

"You, I'm afraid, Mr. Channing."

Channing laughed. "You'd have to get in line for that. There're so many people who don't care for me. They'd have to wait. What's the nature of this trouble you're going to give me?"

"I want you to buy my half interest in the Silver Dollar."

"Why, I thought your sister and brother-in-law owned that."

"My mother divided it before she died. It was in the will. We each got half interest. But she married Millard, and she found out pretty quickly he was just interested in getting her half of the business away and then mine."

This did surprise Channing. "Why would it be trouble for me?"

"Because if you bought my half, you'd be a partner with Billaud, and he can be troublesome. He's a mean, cruel man."

Channing said mildly, "No, I don't think so, Raina. If anyone has trouble, he'll have it with me. How much would you want for half of the place?"

"I don't know what it's worth, but I must have two thousand dollars cash to get away from here."

"It's worth more than that," Channing said.

"I mean I want the money right now, and I want it in cash."

"You mean today?"

"I mean in one hour."

Channing said, "Everybody expects lawyers to cheat their clients. I wouldn't want you to think that. Half of that place is worth at least three thousand."

"I know, but I just want enough to get away, and I want you to get paid for your service. Will you do it, please?"

"You want to tell me anything else about your plan?"

"I'm going to find my father. All I have is a letter with his picture that came some time ago from Arkansas. It was written to my mother, but she had died by the time it got here. I found it by accident. He asked her to let him come and see me, but she never told me about it."

"All right. I'll help you. Now let's talk about this." They talked for fifteen minutes, and in the end he went to the safe and got some cash out. "Most of this is in small bills. That'll help. Now you'll have to sign a paper. Let me make one out."

Raina waited while he wrote out a paper, and then he had two men come in whom she didn't know. He didn't tell the men what the paper said. "Just witness this signature." He dismissed them, and as soon as they left the room, he said, "Here's your money, Raina. Go with God."

"Thank you, Mr. Channing. I'll think of you often when I get away. You've been very kind to me."

She left the office and went at once to a small house on the outskirts of town. She knocked on the door, and it was opened almost at once by Antoine Doucett. He was a slim man with dark hair and black eyes. Unlike most of the men in the area, he had always treated her with respect. "I need your help, Antoine."

"Surely. Won't you come in?"

"Are Lena or the kids in the house?"

"No. She's away for a few days with our kids visiting her parents."

"All right." Raina entered and said, "I want you to help me get away." She went on to explain how she was running from Billaud.

Antoine's face darkened. "He is a cruel man. He cheated me out of my money on that stallion I sold him. But Billaud won't let you go."

"He won't know it. I'll pay you for this, but I want you to go buy a wagon and a team." She went on, giving him instructions about where to put it, and told him that she would be leaving late that night and needed him to be waiting for her with the wagon and team. "And another thing, it must be loaded with hay."

"That will not be hard. It's bad weather to be traveling though."

"But it'll be bad weather for those who try to find me, too. I appreciate this, Antoine."

"That's what friends are for. Don't worry. I know where I can get a wagon and team cheap." She gave him cash and then left. She went at once back to the Silver Dollar and started cooking breakfast. That day she made everything as usual. She cooked and served and managed to stay away from Billaud all day long. Finally night came, and she asked Roxie, "Where's Millard gone?"

"He's after some woman. He won't be back until tomorrow probably. I wish he'd stay gone forever."

Raina went up to her room and gathered together what she wanted to take. She didn't have a suitcase, so she tied her things in a bundle using a blanket. She did not have many clothes anyway, but she did throw in six of the small romance novels that she loved especially.

She sneaked down and got a bottle of whiskey and went to the place where Roxie kept the medicine. She found a bottle of the laudanum they all used when they had aches and pain and poured part of the whiskey out and filled it to the top with the strong sedative.

Finally the saloon grew quiet. She looked at the clock and saw that it was after midnight and the town was shut down in the midst of the storm. Quickly she left the saloon and went to the jail. She knocked on the door.

A voice said, "Who's there?"

"It's me, Ben. Open the door."

The door opened, and Ben stared at her. "What are you doing out this late?"

"Why, I've been having a birthday party, Ben. I've come by to get you to celebrate with me." She held a bottle up.

Ben Hogan's eyes livened. "Come on in out of the cold!" he exclaimed.

"Get us some glasses. We're going to have a good time."

Getting Ben Hogan drunk was the simplest part of the whole plan. He drank quickly, gulping the whiskey down. She had been pretending to drink with him but actually did not swallow any.

Finally his eyes began to shut. He said, "I don't feel so good, Raina."

"You sick?"

"I think so."

"Well, here. Lie down on this cot. You'll feel better in a minute." She helped him over to the cot.

He practically collapsed. He put his feet up and began snoring, his mouth open wide.

Quickly Raina got the key off the wall, entered the jail section, and saw that the prisoner was waiting for her. "We've got to hurry," she said. "Get as far away as we can." She unlocked the door, and he stepped outside.

His face was flushed, but he smiled and said, "If this works, it will be a miracle. I've got to have my gun." He found his gun and gun belt, strapped it on, and said, "What now?"

"Come along. We've got to be away from this town as soon as we can."

She led him down the alley to Antoine's house. She was glad to see, even in the darkness, that Antoine had lit a lantern and was standing there in front of the house.

"That you, Raina?"

"It's me. And this is the man I told you about."

"You're the fellow that was in jail?"

"That's right. I'm Tyler Kincaid."

"He's taking me away from here, Antoine. You get everything fixed?"

"Sure did. I built a little kind of a box on the wagon. You get in there and shut the door. It'll be pretty dark, but you don't have to stay in there too long, I hope. And here, I had this much left over from the money you gave me."

"You keep it, Antoine."

"I'm going to drive you to my cousin's house. I'll borrow a horse from him to get back here."

Raina nodded. "Thanks so much for doing this for me."

"It's no problem. I'm glad to help you get away from a man

like Billaud. I just wish you had come to me sooner."

"I never saw a way out until now."

Antoine looked up at the continuing storm. "You were right about the weather. There won't be anybody out looking for you at this time of night and in all of this." Antoine turned to the bed of the wagon, scraped some of the hay away, and opened the small door. It was about five feet square. He said, "Put your blankets in there, and I brought some extra ones. It's going to be cold tonight."

Ty stared at the hiding place and smiled. "Well, I never done anything like this. You want to go first, Miss Raina, I believe is your name?"

"Yes." She got in, and they spread the blankets around to make the floor somewhat softer and then wrapped up in them.

"I'll stop when we get to my cousin's house. If somebody stops me, just don't pay any attention. But I don't think they will. They don't know you're out, do they, Kincaid?"

"No."

Antoine shut the door, and they heard him piling loose hay over it. Then the wagon sagged as the young man got into the seat, and the wagon jerked as the horses pulled out.

"Are you scared being here in the dark with no light at all?" Kincaid asked.

"There are things that are scarier than this."

Kincaid replied, "I guess you've had it pretty hard."

"I can tell you know why I have to get away. My brother-in-law that's married to my sister. He—he's been after me for a long time, ever since I was fifteen. He's going to get me, too, one way or another. I've got to get away."

"Well, we're on our way. I guess Billaud's a bad man to cross."

There was silence for a time, and finally Raina said, "God will take care of us."

"Well, that's a good thing to think. But why do you trust me?"

The wagon jolted and threw her against him. He made no attempt to touch her, and she immediately moved away. "I have nobody else, Kincaid."

The wagon rumbled on, and both of the passengers inside the small box wrapped up and kept warm under the hay and with their covers.

Raina wondered if she had done the right thing. Finally she asked, "*Can* I trust you?"

"You've just about saved my life. I'm not much good, but I always pay my debts, so yes, you can trust me."

"I've not had much luck with men being honest with me."

"Sorry to hear that, but I promise you I'll keep my word to you. Not too many people would have helped me the way you have."

They both fell silent.

Once the wagon stopped, and Raina whispered, "I hope it's not the sheriff."

"Not likely in this kind of weather."

Raina held her breath, but then the wagon lurched on. "Guess we're all right." Raina heard Ty's uncontrolled coughing. "We need to get you to a doctor."

"I'll be all right," he muttered, but Raina knew a little about sickness and wondered if he would live long enough to get her to the territory.

CHAPTER 5

Even though Kincaid could feel the wagon swaying and hear the whistling of the wind, he knew that his fever was rising. His forehead was beginning to feel like a furnace.

He longed to be out of the rather small cocoon where they were hidden from the eyes of men. Close places had always troubled him, and this was a tight one and pitch black, with trouble on the outside. Everything was wrong with it.

"What's the matter, Kincaid?" Raina's voice was soft in the darkness.

He said nothing except, "Well, this fever of mine's going up."

The wagon jolted on and suddenly Ty felt her move closer to him, felt her hand on his shoulder and then up on his forehead. "You're burning up with fever. Here. You need to drink all the water you can."

They had put two water bottles in the hiding place, and now Ty groped for one and felt it. It was cold, but his lips were cracked and parched with the fever. He drank all he could hold, put the top on, and murmured, "That was good."

"Maybe we need to get out of this thing. We may be safe now."

"I don't think so. We'll wait until we get to Antoine's cousin's place. That ought to be good enough."

"I wish this storm had held up. It sounds as if it's getting worse."

The wagon rolled on, and Kincaid continued coughing at times.

Then he heard her say, "Here. Let's wet this handkerchief and put it on your face."

"All right." He waited until she had moistened the large handkerchief that she wore around her neck and began to bathe his face with it. "Feels good," he muttered. "I would have to pick this time to be sick."

"You didn't pick it. Sickness just comes on."

From time to time Raina moistened the handkerchief. It would grow almost hot from the fever that was running through him. "What's your plan after we get out of this thing, Ty?"

"We'll immediately head for Indian Territory."

"It might be hard to get there, don't you think?"

"I expect so. It's an out-of-the-way place. I'm hoping we can catch a steamboat at Baton Rouge."

"Does the Mississippi River go all the way to Fort Smith?"

"No, we'd have to get off where the Arkansas River feeds into the Mississippi, but steamboats go up the Arkansas all the way into Fort Smith. The trouble is I don't know if we can do that."

"Why not, Ty?"

"I think Sheriff Farmer will send out word with our descriptions. We'll have to sneak in somehow." He suddenly hacked a raw cough.

She said, "You're so sick. I'm afraid."

"I'll be all right. I've been sick before."

Sometime later Raina heard Antoine say, "Whoa!" and the wagon ceased to heave and pitch. "Here we are, Ty." She got no answer and realized that he was asleep. "Ty, wake up!"

Ty came awake slowly, and his voice was thin. "Are we here?"

"Yes. Antoine will let us out now."

A few minutes later they heard the scraping at the door of their hiding place and then it opened. A freezing blast of air mixed with snow swirled in, and Kincaid murmured, "That's real winter there."

The two got out, and Raina said, "You did a good job, Antoine."

"Well, come in to my cousin's house and get warm, and I'll fix you something to eat."

It was a welcome break for both of them. They went inside, and Raina saw a heavyset woman with black eyes and a man who looked somewhat like Antoine.

Antoine said, "Give them something to eat. They'll be moving on."

"We don't have much."

"Anything. Heat up some beans or bacon or whatever you can find."

"We've got some ham and some corn."

"That'll be good."

Thirty minutes later the fugitives were standing beside the wagon. The wind was rising now. It was winding around the house corners, and it had blown down the chimney, making the smoke whirl inside the house.

The whole world was cold, and Raina saw that Ty was using all his strength just to hold on to the wagon. "Get on into the wagon, Ty. I'll drive. We'll cover up with these blankets." She turned to Antoine and said, "Thank you, Antoine. You may have saved our lives. Stay out of Sheriff Farmer's way though."

"You do the same. But he won't likely be out in this kind of weather. Everyone will just think I went to see my wife and kids overnight. I'll be fine."

Raina climbed into the wagon and picked up the lines. She had driven a few times. The horses were sluggish, so she took the whip and touched them with it. They pulled forward, throwing her back into the seat. "You all right, Ty?"

"Sure."

"Wrap up in these blankets. It's getting worse all the time."

As they moved on, Raina saw that Ty's head was nodding. *He looks terrible*, she thought. *I've got to get him in some shelter.*

They drove for a while in the driving wind, and the weather was getting worse.

"Ty, there's a house."

"We probably don't need to stop there. If anyone is tracking us, they would stop and ask at houses about us."

"No, it's vacant. Antoine told me about it. Folks sold out last week, and it's for sale, so it'll be abandoned. Nobody will be out looking at a house to buy in this storm. And there's a barn to put the team in."

"All right."

Raina drove the team up to the barn, got out, and had to struggle to open the doors that were crammed with snow. She did get them open wide enough and drove the team in. She noted that Ty was only able to fall out and hang on to the side of the wagon.

"Look, Ty. They left some feed here. The horses will need it. Let's go in, and I'll come back later."

"I wish I was more help. I hate being sick."

"It'll pass." The two of them made for the house, and Raina said, "Look. They've got a lot of firewood stacked up against the side of the house here."

"We'll probably need it in this storm."

When they went inside, the faint light came through the windows, but there was a lantern with coal oil in it. Raina lit it and set it on the table. "Here. You come on in and lie down. I'm going to get a fire started."

"Let me do that."

"No, you lie down. We've got to take care of you."

"Whatever you say."

Raina was glad that the wood box was filled. There was even some rich pine kindling there. She got the fire started, and while it was catching she went out and fed the horses and unhitched them. Going back to the house, she looked in the wagon and got the box of groceries and took it inside. The snow was falling thick now so that she could barely see the house. She stepped inside and felt immediately the difference that the small fire had made. *I've got to be careful with the wood. It's got to last.*

She went over to the stove and got out the frying pan and a saucepan. She quickly cooked some grits, added condensed milk and some sugar, and then she fried up some ham and added two eggs. She fixed a plate for Ty and said, "Just stay in your bed. You can eat there."

"I can get up."

"No need to. Here." She watched him struggle in the bunk,

leaning back against the wall. His face was flushed, and his eyes were bleary. When he took the food, his hands trembled, but she said nothing. She ate her meal and watched as he tried to get some down. "You need to drink all the water you can."

"I don't know why I'm not eating like I should."

"Fever does that. Especially pneumonia."

"Well, it's bad news if I've got that. I think more people die of it than live through it. Can't eat any more." He handed her the plate.

She saved the food. She then saw that he had slumped back. A spirit of fear came to her. She was alone in the middle of a snowstorm such as she had never known. She saw that Ty was unconscious. His breathing was irregular, and the violent coughing came at fairly regular intervals.

I got Ty into this, she thought. *I wish I hadn't. He may die here. . . .* The thought frightened her, and she tried to pray, but she was not a woman of prayer and could only say the Lord's Prayer that she had memorized. It didn't seem right, but she didn't know what else to do.

She rationed out the fire, built it up, and put a pallet on the floor. She lay down on it, wrapped up in two other blankets after covering Ty. The warmth of the cabin soon got to her. She tried to pray again but failed and dozed off to sleep.

Raina was awakened by the coldness of the room. The fire had died down. She shivered, got up, and built up the fire again.

Going over to the bunk, she looked down and said, "Ty, are you all right?"

He did not stir nor speak.

She saw that his lips were crusted over, and his breathing had a frightening rattle to it. She had seen pneumonia before, and to be alone with a dying man and no one to help was the scariest moment of her life.

She remembered that the horses needed water, and taking a bucket she went outside and returned. She filled a dishpan with snow until it was full then set it on the stove. As the snow began to melt, she stirred it to hurry the process. Finally she got a large fruit jar and began to dip it out into the bucket. It took her four trips to get the horses satisfied, and she had to keep on heating the snow as it was the only water available.

She returned to her makeshift bed and wrapped up in the blankets, continually repeating the Lord's Prayer as she slipped into a fitful sleep.

The storm went on for two more days, and it was a Herculean struggle for Raina to exist. She had to keep the horses watered and fed, and just getting to the barn took a mammoth effort. When she came back each time, she was so weak she had to sit down and pant like a dog. Keeping the fire going with what wood was available was also a chore. Each time she had to go break the firewood loose where it was frozen and bring it into the house so it would thaw out before it could burn.

Her worst problem, though, was with Ty. She knew for sure now that he had pneumonia, and there was nothing she could do for him except to help him sweat it out. She would warm the blanket at the stove and put it on him. He tried to fight her for he was blazing with the fever, but there was nothing else she could do.

She had brought some of her romance novels. On one of her return trips from the barn, she had brought one inside. It was called *Ivanhoe* and was written by Sir Walter Scott. She had read it more than once, but now she sat down and passed the time reading. There was a sufficient supply of coal oil to keep the lantern burning dimly, and she read the story of the knight and the fair lady and the dark lady again. Finally she closed her eyes and held the book to her breast. *I wish life was like that. That some man would come along and care for me and tell me the things I want to hear, but I don't think that will ever happen.*

On the third day, the wind dropped and the snow stopped falling out of the sky. She went over to Ty and said, "The storm is falling away, Ty." She saw that he was unconscious, but he was burning up. She pulled the cover back, wet some cloths in the dishpan where she melted the snow, and covered his body as best she could. The cloths grew almost hot to the touch, and she dipped them again into the cold water. Finally the fever came down, and he fell into what seemed like a normal sleep.

Once again Raina tried to pray, but it was a failure. "I wish I knew God," she whispered, "but I don't. So God, hear somebody's prayer. Help this man and help me to get out of this place." She waited for some kind of answer, but all she heard was the silence and the crackling of wood in the stove. She said wearily, "It'll just have to be like it is."

She sat down beside Ty, picked up his hand, and held it. She stayed that way for a long time. She felt alone. . .without a future, with a bad past, and no present. Tears began to roll down her cheeks, and she gave in to the sorrow and grief that had been building up. As the storm abated outside, so her spirit seemed to grow weak and weary.

CHAPTER 6

The day had passed and the night, and now getting up from the floor Raina saw that the fire was practically down. The room was freezing cold, and she had to start with the few pieces of kindling she had made by breaking one of the drawers to a small cabinet. As soon as she got a blaze going, she picked the smallest bit of firewood and laid it carefully and then added two more pieces on top, leaving room for it to draw. The sight of the yellow flames flickering and the sound of the crackling was cheerful.

She rose and went to the door. She opened it, looked outside. She felt smothered somehow by the coldness, the terrible, awful coldness of the weather. She shut the door then laid her hand against it. It made a solid wall of walnut, but it was a feeble thing against the onslaught of the bitter cold.

She listened closely and heard the wind rising again. It whirled around the house corners and blew down the chimney, making the stove smoke. She felt the chill bite into her shoulders, and with the fire burning it only made the temperature bearable.

She knew she had to go make snow water. Finally when she went out, she found the horses stamping. They looked pitiful to her. She fed them from the grain that had been left and some of the hay. She gave them two buckets of water each and then went back inside. She took the dishpan and made enough snow water to fill buckets. Then there was nothing left to do.

Finally she saw Ty turning from one side to the other and coughing. "Are you all right, Ty?" she said.

"It's cold."

"Let me wrap you up in another blanket." She took one of her own blankets, put it over him, and tucked it in closely so that the air could not get through. She had thought to put one of the blankets underneath him so that the cold rising would be barricaded off. "I'm gonna fix you something to eat, Ty."

"Not hungry."

She ignored his words and cut off two slices of ham and made more of the oatmeal from their diminishing supplies. There was a little piece of pork fat, and it made the skillet greasy. The ham sizzled in it as she warmed a small skillet full of the oatmeal. She poured it onto a plate, went over, and said, "Sit up, Ty. You've got to eat." He said nothing, and she helped him into a sitting position, and then she fed him. "How do you feel, Ty?"

"Rotten." He opened his eyes and stared at her. His eyes seemed to be hollow, and he whispered huskily, "I'm no help to you, Raina."

"That's all right. We're going to make it."

Ty said, "That's what Jim said, but he didn't."

She got up and put two small logs on the fire. "I can't use up all the firewood, but you know, Ty, I think it's warmer on the floor."

His teeth were chattering, and she pulled the blanket off, made a thick fold, and said, "Come on. Lie down here." She helped him out of the small bed.

He lay down as close to the stove as she dared allow, and then she covered him up with all the blankets. "That feels good," he whispered. His eyes shut.

She said, "Are you thirsty?"

"Yes, I feel like I need water all the way through me." Indeed, his lips were chapped, and when she fed him he sipped the water gratefully. When he had drunk enough, he laid his head back and whispered, "I wish I could help you, Raina."

"We'll be all right."

"I'm not sure about that."

The day passed, the night, and another day and another night. The woodpile was going down alarmingly, but she could not afford to have no fire. It had helped some to put Ty on the floor, for the heat radiated outside the woodstove for a few feet. Finally she lay down with him, and the warmth of her own body seemed to help him.

Later that day she went outside, and to her surprise she heard a faint sound. She looked over and saw a hen staggering out of a small building. She walked over to the building, looked inside, and saw that there were four more, but they were skinny and all trembling with the cold. She picked up the one hen, shut the door, and taking a sharp knife, cut its head off. She went to the barn and got some of the feed for the horses and scattered it inside for the chickens, and while she was there she found just outside that there was some cracked corn. It could be eaten if it was soaked, but the chickens could eat it, too, and that thrilled her.

She walked inside carrying the chicken and said, "Something good, Ty."

"What's that?"

"There are five chickens out there. We're going to have us a nice chicken stew."

She worked hard making the stew, which was really nothing more than chicken soup. She dressed the chicken and boiled it. For the next day they ate chicken, chicken, and chicken, even the gizzard and the liver.

The food seemed to help Ty, for his eyes grew brighter, and he said, "How many chickens did you say there were?"

"There's four more out there, so we can last a week on that."

"I feel sorry for the poor chickens."

I feel sorry for us, Raina wanted to say, but she did not. She watered the horses, fed them, and saw that the feed was going down rapidly. *What will we do if the feed goes and the horses die?*

The next day she went out, and the chickens were huddled in a far corner. Their feathers were drooping, and their eyes were glazed over, but they were alive. She had found a narrow pan and knew they must be thirsty, so she took the bucket of water and the pan and filled it. One of the chickens came over at once, clucking feebly, and began to peck at the water, and then the others came. "You poor things. You're starving, aren't you? I'm afraid you're going to have to die for us." She realized she had never felt sorry for a chicken before, and she had had fried chicken all her life. Finally she left and went back.

Ty was sitting up in bed. "You know you could bring those chickens in here. It's warmer than it is in that henhouse."

"I think you're right, Ty." At once she left, and it took her four trips, but the chickens were inside. She brought some of the feed and the pan out, and soon the warmth of the fire helped the birds. One of them seemed to be dying, and she managed to pour a little water down its throat. The bird began to perk up and finally ate a little.

"How much firewood is left, Raina?"

"About half of it."

"How long do you think it will last?"

"Well, it all depends. We can't have big roaring fires like I'd like to have."

"No, but this cabin and that firewood is saving our lives and now those of the chickens." His voice was somewhat clearer, and she moved closer and put her hand on his forehead. "Your fever's about gone!" she exclaimed. "That's wonderful."

"Well, I do feel better."

"Could you eat some more chicken soup?"

"I believe I could."

She stirred up the fire and put the pan right on the coals from the front where she usually loaded it. Soon the soup was bubbling, a full stew pan. She poured two bowls of the soup, went over to Ty, and said, "Can you feed yourself?"

"I think so."

She gave him one bowl and a spoon, and then she took the other. "This is good," she said.

"Sure is. I thank the Lord for those chickens." He hesitated then said, "That's what my friend would have said. Jim Adams. He always believed in the Lord, even when things were at the worst."

"Have you known him long?"

"Just a few months. We worked on the railroad together." He

then told her how they had been captured by the army and thrown into a prison. He ended the story by saying, "He gave his life for me, Raina. He could have gotten away if he had left me there, but he didn't do it."

"What a good man he must have been."

He suddenly changed the subject. "That wind's picking up."

She had finished her soup, and she went over to the door and cracked it. "It's blowing hard. I don't think—" She suddenly stopped.

Ty asked, "What is it?"

"There's a deer out there. He's coming this way."

"You'll have to shoot him, Raina."

"I'm not much good."

"There's that shotgun. You can't miss."

"All right, Ty, if you say so."

"Bring me the shotgun."

She took it to him.

He checked the load and said, "Get as close as you can and pull one trigger. If he doesn't fall, pull the other one."

"All right, Ty." Raina took the shotgun, moved to the door, and closed it behind her. She half expected to see the deer run away. The poor creature was weak and did not seem to see her. She walked on the snow, and when she was no more than five feet away she lifted the gun. She pulled the trigger. The deer was knocked backward. It lay there bleeding in the snow. Raina felt tears come into her eyes, but she knew that this was life or death. She took the shotgun inside and said, "It's down."

"I wish I could help you dress it."

"I helped my brother-in-law dress a deer once. I think I can do it. I'll cut off some steaks and bring them in. Then I'll get the rest of it."

The deer was indeed lank and had lost most of the fat, but it was the closest thing to a feast that they had had. She worked hard getting the deer cut up, and finally she had all the meat inside. She was panting with fatigue. Ty had fallen asleep again. She put the meat over to one side of the cabin and cut it into smaller pieces so she could fry it.

When Ty woke up a few hours later, she told him what she had done. "We're gonna have a steak now. I cut a couple out." She put two pieces of small wood in the stove, and when it got popping she took the two steaks and put them in the large frying pan. They sizzled for a while.

Ty said, "That smells better than anything I've ever eaten."

Indeed it was good. The two of them ate slowly, chewing the tough meat.

"Did you save the liver?" he asked.

"Yes, I did."

"It would make a good soup. The liver is the best part of a deer, I think."

"We'll have that for supper."

They sat there with the odd sensation of being full and not hungry.

"You know we've got enough food here for a couple of weeks if we take it easy," Ty said. His voice was thin, and his weight loss was obvious by the hollows in his cheeks and in his eyes.

"We'll be all right. I think your friend was right."

"He said God was going to get us out of it. I never believed him. I guess I need to now."

They were quiet for a time, and he slept. When he woke up she left him and looked outside. "I've never felt cold like this," Raina said.

"I did once, up north in Michigan. Went up to work as a timberman, but I was no good at it. It got even colder there."

The next three days passed without incident. Raina had found the well and was able to get water from it. She fed the horses and watered them and was glad to see that there was still a bag of feed that would last another week or maybe two on short rations.

The deer had been thin, but she used every bit of it, and they had fresh meat every night.

A couple of days passed, and their supplies were low.

Ty had awakened that morning and taken a deep breath. "My lungs feel good," he said.

"Oh, Ty, that's wonderful."

"Let me get out of this bed and sit up like a human being."

She helped him out of bed, but he didn't really need it. She saw that there were hollows in his throat where he had lost weight. "Our wood's not going to last much longer," she said.

"Well, now that I'm strong we can get out of here. How are the horses?"

"I've kept them on low rations, but they look strong."

"We'll need 'em to get us out of this place."

"I expect so." She had sat down on the floor, soaking up the meager heat the stove threw off. "Do you think God had anything to do with leading us to this place?"

Ty looked at her and said, "We'd be dead if we hadn't found it.

And then that deer coming and the chickens. . . Makes me think God is in some things."

"I think so, too."

The two sat there quietly talking, and he said, "Give me two more days and we can go. As long as no more bad weather comes."

They waited the two days, and the weather was clearer. "We can go now. We'd better take any supplies left, including food for the horses. We should also kill the last chicken and take it. Don't know how long it will take us to get to Baton Rouge."

"Well, the sun's shining. I think God has helped us," Raina said. "I'm thankful that we made it."

Ty suddenly turned and faced her. "You saved my life, Raina. Thank you for that. I hardly think I'm worth saving, but you did it."

Raina felt a warmth. She had learned to trust this man, and in his weakness he had revealed that he was a good man. She had not really doubted it before, but now she knew it beyond any doubt. "I'm glad for both of us."

The sun was shining even brighter as they left. Ty had managed to hitch the horses to the wagon, and they had watered and fed them. As they left the cabin, they got into the wagon, and Ty looked back. He stared at the house and shook his head. "I'll never forget that place, Raina."

"Neither will I. Thank God for that house."

"Amen," Ty said. "I'll say amen to that."

CHAPTER 7

A loud screeching noise brought Raina out of a fitful sleep. She sat straight up in bed and looked around wildly for a moment, then realized the sound came from the street below. The room was cold, but she threw the cover back and dressed in her warmest clothes. As she dressed, she looked down where Ty had slept, and a start of fear ran along her nerves. *What if he's left me?* The thought frightened her more than she had thought it would, for she realized that she was helpless without him. As soon as she was dressed, she began pacing the floor. She was ordinarily able to handle a crisis, but the strain of the storm, the imminence of possibly freezing to death, and the crisis of running away from all she knew to some destiny that she could not even think of—had all worn her down.

Finally she stopped and walked over to the window. The street was muddy, and a man was driving a wagon pulled by four mules. He was striking them steadily and methodically with a whip. She could hear his curses clearly.

She roamed the room restlessly, then finally she walked over to her baggage and pulled out a copy of one of the romances she loved so dearly. She had read it at least five times, but she found some sort of comfort in pulling the blankets off the bed, wrapping them around her, and reading the story again. It was a story she loved about a young girl who was pursued by an evil man. She snuggled deeper into the cocoon she had made out of blankets, and as always, she was able to turn her mind away from the immediate and very real problems into the world of fiction.

I read too much, and I know these stories aren't true, she thought. *But it gives me some sort of pleasure. I don't see anything wrong with it.* Her sister had criticized her endlessly about reading what she called *trash*, but Raina had paid her no mind at all.

She was so deeply engrossed in the story she paid little heed to the footsteps, for it was apparently busy in the hallway. But then she heard the two knocks, a hesitation, then three knocks. She came out of the chair quickly, throwing the blankets back on the bed, and tossed the book back into the box she had taken it from.

She got to the door, unlocked it, and opening it, she stepped back. She had no idea what to say to Ty. He looked tired, and the sickness had worn him down. He had not shaved so he looked scraggly and rough. "Come in," she said. "But it's cold in here."

"Well, we'll be leaving anyway." Ty stepped inside, glanced at the bed for a moment then back to her. "We're going on. We're not too far from the Mississippi River. There's a little town on the bank there. We can sell the wagon and the team, and we'll take the boat up to where the Arkansas feeds into the big river."

"What if somebody hears about us and recognizes us?"

"They'll be looking for a couple. I'll get the tickets, and I'll go in by myself. There's always a lot of activity on those boats when they pull out. People leaving, others hurrying on. You just hide yourself in there. The cabin is room number 206."

"Do you really think that we'll be safe?"

"I think so. When you get in the cabin, I'll get some food and bring it to you. We won't be seen together."

"All right, Ty," she said timidly. "You've done well."

"We'll be all right," he said finally. He shrugged his shoulders. "I'll carry your stuff down to the wagon."

Thirty minutes later they were eating a breakfast of ham and eggs and homemade bread in the single restaurant the town possessed. After they finished their meal, they went outside. She climbed into the wagon, and he mounted to sit beside her.

He picked up the lines, slapped the horses' backs, and the team at once lurched forward. "If I got it right, we ought to be at the river sometime before noon."

Raina said quietly, "It's been hard on you. You're not fully recovered yet with that sickness you had."

"I'm all right."

They stopped once to rest the horses and then proceeded at an even pace. When they reached the river town, Raina saw it was even worse than the one where they had spent the night.

He nodded toward a small steamboat tied up at the wharf. "That's the ship, I expect. I'll go find out about the rooms. You stay here in the wagon."

"All right, Ty."

Raina sat in the wagon watching him move away. He was moving slowly, and she knew that he had lost some of the vitality that she had first noticed in him. Sickness would do that. The fever had drained him, but he doggedly moved forward.

He was back in thirty minutes. He said, "I'll show you the rooms up on the second deck. When you get in there, I'll bring you food."

"Thank you, Ty."

He hesitated, then for the first time that morning lifted his eyes and stared at her. "You won't have to worry about me bothering you again, Raina."

Raina was on the verge of apologizing, but his manner was so stiff she could only say, "Thank you, Ty."

"Almost time for the boat to leave, Raina," Ty said. He had sold the wagon and the mules and bought a trunk that could carry more of their things in it. He stood beside it now down on the wharf and said, "I don't think there's any danger. We'll go on together."

"All right."

She was relieved when he picked up the trunk. She carried the valise. She had to struggle to get up to the second deck, but when they got to the room and he shoved the door open, he stepped back and let her go in first.

It wasn't much of a room, but the ship was rough and years past its youth. It might have been finely finished at one time, but now everything looked worn and pitiful.

Putting the trunk down, he said, "We'll be leaving right away. Maybe you ought to stay in here until I come for you."

"I will."

"There's a lock on the door. Don't let anybody come in until I knock like I did before. We'll go eat after we're under way."

"Where will you sleep?"

"There was an extra room. Somebody canceled their trip."

The trip up the Mississippi had been tense at first. Raina had been terrified that they would be caught, that Farmer had put arrest papers out on them. But the boat was small, the passengers were few, and nobody paid attention to them. They had their breakfast, the noon meal, and then there was nothing to do.

Ty stayed on deck mostly, up in the bow looking ahead, his eyes searching the banks. She could not tell what he was thinking, but she was low-spirited.

The boat stopped several times as it went up the Mississippi, taking on passengers and letting off some. The tension left her as she became less and less worried about getting caught.

Most of the time she read one of her romance novels. She stayed for long hours in the room and from time to time would take a break.

Once Ty had come to get her in the middle of the afternoon and said, "The cook's just made some fresh donuts. Let's go treat ourselves."

"That sounds good. I always love donuts." The two left the cabin and walked down to the kitchen.

The cook, a fat, greasy-looking man with a broad smile, winked at them. "You smell them donuts, do ya?"

"I can resist anything except temptation and fresh donuts." Ty smiled.

"Well, here. Sink your teeth into one of these, and you, too, ma'am. I'll have to tell ya I'm renowned for my donuts."

Raina bit into the donut. "These are so good!"

"My ma taught me how to make donuts. Never thought I'd

wind up bein' a cook, but there are worse things to be."

They ate two of the donuts apiece with fresh coffee, then she said, "I think I'll go up to the front."

"Pretty cold still. That breeze is stiff."

"I don't mind."

Ty followed Raina as she moved toward the bow. He watched as she put her hands on the railing and stared out at the broad Mississippi.

She stood for a long time. The breeze was cold, and she shivered a little.

He said, "You ought to wear a heavier coat."

"It's all right. I don't mind. It's good to be out here."

They stood together, and from time to time one of them would notice something on the bank. Mostly it was nothing but forest and cotton fields right up to the river itself. "Mighty flat country," Ty said. "I always liked to see hills and mountains."

"I've never really seen any big ones."

"You'll see some up around Fort Smith. That's Ozark country up there. Some of it's right pretty. Oklahoma's got pretty things and ugly things."

Raina was quick to ask what he was expecting next.

"The next thing is we'll get off this boat and find a smaller one going up the Arkansas."

"Does it go all the way to Fort Smith?"

"Well, there will probably be some stops, but yes, pretty well. What will you do when we reach Fort Smith, Raina?"

"I'm going to look for my father."

He turned to study her face in the growing dusk and was once again impressed with the qualities he saw in her. Her hair was raven black, but her eyes were blue and made a pleasing contrast. She was, as far as he knew, as thoroughly alone in the world as if there were no other thing alive on the planet. He knew she was hungry for color and warmth, and he had seen the solace she seemed to take from her romances. Here in the falling darkness a spirit glowed in her like live coals, but as always, she was on guard.

She looked at him silently, and a woman's silence could mean many things, Ty knew. He was not sure what it meant in Raina, but it lay on his own solitary thinking. When she drew away, there was a curtain of reserve, and he suddenly felt that she was the kind of woman who could, if necessary, draw a revolver and shoot a man down and not go to pieces afterward. He had seen her courage and willingness to face danger, and he knew that she had a temper that could swing to extremes of laughter and then turn instantly to softness or anger.

He could not help but appreciate the supple lines of her body. She was just past the stage that follows girlhood, and he realized, for all her youth, she was a beautiful and robust woman with a woman's soft depth and a woman's spirit and a woman's fire. "What if you find your dad and he's not a good man?"

"I don't know. I don't have any other plan."

"Well, I guess we better turn in." Raina nodded in agreement, and Ty escorted her to her room before going to his own.

A restlessness settled over Ty. He finally left his room and moved toward Raina's. Seeing a light through the crack at the bottom of her door, he knocked.

Raina opened the door slightly. "What is it, Ty?"

"I couldn't go to sleep and wanted some company. But if you

want to go to bed, I'll leave you alone."

"No, that's all right. Come on in."

Ty entered the room. He saw that Raina had been reading one of her books and asked her about it.

She began to tell him the plot. He got lost in her words and in the way her eyes lit up when she talked about one of her stories.

Ty saw that she was only wearing a thin robe over her nightgown. The beauty that he had ignored struck him hard, like a raw force. She was looking up at him, her lips slightly opened. Ty had been under pressure for a long time, and now as Raina smiled, he felt a sudden gust of freedom. He was aware of his vow to this young woman, and it had not been difficult to keep himself from even thinking of her as a woman—but now as the desires of a lonely man drew him to beauty, he suddenly felt a sense of joy.

He made no conscious decision, but without thinking he reached for her with a suddenness that caught them both by surprise. Her firm body came against him, and old hungers awoke with a force that shocked him. He lowered his head and kissed her, again without thought, and at that moment she was for him like cool water to a thirsty man.

Raina surrendered herself to Ty's sudden embrace too easily. She was a woman of strong emotions, but a hard life had forced her to keep them under iron control. Now, however, as his lips pressed against hers, she was aware of a passion that shook her. She had longed for love from a man, and the long hours she had spent caring for Ty had gone deeper into her spirit than she had suspected.

Perhaps if Ty had released her at once, the kiss would not have struck Raina so hard. It might even have been a moment for her to treasure, for even in that instant she sensed in his caress something different from the crude advances that she had spent a lifetime avoiding.

Then she felt a flash of anger—mixed with disappointment—and her self-defense flared. He was a strong man, and she was alone and in his power, just the kind of situation she'd learned to avoid. She struck Ty in the chest and cried out, "Leave me alone!"

Ty was shocked and started to respond. "Raina. . ."

Raina was shaking, and her emotions were a mixture of fear and loathing. He tried to explain, but she was beyond listening and moved away from him until her back was against the bulkhead as she cried, "You're no different from all other men, Tyler Kincaid!"

Ty said, "Raina, it was just a kiss. Nothing more."

She crossed her arms in a defensive gesture, and her tone was hard as steel. "I've heard that before."

Ty stared at her for some time with a sad look on his face. Then he lowered his head and said flatly, "I'll see you tomorrow, Raina."

Raina saw the determined look on Ty's face as he turned and left the room. She began to tremble and paced the floor for a time before finally getting into bed.

She lay awake, unable to forget the encounter with Ty. She had a fleeting thought that maybe she'd misjudged him, but her old defenses returned in strength. *He's just like the others!* She finally fell into a fitful sleep with the sense that her future lay before her like a black tunnel whose end she could not see.

Raina woke with a start, and at once the incident with Ty flooded her mind. *I'm all alone now!* She knew that she and Ty had lost something, and the sense of loss was sharp.

She shook off the depressing thoughts, then rose and dressed. She was startled by a knock at the door.

It was Ty, but the sight of him was troubling. His features were stern. "We have to have breakfast," he said, his voice revealing nothing.

Raina hesitated and said, "I'm sorry I spoke to you so sharply last night, Ty."

"The fault was mine, not yours. It won't happen again." His voice was flat.

Raina went with him to the dining room, and the meal was a misery for her. Ty didn't speak, and it was all she could do to swallow the food. When they rose, Raina followed him, hoping they could talk, but the glance she got of his features convinced her that they were now two strangers with nothing to say to one another.

"We're there, Raina."

Raina was in the stateroom. She heard Ty's knock and opened the door at once. "Do we get off now?"

"Well, we'll get our things together. It won't be long."

"Here. Take the money."

"No, you keep it. You'll have to find a place to live."

After they had packed their few belongings, Ty carried the trunk up and they moved their baggage. Finally they sidled into a wharf, and a plank board was let down. He shouldered the trunk, and she followed him off the boat.

When they got on land, he put it down and turned to face her. "We'll have to find you a place to live."

"I have to thank you."

"No, I'm in your debt. I'd have been in prison if it hadn't been for you." He hesitated and pulled off his hat and ran his hand through his coarse black hair. His face looked rough, but she had learned that the roughness was all in the outer man. "I'll be around, Raina. If you need me, let me know."

"That's good of you, Ty. But I hope I don't have to call on anyone."

"Come on. I'll carry your trunk."

It did not take long to find housing for there were several boardinghouses. The first three had no rooms, but at the fourth one, the landlady had two available. Raina chose one.

When he carried her trunk upstairs, he took his hat off and said, "I'll be going."

She hesitated then put out her hand.

He was surprised but took it.

She was aware of the bluntness and the strength of his grip. "Good-bye, Ty."

Ty was shocked at her gesture, but he said, "We'll be seeing each other."

Raina watched as he turned and left the room. She felt a sense of loneliness. He had been her hope of protection, and now he was gone, forever, she was convinced.

She went to the window and saw him walk away. Suddenly she was filled with a sense of loss and was terrified at what lay before her.

PART TWO

CHAPTER 8

Raina awoke when the storm that had been threatening the day before finally broke. A boom of thunder brought her awake, grasping at the bed covering as if for safety. She was very afraid, and for a moment could not think where she was. Finally a drum of thunder came to her.

She got up and walked to the window. The sky was very dark, and the wind was blowing hard. She stood looking out while the thunder clapped loudly and sharply and reverberated endlessly, rolling off into the distance. She wanted to go back to bed, for the weather had turned cold, but she knew she would not sleep through the storm.

She looked out the window and blinked as the lightning forked in the sky. It seemed to grab at the ground and burn and leap upward, crackling. While the thunder boomed and struck her ears, the bright streak blinded her eyes. Then the rain started, a few drops and then increasing as if someone had poured a huge bucket of water over the town.

Finally Raina went back to bed and managed to sleep until dawn. She got up, shivered, and quickly put on the warmest clothes she had. When she was fully dressed, she went to the window and stared out.

On the damp ground a flight of sparrows were searching for food. Taking a piece of a sandwich that she had had the night before, she tossed it out. Immediately the birds began to fight over it, and she remembered a romance she had read and a character who had said, "Birds in their nest agree, so why can't we?" And through her mind came the thought, *No, no, even birds have fights.*

She lit the lamp. The room was dark with the one tiny window. The yellow blaze, small as it was, cast its glow on the darkness of the room. She went to the washstand and discovered that there was a film of ice on the water in the pitcher. She broke it with her fist and poured the basin half full. She forced herself to wash in the cold water, then she looked up and saw that her hair was not as neat as she usually kept it.

She thought of a set of mother-of-pearl combs and a brush that had been her mother's—and hers. It was all she'd had of her mother's, and she felt the loss of it. She had misplaced them or someone had taken them. In any case, it was one of the many things that she had lost, and it made her sad. She felt dirty. Her clothes were filthy. She always hated that, but there was no other choice.

When she was fully dressed she sat down on the bed, and fear swept over her like waves. She thought abruptly of Ty and was disturbed to find that she missed him. She couldn't help but think of their time in the cabin and how they had been so close.

Then another thought came to her of the time he had kissed her and how she had lashed out at him. *I wish I could do it over again. He wasn't that bad. It was my foolishness.*

She tried to brush the thoughts away but had little success. Finally she stood and gave up on her hair. She took one more look out the window and saw that the morning was white with frost. The trees outside stood stiffly as if reaching for something they could not have, and some of the roofs were lightly quilted with frost. At that same moment the wind began to utter a long, low whine from the eaves of the building, and tiny flakes of snow began to dance before her eyes. This disturbed her, so quickly she went downstairs to the kitchen.

Mrs. Mullins, the lady who owned the house, said, "You're just in time for breakfast. I've got some biscuits made."

"Oh, I can fix my own breakfast, Mrs. Mullins."

"That would be a help."

Raina found a basket full of eggs, and being hungrier than usual took two of them and three slices of thick bacon. She turned the bacon over until it was well done and then made her eggs over lightly. There was a jar of some sort of jelly on the table, rather dark. She tried it and found that it was delicious. "This is good fig preserves."

Mrs. Mullins was a large woman with lines of fatigue in her face from running a boardinghouse. "My husband planted that tree. We always had a good crop of figs." She made a face and shook her head. "It was the only thing he could ever do well. No farmer at all." She poured herself a cup of coffee and filled Raina's cup again. "Have you come far?"

"Yes, pretty much."

"Well, you picked bad weather to travel in. You got business in Fort Smith?"

"One thing I have to do is find my father. I'll show you a picture of him. I only have one. His name is Ed Vernay."

"Well, I don't believe I know the man, but you can ask around and somebody's probably heard of him around here. He's in this part of the world, you say?"

"The last I heard—which has been quite awhile ago."

"Well, are you going to stay here long?"

"I don't have much money."

"Well, there's a Chinese man here who does washing. Your clothes probably need it after that long travel."

"Oh, I couldn't afford to hire somebody."

"Why, you can use my tubs. You'll have to heat the water on the stove before I start cooking lunch."

"Thank you, Mrs. Mullins." The kindness of the woman pleased her, and she spent the next hour heating water and washing all of her clothes. She asked Mrs. Mullins if she could hang them close to the fire.

She said, "For the next hour you can, then I have to start cooking dinner."

After she washed her clothes, she borrowed Mrs. Mullins's iron and pressed them.

Two of her boarders came in, rough-looking men, and one of them winked at the other one and said, "Hey, sweetie, how about you and me goin' out tonight?"

Mrs. Mullins entered as he spoke and said, "That's enough out of you, Bill. Leave this lady alone."

Both of the men laughed, not at all intimidated. "We'll be

back. We'll work on that goin' out together."

When the two men left, Raina said, "Thank you for taking up for me."

"Well, what are you aiming to do now?"

"Well, I'll start trying to find my father."

"How will you do that?"

Raina suddenly realized she had no idea about how to find a man who had disappeared from her own life years before. "I don't know," she said. "I'll just have to start asking around."

"That won't be easy," Mrs. Mullins said. "People comin' and goin' here all the time. Most of 'em is trash and wouldn't help you unless there was money in it for them."

"I don't have enough money for a reward."

"I didn't reckon so. Just didn't want you to get your hopes up."

Raina shook her head. "I don't have much hope, but I have to try to find my dad. I don't have anyone else."

"Sad to have no folks."

"Do you have a family, Mrs. Mullins?"

"Me and my man had five children—but two of them died and the others went off."

"You don't know where they are?"

"No, I wished I did."

The two talked for a while, and then Mrs. Mullins said, "You ort to go to the hanging."

"A hanging? Why would I go there?"

"Why, you might see your pa there."

It was a thought that never would have occurred to Raina, but she decided at once that she would go. *I might not know him if I saw him. All I have is this one picture, and he's a lot older now.* She got her coat and left the boardinghouse.

The flakes of snow had fallen enough to whiten the ground. As Raina walked down the main street of Fort Smith, she was not overly impressed. It was not a beautiful town. The main street had businesses on both sides, usually in framed buildings, many of them unpainted. The bank itself was made out of brick, as was the courthouse, but aside from them, the buildings were mostly warping lumber.

She had almost reached the end of the street, and she saw a crowd had gathered. They were talking loudly. She went closer to watch.

A woman stood next to her. She was wearing a scanty-looking dress and over it a coat not fastened in the front. The woman turned to her. She had a hard look about her. Her early beauty had faded. "Do you know the fellow?"

"What fellow?"

"The one being hanged."

"No, I'm new to town. Who is he?"

"Mack Wilford. He killed his wife and her cousin and a marshal who came to arrest him. Ought to be a good one. Mack's a tough man." She laughed shrilly and said, "We'll see how tough he is with a rope around his neck."

Raina had nothing to say to this. She had never seen a hanging and suddenly had an impulse to leave, but for some reason she stood in place waiting to see what would happen.

"My name's Alice."

"I'm Raina."

"So you're new around here. . . ."

"Yes, I just got in town yesterday. I'm looking for my father.

I've lost touch with him, but I know he's somewhere here in the territory." She reached down in her reticule and pulled out the picture. "This is him. You ever see him?"

"Nope," Alice said, "but to a dance hall girl, all men look alike—" She broke off suddenly and glanced up. "Look, there's the judge."

Raina looked up and saw a dignified-looking man standing in the second-story window. The window was up, and he ignored the cold weather.

"Who's that?"

"That's Judge Parker. They call him the Hanging Judge."

"Don't all judges hang people from time to time?"

"Not as many as Parker. He never misses a hanging. He must have hanged forty men. How do you think a man would feel if he hanged forty men?"

"Pretty bad I would imagine."

"Look, there's Jack Maledon."

"Who's Maledon?" Raina asked.

"He's the hangman. See, he's got that rope. He went all the way to Saint Louis to get the rope he uses to hang men. He's very fussy about his job."

Maledon was a small man with a large, long-pointed beard. His eyes were a cold gray, and he appeared to be completely uninterested in what was going on.

"He tries to pretend he don't like it, but he does. One time they hanged six men all at the same time. They made quite a racket when they pulled the trapdoor. See that scaffold there? They can hang as many as eight men at once. I doubt if there's another gallows like that in the whole country."

"I don't see how a man could live with himself knowing he had hanged men like that."

Alice laughed again, her voice shrill and yet without humor. "Can you imagine when he goes home and his wife says, 'How was your day, Jack?' 'Oh,' Jack would say, 'I only hung two. Not a very good day.'"

"Look, that must be the man they're going to hang."

Everyone in the crowd began to murmur as a man came out. His hands were tied behind his back, and he was kicking and cursing at the two jailers who dragged him out.

One of them said loudly enough to be heard, "Now Mack, be nice."

"Be nice nothin'!" Mack Wilford cursed the jailers, Maledon, the judge, and the people who were watching. He was practically dragged up the stairs and held in place.

Maledon came forward with a hangman's noose in his hand, pulled a black mask over Wilford's face, and then adjusted the rope.

"I often wonder why they do that," Alice said. "What don't they want 'em to see?"

Raina watched in horror as Maledon tightened the noose so that it was just under the man's left ear. He stepped back then and without warning pulled the switch. The trapdoor opened beneath Wilford's feet. He shot downward, and she heard plainly the snapping of his neck.

"Well, he was a tough one," Alice said. "Some of them faint."

The execution sickened Raina. She turned to leave.

Alice said, "You go see the judge. He knows lots of people. He may know where your pa is."

"Thank you, Alice." Raina left and made her way to the courthouse. The crowd was dispersing. She walked in and asked a man who was also entering, "Where would I find Judge Parker's office?"

The man was not imposing. He had a pair of direct blue eyes and a mustache and a big pistol on his side. "Well, it's upstairs, but you won't be able to see him now. He's behind with his court. You can try later."

"Do you know him?"

"Yes, ma'am. My name's Heck Thomas. I'm the chief marshal."

"I'm here looking for my father. Would you look at this picture to see if you've seen him?"

Heck waited while she pulled out the photograph, and he stared at it. "No ma'am, I don't recognize him, but that don't mean I ain't seen him. There are so many folks here, and I see lots of 'em. If I see a face on a Wanted poster, I don't forget it, but I don't recollect your pa. You got any copies of this picture?"

"No, I don't."

"There's a picture man here. Takes portraits, you know. He could probably make some copies. You could pass 'em around. I got a hundred and fifty marshals, and they see lots of folks."

"Could I see the judge later?"

"I 'spect so. He's a mighty polite man, and he'll help you if he can. What's your name, miss?"

"Raina Vernay."

"Right pretty name, Miss Vernay. You come on back. I'll mention it to the judge."

"Thank you, Mr. Thomas."

Raina made her way back to the boardinghouse, not knowing what else to do.

Mrs. Mullins had a harried look. "My helper is sick and will not be able to assist me for a while. Can't pay much, but if you want to help me with the cooking, you can get your meal and fix up a storage room in the attic. That is, if you'll help me with the cooking and maybe some cleaning."

"I'll be glad to do that." The work did not sound terribly hard, and Raina was a fine cook. She peeled the potatoes and baked the bread.

That night, Mrs. Mullins, whose first name was Emma, said with satisfaction, "You'll do real well, Raina."

Later Raina served the table. There were eight men there. One man, about as rude and dirty as a man can get, made a remark equally rude.

Emma Mullins said, "Jack, if you can't be decent, you can get out and find someplace else to stay."

"Didn't mean nothin', Emma."

Mrs. Mullins said, "Miss Raina, show 'em your pa's picture."

Instantly she went to get her bag, got the picture, and passed it around. They all examined it but said they didn't know him.

The lack of response dampened her spirit. She helped Emma clean up.

The old woman then took her upstairs to the attic. The room was small, but it did have a window. It had a bed but lots of junk. "This is a catchall. I've got another place you can store all this stuff. You might make it fairly presentable. You'll need some bedding though. I can fix you up with that."

"Thank you, Emma. I appreciate your help. I feel kind of lonesome here. No people, no friends."

"Oh, you'll make lots of friends. These men are great at makin' friends with pretty women," she said sarcastically.

For most of the next day, Raina did her best with the room. It was indeed dirty and full of dust, and by the time she had moved out all of the extra stuff, washed the window, swept the floor, beaten out the rug that covered part of it, moved in her things, and fixed the bed, she was tired.

The room was cold so she put on her warmest clothes, lit the lantern by the bed, and then picked up one of the romances she had brought with her. She got in the bed and pulled the blankets over her and read the old romance again.

Finally it was time to go help Mrs. Mullins. She got up and went downstairs. She peeled potatoes, fried ham, shelled peas, and made coffee.

At the meal, the men were pretty much the same except there were two new faces. She showed them her father's picture, but neither of them had seen him.

After the meal was over and she had helped Emma with the dishes, she said, "I'm tired. I think I'll go to bed."

"Why don't you have some coffee before you go. It'll warm you up."

"Thank you, Emma." She drank the coffee, chatting with Mrs. Mullins.

She then went upstairs and, not bothering to undress, simply pulled off her shoes and got under the covers. She read some more of the novel but found it strangely unsatisfying this time. She realized she was longing for a real romance, one that provided more than those she read about in the pages of her books.

CHAPTER 9

A fly crawled across Ty's face, and he slapped at it unconsciously. The straw that he had slept in fitfully all night exuded a rank odor. Slowly Ty brushed his hand across his face and then opened his eyes to see the sunlight coming through a crack in the roof, putting a bar of yellow illumination on the livery stable.

Slowly he rose up to a sitting position, reached over his head, and stretched his muscles. The straw had been better than sleeping on the floor, but not a great deal. The lack of a bath troubled him, and he reached up and tried to scratch between his shoulder blades but did so ineffectually.

He got to his feet noting that his wardrobe was sparse. His jeans were worn and patched over the left knee, white with many washings. He dusted himself off as best he could.

Reaching into his pocket, he found a dollar and twenty-seven cents. He stared at the money as if by observing it he could make it multiply itself, then shook his head dolefully and stuck it back in his pocket. He took off his shirt and shook it violently, getting the straw and the dust out of it. He put it back on and buttoned it. Then he picked up his coat and shrugged it on. It had been an expensive coat at one time, but that was many years ago. Now it was merely shabby and did little to cut out the cold. His hat was hanging from a nail in the rafters, and he plucked it off and jammed it on over his head. Slowly he left, and not seeing anybody in charge of the livery stable, he filed it in his mind that he might have to come back and spend another miserable night in the straw.

He walked along the boardwalk, noting that the town was only gradually coming to life. A few stores were now opening up, and glancing up, Ty saw that a darkness lingered beneath the stars.

He moved slowly and noticed the sun was just beginning to glow in the eastern sky. He passed by some birds that were noisy with a wild joy, twittering and calling. They were not yet singing but ecstatically greeting the day.

Sunlight soon ran fresh and fine throughout the town, flashing against the windowpanes and cutting long, sharp shadows against the dusty velvety carpet. "Going to be cold today," Ty muttered, but it was not a complaint. He had expected no less.

He reached a café and was glad to see that it was open. When he entered, he saw that he was the only customer. He sat down at one of the tables covered with a dingy red-and-white-checked tablecloth.

A woman came over. She was past her prime but still attractive, somewhat overweight but with a figure that drew men's eyes. "What'll you have, hon?"

"I guess bacon and eggs, if you have it."

"Sure do and some fresh biscuits, and how about some coffee?"

"That sounds good to me."

"Be right back." He watched as she left, swaying in a practiced gait that she had obviously assumed would attract men's attention.

As soon as she disappeared through a swinging door, Ty leaned back and closed his eyes. The night had been fitful, and he had slept little. Now he felt the grim arm of weariness and despondency drawing him in. He was not a man who gave in easily to such things, and finally he put the matter out of his mind. *I'll get out of this somehow,* he thought. *I always do.*

Ten minutes later the woman brought out a platter of eggs and bacon and a cup of coffee. "I'll get your biscuits, hon."

"Thanks. That will be just fine." He began to eat slowly.

When she brought the biscuits, she had a chunk of butter on a saucer. "This is fresh butter. Just put some of that on them biscuits, and I'll bring you some jelly to go with it. Blackberry jelly, I think."

"That would go down real well."

She turned to leave, then stopped to turn and face him. She flirted with him wantonly. Ty knew that she was one of the many women he had met who outlasted their first flush of beauty and began to degenerate.

He answered, but mostly he paid attention to the food. He ate slowly, chewing as well as he could, and he did find that the biscuits with the blackberry jelly and butter were as good as any he had ever had. When he had finished, he asked, "What do I owe you?"

"Seventy-five cents, I guess."

He put a dollar down, smiled at her, and nodded. "Mighty good food," he said.

"I get off at six o'clock."

"Maybe I'll see you then."

"I hope so, hon."

Leaving the café, Ty walked down the plank boardwalk. The earth began to warm up, not a great deal, but it was better than the coldness of the livery stable. He was thinking about what to do next when he saw a man wearing a star leaning back against the wall of a two-story building. Glancing up, he saw the sign said CITY HALL. Slowing down, he walked over and said, "Howdy."

"Hi there. Gonna be warmer I reckon today."

"I'm new in town. Come a long way. I'd like to be one of Judge Parker's marshals."

"I'm Frank Dillinger. I'm one of the marshals." A gloominess occupied the man and marked his face with a doleful expression. "You better think on that."

"Why had I better do that?"

"Why, it's a dangerous line of work." Dillinger reached into his pocket, pulled out a plug, took a bite, and stared at the remains joylessly. "Mighty dangerous work. The judge used to have two hundred marshals. Over fifty of 'em have been killed. Dangerous line of work."

"Well, I guess I'm ready for that."

"Your choice." Dillinger shrugged. "The judge's always lookin' to hire more marshals but can't find many who can do the job."

"What kind of qualifications is he looking for?" Ty smiled.

"Somebody that's tough. I guess that's the biggest thing. Bein' smart don't help a lot. Got to be tough to be a marshal these days. Just last week there was two of our men got waylaid and shot not ten miles out of town. They never even seen the killer, I reckon. Nobody knows why they was killed, but you make enemies in this line of work."

"Well, I'd like to see the judge."

"Guess you'd better wait until after the hanging. He's in a bad mood on hanging days."

"What time will the hanging be?"

"I think this one will be at ten o'clock. You'll see the judge standing up in that second-story window. He never misses a hanging."

"Pretty hard man?"

"Hard as you ever seen. I guess I'd feel kind of jumpy myself if I'd hanged forty men. I wonder what he thinks about at night. . . ."

"Probably about the next forty men." Ty walked away from the courthouse and stopped long enough to take a free cup of coffee from the blacksmith's shop. He was watching the blacksmith shoe a fine black stallion, and he commented, "I never could do that. It takes a special man to be a blacksmith."

Tim Carver, the blacksmith, was a bulky middle-aged man. He grinned and said, "You've got to have not much sense and tough muscles. That's about it."

The two fell into a conversation about the art of shoeing a horse. A crowd began gathering.

"It looks like that hanging is about ready to take place," the blacksmith said. "Sure hate to see it."

"Do you watch 'em?"

"No sir, not me! I got bad enough dreams without some of them comin' into it. Most people do though."

The blacksmith was correct, because by the time ten o'clock rolled around, a large crowd was gathered around the gallows.

Ty had no interest in seeing a hanging. He had seen two and had not liked either one—but he was shocked to see Raina. She was standing back in the crowd. His eyes fell on her, but he didn't move toward her.

He was aware that a man had moved in beside him and turned to see a well-built individual wearing a gray suit and a fancy checkered vest. "You new in town?" He had a pair of intense gray eyes and was watching Ty carefully.

"Just got in."

"I'm Sid Driver. I own the Lucky Star Saloon. Come on over and try your luck."

"No, I won't be doin' that. I'm flat broke."

"You lookin' for work?"

"I'm hoping to get a marshal's badge."

Driver shook his head. "Better you than me. Lots of danger and low pay. But come in when you can afford to lose a dollar or two."

"I may do that."

The hanging had been perfunctory. One of them was already dead, and the one who did the shooting was soon dead at the end of a rope.

Looking up, Ty saw Judge Parker staring down. *I wonder what a man thinks that's killed forty men with a rope. Not for me.* He made his way back to the courthouse and found another man he had not seen before.

He was a small man, a careless dresser, with intense blue eyes and light brown hair. "Howdy," he said. "What can I do for you?"

"I'd like to see the judge if I can. I'd like to get on as one of his marshals."

"I don't think you'll have much luck right now. The judge always gets behind on hangin' days. Come back though about maybe three o'clock in the afternoon, and you can see him."

"My name's Ty Kincaid."

"Heck Thomas. Glad to know you, Kincaid. You just get into town?"

"Yes, sure did."

"You ever done any law work?"

"A little bit. I soldiered some. I was a deputy in Texas. Can't say I was the best they had, but I did my job."

Thomas grinned and sent a stream of tobacco juice to the floor. "Wal, that's all a mule can do, ain't it?"

"Guess that's right."

"Well, come on back around three o'clock."

Having nothing to do for the rest of the day, Ty Kincaid went into the Lucky Star. He had enough for one beer, and he nursed it along.

The bartender wiped in front of him and said, "Have one of them sandwiches."

"Thanks. I believe I will."

The sandwich was good, and Ty ate two of them. He was finishing the second one when a woman came over.

"Hello, I'm Marie."

"Sorry, Marie, I'm broke."

"Well, that's too bad."

At that instant a big, rough-looking man came over and took Marie's arm. She cried out.

Ty could never stand to see a woman mistreated. He put the stein of beer down and turned to face the big man. "Turn loose of her arm and be on your way."

Somebody said, "You better look out. That's Hal Carson."

"I don't care who he is," Ty said lightly. He stood with his feet slightly apart, ready for anything Carson might offer.

He looked like a drunk and had been drinking, but he had a neck as thick as any that Ty had ever seen. He sneered at Ty and squeezed the woman's arm.

Ty reached out and struck him in the throat.

Carson backed up coughing and gagging, but he came back ready for a fight.

Ty didn't need any more bruises or cuts. He pulled his gun with a lightning draw and hit Carson over the head.

When the man went down, his head split. Finally he crawled to his feet, blood running down both sides of his nose.

Ty said, "You can either leave or I'll shoot your knee off and you can crawl around for the rest of your life."

Sid Driver had come over at that moment. "You better move on, Hal. Maybe you can come back later."

Carson wiped the blood off his face, smearing it and making a worse mess. "You won't always have that gun," he gasped.

"I'll always have the gun, Hal. I sleep with it."

As Carson walked away, Sid said, "You better watch out. He's a pretty mean fellow. He'll try again."

"He'd better not."

Marie had not moved. She was rubbing her arm and said, "Thanks. I'll buy you a drink."

"Drinks on the house for you two." Sid smiled.

Ty refused the offered drink as it was almost time to meet the judge.

Sid walked back to his table, and Ty heard him say to his bouncer, "Pretty fast, isn't he, Jack?"

Jack shook his head. "I ain't seen a draw that fast since Slinger Dunn went down. He could have stopped Carson's clock real easy."

Ty grinned as he left the Lucky Star to go meet with the judge. He was back at the courthouse by three o'clock as Heck Thomas had suggested.

Heck immediately motioned for Ty to follow him. Heck led Ty up to Parker's office on the second floor and without knocking opened the door.

Ty could see from the door that the judge looked tired. It was well known that he took his cases seriously, and after a hanging he was always in bad spirits.

"A fellow wants to see you, Judge," Heck began.

"I'm too tired. What does he want?"

"Wants to be a marshal."

Judge Isaac Parker was a tall man, well built, with an aristocratic face. He had served as a lawyer and as a judge. He was now in Indian Territory as appointed by the government, and his rule was law. He had lost many men. It was a rough and dangerous world he sent them out into. "Well, what does he look like?"

"Well, he roughed up Hal Carson. That ought to count for somethin'."

Ty was surprised Heck had already heard about his confrontation in the Lucky Star. He was also embarrassed by the chief marshal's praise.

"Send him in, Heck."

Heck motioned for Ty to enter. "Come on. The judge will see you."

Ty walked through the door with Parker's name on it.

Judge Parker said at once, "I understand you want to apply for a job a marshal."

"My name's Ty Kincaid, Judge Parker. I guess that's right."

"Well, you realize it ain't like sellin' peanuts at a circus."

The judge's rough attempt at humor amused Ty. "I never thought it was. I know you lose men."

"Tell me why I should hire you."

"Well, I served as a peace officer in Fort Worth, Texas, quite some time ago. I reckon the sheriff there would give me a recommendation if you wrote him a letter."

"So you've done some law work."

"Yes, a little."

"What else?"

"Well, to be honest, I should tell you that I worked for a time in Mexico and was arrested falsely for being a revolutionist. I escaped with the help of a friend and ended up in Louisiana, where I was taken to jail by a sheriff who recognized me from a Wanted poster. I escaped from there, too, and made my way here. I know you can have me put in jail right now, but I really want to serve as a marshal. I promise to uphold the law the best I can."

The judge stroked his chin. "I thought I recognized your name. I heard a wanted man was on the loose named Ty Kincaid. Well, I can take care of that if I decide to hire you." Parker remained silent as he sat thinking. "All right. I'm gonna take you on tentatively until I hear from the sheriff you worked for and check into that Mexico business. What's his name?"

"Bud Zeller."

"Why, I know Bud. If he'll recommend you, that's all I need. I hate to write letters. You give me your word that this is the truth?"

"No need to lie, Judge."

Heck had come in and picked up on the last of this. "I expect you're broke. I've got a spare bed at my place. You can bunk there until you get a payday."

"Thanks, Judge. And I'll take you up on that, Heck."

He followed Heck out the door, and they went down the street and turned the corner. Heck paused in front of a small house and said, "I'll expect you to help with the expenses when you get paid." He unlocked the door and walked inside. "There are two bedrooms. You can take the one over there. It's got a stove. Can you cook?"

"Ham and eggs."

"That's about my speed, too. I get most of my meals from the Chinese. They're the best cooks." He turned and stared at Ty carefully. He was obviously accustomed to judging men in his line of work. "You ever kilt a man, Kincaid?"

"Yes."

"How'd it feel?"

"Not good."

Heck grinned and shook his head. "You get used to it riding for the judge. Here. I'm giving you twenty dollars out of my pocket. You can give it back when you get paid. Go buy some better clothes. You look like a bum."

"I'll do that."

Ty was leaving when he ran into two more marshals. One of them introduced himself as Larry Dolby. He was a tall man in his midthirties with blond hair and faded blue eyes. He introduced his companion as Gale Young. He was ironically a younger man in his early twenties.

"We're happy to know you. Didn't get your name."

"Ty Kincaid."

"Well, I'm glad you're here," Young said.

"Why's that?"

Young grinned. "Now I ain't the newest man around here. You are."

"You better watch out for this fellow," Dolby said and winked at Ty. "He's a bad man around women."

"I'll keep an eye on him."

Young said, "He's teasin' me, but that's the truth. I ain't no good with women."

"That's probably a good thing," Ty replied. "Well, I have to go buy some clothes. Marshals ought to be dressed right."

Young grinned and said, "Don't know about that. Ain't none of us won prizes in the fine clothes contest. Look at what I'm wearing." Indeed, the marshal was wearing a pair of pants with patches and a shirt that was much too large for him.

"Why don't you buy some nicer ones?"

Larry sniffed. " 'Cause he lost his money playing poker 'fore he could get to the general store. Maybe you better lend him enough to buy something nice."

"Wish I could, but I don't have much. And I'll be as ragged as you are, Gale, before long."

"We'll be a matched set then. See you later, Ty."

Ty left the two marshals behind as he headed out to buy some new clothes. He was thrilled to be counted as one of Judge Parker's marshals and determined to be one of the best in the territory.

CHAPTER 10

The sun was peering over the western mountain range, casting a pink tint along the lower edge of the sky. Overhead, clouds were beginning to form, and there was a feeling of colder weather in the air.

"I don't know why we have to get up so quick."

A group was gathered around the campfire, watching as Joshua Hayes flipped a pancake in the air and caught it in his pan. Hayes was a small man with faded blue eyes. He was worn by what appeared to be hard labor, and now he said, "Come and get it. I've got one for each of you. I learned to cook with three pans when I was no more than fifteen years old."

Aaron Jordan, a big man with black hair and brown eyes, came over and picked the pancake out of one of the pans. "It looks good, Joshua."

"Bless the Lord for good pancakes."

Aaron Jordan grinned. "I believe you'd bless the Lord if you broke your leg."

"As a matter of fact I did, Mr. Jordan. Broke my leg in two places, and all I could do was thank the Lord for it."

"I don't believe all your stories." Leoma Jordan, Aaron's daughter, had come up and removed a pancake and poured syrup over it. She took a bite and chewed. "I think you make up all these stories about how God takes care of you."

"No, I don't make up nothin' about that. Now I do get a little bit wild with my huntin' stories." He poured batter into Leoma's frying pan and watched as it spread out into a perfect circle.

Lottie, Aaron's wife, was a blond woman still pretty despite her forty-three years. "I been thinking about what Oscar Manning told us about this ranch we bought. He made it sound—I don't know—dangerous."

Aaron chewed thoughtfully on his pancake, swallowed, and shook his head. "No," he said, "there're seven of us. We can defend ourselves. I know this is Oklahoma Territory, but we've got enough gun power here to keep the bandits off."

"I don't care. I don't think he told us the truth about this. He sold out too cheap."

Leoma spoke up. "Manning was pretty tired of the ranch. He seemed like a hard man. I wouldn't think he would give up that easily."

"Well, he was a hard man," Ash said, "but he didn't have no family like we've got." Ash was the older son of Aaron and Lottie. He was one inch over six feet tall with black hair and dark eyes. He gulped his breakfast down and said, "How about another pancake, Joshua?"

"Just one minute, boy." He flipped it in the air and caught it and said, "When it bubbles on top it's ready to turn over."

"Pa, I think you ought to go ahead and see what's up ahead of us here. We don't really know where this ranch is for sure."

"Well, I think it's true," Aaron said, "that he had no family to help him. Just sorry drunks he couldn't depend on."

Ash poured more molasses over his pancake and cut it up with a knife at his side. He speared a large chunk, stuck it in his mouth, and chewed it, saying, "I figure we can handle a bunch of drunk Indians and these so-called outlaws that make their home in the Indian Nation." He gave Mingan a sly grin. "Reckon we'll have any trouble with your kinfolk, Mingan?"

Mingan had made another fire and was cooking his own pancakes. He was a tall man, lean but strong. He had jet-black hair, obsidian eyes, and a coppery complexion. His Indian blood showed, but only slightly. "If there are any Comanches come to get our scalps, I'll let you take care of them, Ash."

"You think they're pretty tough?" Ash demanded.

Mingan stirred up the fire, added another few sticks, and put the pan on. "I was working for old man Henderson who was taking a herd across Texas up north. One morning we woke up and found three men dead. They all had their throats cut. We never heard a sound."

"What'd you do?" Leoma asked, her eyes wide with shock.

"Old man Henderson turned the herd around, and we scooted back where we came from. Scared him to death, the old man."

"You a Comanche, Mingan?" Ash said.

"Not really. Just a quarter." He got up and turned to stare off into the distance. Finally he said, "You can cook the rest of these pancakes, Nelson."

Nelson Fox, called Nelly for short, was the smallest man, with brown hair and brown eyes. He was the best man with cattle. Good with horses, too.

"I'd hate to meet up with any of those Comanches." Harry Littleton stood beside him. He was only five-eight with tow hair and blue eyes. He wasn't as tough as the other men, but he was a faithful hand.

"I don't think Mingan's so tough," Ash said.

"He's the best shot we've got with a rifle, a handgun, or a knife," Benny said. He was the younger of the Jordan boys at only nineteen.

The talk ran around the campfire, and when they were through, Aaron said, "Let's get this herd started. We've got to get up to Fort Smith before dark."

Leoma saddled her mare and came to ride beside Benny, who was her favorite. "Don't pay any attention to Ash, Benny. He just likes to brag."

"I wish I was as tough as he is."

She leaned over and slapped him on the arm. "You're sweeter than he is. I'll tell you what. I'll find you a nice girl to fall in love with."

"Good." Benny grinned at her. He had a good grin. He was a pleasant-looking young man. "And I'll find you a marshal who's rich and handsome."

"You do that, Benny." Leoma smiled. "Find one who can write love poems and sing me romantic songs. That's what I'm looking for."

"Somehow I don't think these marshals are too romantic," Benny said, growing more sober. "They're a pretty tough bunch from what I hear. Well, let's get this herd moving."

Soon the air was full of dust made by the herd of cattle. With the hands and Aaron and his two sons, they had no trouble heading them. They crossed a small stream once and let the cattle and their horses water.

Aaron shook his head. "We ought to be getting close to Fort Smith pretty soon."

Mingan was riding by. "Sir, it's right over there. Don't you see that smoke?"

All of them turned, but none of them saw anything.

Ash scowled. "I don't think you see anything. You just like to brag on having good eyes like most Indians."

Mingan said nothing but shrugged and spurred his horse away.

Heck exited the jail and stopped. He looked down the street. "Looky there, Judge."

Parker was right behind him, and he stopped behind him. "Looks like a herd coming in. By the way, how's that new man going to work out?"

"I think he's gonna be a good one. He arrested Big Henry and put him in jail."

"Did Henry go easy? He's a pretty rough cob."

"Ty had to slap him on the head with the barrel of his six-gun."

"Good." He looked down the street and said, "They can't bring those cattle through the middle of town. Go head 'em off, Heck. Tell 'em to go around town. Wait outside."

Heck nodded quickly and mounted his sorrel and rode toward where the herd was approaching town.

Aaron Jordan saw a man approaching. "Howdy. What can we do for you?"

"Hello. I'm Chief Marshal Heck Thomas."

"I'm Aaron Jordan. These are my two sons, Ash and Benny. This is my wife, Lottie, and my daughter, Leoma."

"Well, we're glad to see you, Mr. Jordan, but it'd be better if you didn't go down the middle of town. These cattle make a real mess."

The two stood talking while the men got the cattle turned so they would circle the town. Aaron studied Heck, who was the first of the marshals they had seen, and Heck was rather unimpressive to him. Jordan said, "I bought Oscar Manning's ranch."

"Yeah, I heard Oscar sold out."

"Can you tell me how to get to his place? I've got a map, but I can't make much sense out of it."

"Oh, I can do better than that," Heck said. "I'll send one of my men to take you there."

Aaron shook his head. "You don't have to go to that trouble. We can take care of ourselves."

Heck took off his hat, scratched his head, then put his hat back on and pulled out a corncob pipe. It had tobacco in it evidently, for he struck a match on the seat of his pants and got it to draw. "Well, there's kind of a problem."

"A problem? What kind of a problem?"

"Well, Oscar had been leavin' the ranch all by itself, and a couple of pretty tough hairpins. . .well, they've moved into it."

"Why, what do they say?"

"They claim they own the place, but they can't prove it. They'll probably be pretty hard to move. I'd better send a man with you in case they prove aggravatin'." He turned and rode back toward town.

Aaron only had to wait a few minutes. Heck soon returned, another man riding along. "This is Ty Kincaid," Heck said as soon as he reined in beside Aaron. "Ty, this is Mr. Jordan and his family. You remember I showed you Oscar Manning's ranch?"

"Sure, I remember, Heck."

"Well, Mr. Jordan bought the place, but Long Tom Slaughter and Fritz Holder have moved in on it and act like they own it. As a matter of fact, they ran some folks off. They're actin' like it's their ranch. You go along with these folks and move them two out."

"Sure will, Marshal."

"They may argue. If they do, just arrest 'em and bring 'em back to jail."

Aaron Jordan shifted uncomfortably. Ty Kincaid looked a little tougher than Heck, but Aaron thought himself capable of resolving any kind of trouble. "I like to handle my own problems, Marshal Thomas."

"You're gonna have a lot to do starting your new ranch," Ty said. "Besides, Mr. Heck Thomas is my boss, so I have to mind him. I'll lead the way."

Leoma Jordan walked over to where her father was talking to the two marshals. She found the one named Ty rather attractive and allowed her eyes to trail over him as she asked, "How far is the ranch?"

"Oh, about ten miles."

Pa asked, "Any water along the way?"

"Sure is, Mr. Jordan. A nice little river. You can water your stock on the way."

"All right. Thank you, Marshal Thomas. I don't think we'll have any trouble with two men, but I appreciate a guide."

"You let Ty here do the fightin'. That's what he gets paid for."

Pa laughed. "I'm not sure about that, but we'll see."

The men got the cattle turned, and Ty rode along the outer end.

Leoma rode her mare, a paint that was a bit lively and suited her just fine. She moved closer to where Ty was riding and said, "So, you're a marshal."

"Brand-new one."

"That right? You haven't been a marshal long?"

"No, only a month."

"How do you get to be a marshal?"

"Well, some say you've got to get kicked in the head until you lose all your brains." Ty smiled. "I don't think there's any training involved, any special training, that is."

Leoma noticed that his eyes constantly moved from side to side as if he were aware of and alert to danger of some form. She had not seen a man like him before except Mingan perhaps. She studied him carefully. "Is it really dangerous?"

"It is. The worst men in the world are in the Oklahoma Territory."

"Why do they come here?"

"They get into trouble. They get run out of other places by posses and marshals. They come here to Indian Territory, and nobody can come after 'em except one of Judge Parker's marshals like me."

"What'd you do before you became a marshal?"

"Soldiered for a while. Was a peace officer in Dallas. Did a little prospecting. Didn't make my mark in any of 'em." His lips tipped into a grin.

Leoma was aware that he was a man of rough and durable parts, like a machine intended for hard usage. There was no fineness or smoothness about him. His long mouth was expressive only when he smiled. He had the blackest of hair lying in long chunks on his head, and his eyes were sharp and gray, well bedded in their sockets. He was, she guessed, at least six feet tall, long of arms and meaty of legs with a chest that had breadth rather than thickness. She was impressed by him, which was unusual, for men usually did not impress her. However, she sensed these marshals were a different breed.

"What about you folks? Where are you from?" Ty asked.

"Lately from Texas. Dad bought a ranch there, but it was getting crowded. He heard there was plenty of room in the Indian Territory."

"Yeah, plenty of reasons why there's plenty of room."

"You mean it will be dangerous to start a ranch here?"

"I wouldn't try it unless I had plenty of guns to back it up."

"What about you?"

"What about me?" he asked curiously.

"Are you going to be a marshal for the rest of your life?"

"Nope. Your family has been ranching a lot, I take it."

"Dad likes to try different things. He owned a factory for a while. Did well at it. Made enough money we went into ranching. Did well at that, too, but as I said, it was getting crowded there."

"Well, plenty of room out here. I noticed when I rode by your ranch that there was a creek running through it, so you shouldn't run short of water. That's always a problem ranching."

Ty smiled at her. She was a beautiful woman, and he was not at all unaware of it. He appreciated the supple lines of her body. She was in that maturity that follows girlhood. Her features were quick to express her thoughts, and there was a fire in her that made her very attractive to him. It brought out the rich and headlong qualities of a spirit otherwise hidden by the cool reserve of her lips.

"What about you? You got a wife somewhere?" she asked abruptly.

"No wife. Probably a good thing."

"Why would you say that? You don't like women?"

"I don't think marshals should have wives. I hate to think about the women who open the door and find Heck Thomas or one of the other marshals looking sad, and they know that their husbands are dead."

Leoma didn't have a response to this. But she realized this man was tougher than even she had thought. *I wonder what type of husband he would make. . . .*

At about three o'clock, Ty rode up to Aaron Jordan and said, "There's your ranch, Mr. Jordan."

"Looks right nice."

Ty nodded. "Yes, it's kind of gone downhill lately, but it will make a fine home."

"We appreciate you bringing us this far. I guess you can go on back now."

"No, I have to mind Mr. Heck Thomas. He's pretty hard on marshals who don't obey him. Well, let's see what it's like." He raised his voice. "You fellows bring the herd in slow until I find out how things sit around here."

He spurred his horse, and Jordan followed closely. He was aware of two men who had come out. He said as Jordan slowed down, "I think they're your uninvited guests."

"They look pretty tough."

"Most everybody is out here. You want me to handle this?"

"I guess so. I'll back you up."

They rode in and drew up in front of the two men, one of whom had a rifle, the other a gun at his hip. "I'm Ty Kincaid, federal marshal. Who are you fellows?"

"My name's Slaughter. This is Fritz Holder. What do you want, Marshal? We ain't breakin' no laws."

"Afraid you are. You're living on Mr. Jordan's property here. You'll have to pull out."

Slaughter laughed. "We're not pullin' out."

As Slaughter spoke, Ty suddenly pulled out a revolver. He was very still and said, "You can go to jail, or we'll bury you here. Which will it be?"

The two men were armed and dangerous, but both of them ostensibly saw that the gun in Ty Kincaid's hand was steady as a rock.

Ty kept his eyes fixed on them in terrible intensity.

"I ain't shootin'," Holder said and pulled his hand away from the gun.

"Take that gun out and put it on the ground, Holder. Slaughter, you put that shotgun down. Do it now."

The two obeyed. Slaughter said, "We ain't breakin' no laws except trespassin'."

"You want to bring charges against them, Mr. Jordan?"

"No, just get 'em out of here."

"You fellows git," Ty said. "You come back and give these folks any trouble, you'll have me and Heck and a dozen rangers on your trail. Get your stuff and get out."

Aaron motioned for his party to come in. The Indian, Mingan, said to Nelly Fox, "Good thing they gave up. Kincaid's a killer."

"How can you tell?"

"How can you not tell? Didn't you see he would have put 'em down in a flash if they had gone for their guns? He's a hard man, but marshals have to be, I guess."

Ty pretended not to hear the praise. He had found it best in these situations.

The two outlaws soon left with packhorses laden down with their stuff.

Ty led Aaron and his family into their house.

Leoma and Lottie shook their heads. Leoma said, "This place is terrible, Pa. Those two men lived like pigs."

"Well, we've got to clean it up. Might as well get started. You fellows get the cattle settled down and come and help us."

"I don't mind helping a little bit myself," Ty offered. "I'm too late to get back to Fort Smith."

Leoma smiled. "Most men won't do women's work."

Ty shrugged. "Work is work," he said. "A man does what he has to do. In this case it will be easier than some other things I've done. What do you need first, Mrs. Jordan?"

They, along with the hands, all cleaned up the house as well as they could for one night's occupancy. There were bedrooms enough for the family, and Ty slept out in the bunkhouse with the hands.

When everyone was settling down, Benny came out. "We got some coffee on the stove, Mr. Kincaid. Come along with the other guys and get some."

"No mister about it. Just Ty's good enough. And thanks for the offer. I'll come with them."

Benny turned to go but paused. He faced Ty again, a serious expression dominating his face. "Would you have shot those two men?"

"If I had to. That's why I carry a gun. Don't like to use it, but better to have one than not have one and get shot."

"I wish you'd show me how to shoot."

"Well, you've got a gun."

"I never had no lessons though," Benny said. "I'm pretty good with a rifle, but I can't shoot straight with a forty-four."

"Just like pointing your finger," Ty said. "Sure. We'll go out and get some target practice early in the morning."

"Thanks. I appreciate it. Glad you came along." The young man walked away quickly.

A terrible thought came to Kincaid. *That young fellow could get killed. He don't realize how bad these men are in the Indian Nation. None of them realize it. I hope they don't find out the hard way.*

CHAPTER 11

Raina tried to make yellow laundry soap foam but had no luck. For a moment she walked over and looked out the dirty window, and she remembered that Mrs. Mullins had told her they needed to be cleaned as soon as possible. The order came back to her, and she recalled how she had been glad to find a place to sleep and something to eat. But now, looking back on the days she had spent working as a combination maid, cook, and whatever other work needed to be done, she felt the weariness drain into her. For a moment she considered sitting down at the table, but now that the meal was over, she knew that the rest of the work would have to be done.

She lingered at the window for a few more minutes, and she saw a yellow tomcat creeping across the yard. A smile touched her lips as she saw the mockingbird that daily administered a thrashing to the big tom. The cat's head was scarred, and he crept along as if he could make himself invisible to the bird, but the mockingbird rose in the air, took a dive, and uttering a series of bird sounds, hit the yellow tom who didn't even run but rolled up in a ball as close as he could.

"Stupid tomcat." Raina shook her head in disgust. "All you have to do is reach out and grab that bird, and your troubles would be over. I wish mine were that simple."

She was weary with asking people if they had seen her father, and although she had had several copies of the picture of him made, nobody seemed to have any memory of him. *Maybe he's not here at all,* she thought. *Maybe he went somewhere else. He could be anywhere. He could be dead.* She turned away from her depressing thoughts and began cleaning up the dishes. She raked off the scraps onto one plate.

Going back to the window, she opened it and threw the leftovers out. The birds came at once since she had made a habit of this. She watched as some sparrows began to fight over the scraps and smiled. *I guess the birds in this town are just as mean-spirited as the people here—and everywhere else I've been.*

Moving wearily, she transferred all the dishes to the kitchen then straightened up with disgust when she heard the bell attached to the door ring. "Another customer," she muttered. "Now I'll have to cook him a meal. I wonder who it is."

She moved out of the kitchen, and her eyes opened with surprise when she saw that Ty Kincaid had entered and was standing in the middle of the room.

Their eyes met, and he said, "Hello, Raina."

"Hello, Ty."

Ty seemed at a loss, but then he said, "I just came in from a job and the restaurants are all shut down. You think you can fix me something to eat?"

"It won't be much, but I got some leftover steak and some potatoes and some greens, and I think there's some biscuits."

"You got any buttermilk?"

"Yes, I think there's a little of that. Sit down and I'll heat the food up for you."

She moved back into the kitchen and busied herself with putting the meal together. Fortunately the stove was still warm, so the vegetables and the steak were not cold. She filled up a plate and then a large glass with buttermilk, and adding a knife and fork, she moved back into the dining room.

Ty was slumped in the chair, fatigue etched across his features. She thought again what a fine-looking man he was and wondered that he had never married. He had said nothing much about his life, and she had not asked. The plate rattled when she set it in front of him, and he straightened up.

He looked up and grinned at her. "That looks mighty good, Raina. I haven't had anything to eat in nearly two days."

Raina did not respond and turned to go away.

He suddenly stopped her and said, "Raina, you look tired."

"I guess I am. I thought it was hard working in that saloon on the border, but this work is just as hard. At least I'm away from my brother-in-law. As bad as some of the men act toward me here, it is nothing like having Millard always after me."

Ty began to cut up the steak and said, "Sit down and talk to me. I've had no company but my horse."

"What were you doing?" She sat down, felt the weariness leave her, and then said, "Did you go out after an outlaw?"

"Well, there was three of us, and we looked for the fellow we thought held up the bank over in Green Springs, but he had an

123

alibi so we couldn't bring him in."

Raina sat there watching him eat and noticed that he did not gobble his food like most men did. She saw he was watching her closely, and finally he said, "You know, you look like you need a week's vacation with somebody to wait on you."

Raina smiled, but there was a touch of bitterness in it. "I don't have anybody like that."

"Well," Ty mused and took a sip of buttermilk. Putting it down, he wiped his upper lip with a handkerchief that had seen better days. "There's an old saying. Sometimes there's just a good time waiting to happen."

"I'm having trouble believing that, Ty."

He took another bite, chewed it thoughtfully, and said, "You know, I think a lot about my grandfather. He made me read the Bible every day, and sometimes he read it to me. I remember a verse he quoted to me over and over and over again. I don't know where it is in the Bible, but he would have known."

"What does it say?"

"It says, 'In every thing give thanks: for this is the will of God in Christ Jesus concerning you.' "

"That doesn't make any sense to me. In *everything* give thanks? How could you be thankful when something bad happens?"

"Well, hard to say, but I think it has some truth in it."

"Tell me about how something bad turned out to be something good."

"The thing that I remember most was I was working on a ranch in Missouri, and the horse piled me up and broke my leg. I didn't have any money. Didn't really have a place to stay." He smiled slightly.

Raina saw the strength of his features and noted, as she usually did, what a strong character dwelled inside him.

"I thought of that verse, but I didn't believe it."

She leaned forward and put one of her elbows on the table and cupped her chin with her open palm. "Did you do what it said, give thanks?"

"Well, I tried, but I felt like a fool thanking God for a broken leg. I couldn't see anything to be happy about."

"So you didn't believe."

"No, I didn't."

"I don't blame you. I couldn't believe it either."

"Well, there's some more to that story. A week later, when I was still laid up, the fellows I had been working with went out to round up some cattle. A bunch of Comanches caught them. Killed every one of them. Staked 'em out and tortured 'em. If I had been with them, Raina, I would have lost my scalp. I'd be dead."

"That's a good story, but it doesn't always turn out like that."

"No, not always. But you remember when we were in that cabin and I was so sick, and you was having to keep the fire going to keep us from freezing to death?"

"I think of it a lot."

"Well, I bet if Grandpa had been there, he would have found something to thank God for. He was a thankful man. I think the last thing I heard him say was, 'Be sure you thank the Lord for every blessing, Ty.' He really meant it. I've never met a man like him before."

The two sat there talking while Ty finished his meal. Then he stood up, stretched, and said, "You got time to go for a walk?"

"No. I've got to wash these dishes, and then I have to wash some bedclothes."

"It'll be plum dark."

Raina wanted to complain, but she smiled and said, "Well, let's just give thanks that I've got all these dirty dishes and all these dirty sheets and pillowcases."

Ty smiled slightly and shook his head. "I know it sounds foolish, but sometimes it works out okay. Just remember those times in that cabin. I do. I think I'd have died if you hadn't been there to take care of me."

She didn't answer but noted that he was studying her carefully. Moving back to the kitchen, she thought about what he said as she worked on the dirty dishes and then started on the sheets and the pillowcases. "That's foolishness," she muttered. "Being thankful for something bad—I don't believe it."

Three nights later, one of the boarders, a small fellow named Kayo Flynn, tarried after the others had left. Raina was fairly sure that he was going to ask her to go out with him, but she had made a fixed rule not to date any of the men at the boardinghouse. They never gave up hope, but she knew that it was not a good idea.

She was surprised when he said, "Something came up today I thought you'd be interested in, Raina."

"What's that, Kayo?"

"Well, I was ridin' in, and I met a fellow out over by Juno Canyon. We got to talkin'. I've known him awhile, and I showed him the picture of your pa."

A ray of hope enlightened Raina, and she said, "What did he say?"

"Well, he said he wasn't sure. I'll have the man come by and talk to you."

"Oh, that was thoughtful of you, Kayo. I still have hope of finding my dad."

"I don't even remember my pa. I was an orphan. Grew up in an orphanage, but I do know this. He said the fellow was in jail, but you can go by and visit him and ask him."

For the first time in days, a small ray of hope illuminated Raina's mind. She thought about it as she worked all day, and finally when she got the dishes washed from supper, she left without telling Mrs. Mullins. She knew very well the woman would find something for her to do, but she was disappointed when she got to the jail.

The jailer, a tall, lanky man with deeply sunken cheeks, said, "You have to get Judge Parker's permission to visit people in the jail, lady."

"I'll do that. Thank you." She went at once to the courthouse and found Heck Thomas sitting out in front whittling as usual.

"Do you ever make anything out of those sticks you whittle on, Heck?" She smiled. She had learned to like the man. He had a bad reputation of being hard on criminals, but he was cheerful and said, "No, that gets too tedious. I just like to make shavings." He was whittling on a piece of cedar, and the shavings curled off and fell to the floor around his feet. He kicked them aside and said, "What can I do for you, Miss Raina?"

"I was told that I'd have to get Judge Parker's permission to visit somebody in the jail."

"No, that's usually the way, but we don't have to worry about that. Who is it you want to see?"

"His name is Charlie Dean."

"Sure. I know Charlie. We caught him sellin' liquor to the Indians. Catch quite a few that way."

"Kayo Flynn said that Charlie told him he'd possibly seen my father."

"Well, I hope you're right. Folks get lost out here in this part of the world." Heck looked despondent for a moment. "No matter how many criminals we catch and hang, there's always a new crop comin' on. Some of 'em are even women now."

"You've seen them hang women?"

"Sure have. Judge Parker don't show no favoritism to women. You go tell Frank Dillinger, he's in charge of the jail, that I said that you could see Charlie."

"Thank you, Heck."

Raina left and went back to the jail. She found Frank Dillinger eating some biscuits that looked tough enough to kill an ox. "You must be hungry, Frank, to be eating that stuff."

"Well, it was all there was. What can I do for you, Miss Raina?"

"I talked to Heck, and he said you could let me see Charlie Dean."

"Oh yeah. Come on. We've got a room. You don't need to be goin' down to where those no-good criminals are." He led her to a room that had a rickety table and four chairs, all old and looking rather flimsy. "Wait right here, Miss Raina. I'll get Charlie for you. Don't pay much attention to what he says. He's a world champion liar."

"Thank you, Frank. I appreciate that counsel."

Frank left the room.

She sat down in one of the chairs carefully, lest it collapse. She had not waited more than five minutes when she heard footsteps, and the door opened.

Frank and a small man, badly needing a shave and a bath, stepped in. The prisoner's clothes were filthy.

Frank said, "Well, here he is. Charlie, this lady's got some questions for you. You answer her now, you hear me?"

"Will that let me get out of here sooner?"

"You never know. Be nice now. I'll just be right outside the door."

As soon as Dillinger stepped out, Raina said, "I'm looking for my father, Charlie." She reached into her pocket and pulled out the picture she had in an envelope. She removed it and said, "Kayo Flynn said you thought you may have seen him."

"Yeah, I remember talking to Kayo about that. He had a picture like this one." Dean stared at the picture and said, "But no, this ain't the man. One I met was older."

"Oh, this is an old picture. He'd be close to fifty now. What was the man's name?"

"Well, everybody just called him Eddie. He looked older than fifty though."

"Can you tell me where he is?"

"I can tell you where he was. He's with some sheepherders over near Brice Canyon. Here. If you give me a piece of paper, I can draw you a map, but you don't want to be goin' out there by yourself."

"It's dangerous?"

"You bet your bird it is! There's guys out there that would kill you for a quarter."

129

Raina found a scrap piece of paper and a stub of a pencil.

Charlie Dean began to draw a map. "This right here is where we are in Fort Smith. You take the Old Military Road out of here for about ten miles. Then it divides, and you take the left fork. You'll get up into the high country there, and somewhere in that area, that's where I seen him."

Raina questioned him as closely as she could and asked everything she could think of. She didn't feel encouraged because Charlie Dean kept insisting that the man didn't really look like the picture. And besides, Frank Dillinger's warning that Charlie was a liar kept flitting through her mind. "Well, I'd like to pay you, Charlie, for your information, but I don't have any extra money." A thought came to her, and she smiled. "I can cook you a pie though."

"Oh, that's good. What kind?"

"How about apple?"

"My favorite! But listen, you have to get Heck or Frank to say I get it. Some of these guys in here would steal it from me."

Raina had a thought. "Could you possibly take me out there to this place? I don't really know the country."

"Well, I'd be glad to, but I expect I'll be in this jail for at least two or three months or maybe longer."

"Well, I'll get that pie to you very soon, Charlie. Thank you for your help."

"Sure hope you find your pa. A woman needs menfolk to look out for her."

Raina left the jail and started back toward the boardinghouse. She thought constantly about the man called Eddie whom Charlie Dean had described. He had not been very optimistic, but she realized that the picture she had was made when her father was a young man no more than twenty-three or twenty-four years old, and living a hard life could have made it very difficult for anybody to recognize a picture.

She worked steadily trying to think of a way to get to the man. She thought about asking Ty or one of the other marshals, but she held back. She told herself they were too busy with their jobs and probably wouldn't want to help her find her father anyway. She tried to pray but discovered that she had no confidence in that.

The next morning after breakfast, one of the boarders, Sam Terhune, came in late. "Could I have another one of them pancakes, Miss Raina?"

"Sure you can, Sam, and some more bacon, too." She brought in the bacon and the pancakes.

He said, "I hear tell you been tryin' to get someone to take you over to Brice Canyon lookin' for your pa."

"Yes, I have, Sam. Could you do that?"

"Well, I might could." He grinned at her. He was a homely man, but she recognized the lust in his eyes, for she had seen it often enough in other men. "I would expect a little affection for my trouble."

Raina expected no more out of the man. He had a reputation as a womanizer. "Thanks a lot, but I'll find another way." She became depressed after that and went about her work without a smile, but then, Mrs. Mullins did not require smiles, only hard work.

The sun was high in the sky when Ty rode in. He held the lines to a second horse on which a tall man covered in dust was mounted.

"All right, Horace, you can get down now."

Horace Moore had his hands tied behind his back. He had tried to escape once, but Ty had roped him and jerked him off his horse. To make sure he didn't run away again, he had put him back in the saddle and threatened to shoot him if he tried to get away again. With Ty holding the lines, they had come into town, and when they reached the courthouse, Ty found Heck Thomas just emerging.

"Well, you got Horace this time, did you?" Heck said. He had a disgusted look on his face. "What's the charge this time, Ty?"

"He shot Leonard Hoskins's cow. Not a very daring sort of outlaw, is he? You're not Jesse James, are you, Horace?"

Horace gave him a rough look but refused to say anything. "I want a lawyer," he finally grunted.

"Well, we'll put you in the jail for a month or so, and then if you're a good boy, I'll see about getting you a lawyer. Hey Larry, take this bad criminal in and lock him up."

Larry Dolby shrugged and gave Horace a violent jerk on his arms. "Come on. I want to get you in there before you shoot somebody." He dragged the prisoner to the jail.

"Did he give you any trouble, Ty?" Heck asked.

"No, he just smells pretty bad. That's his worst crime, I think."

"Well, you were gone two days. Did you have trouble catchin' up with him?"

"He was hiding out over in the badlands. I was able to track him though. What's going on here in town?"

"Well, I know you're interested in Miss Vernay, ain't that so?"

Instantly Ty looked up. "Yes, she's a friend of mine. What's the matter?"

"Well, the thing is she's got a lead on where her old man might be, over north of where those new folks moved in."

"You mean the Jordans?"

"That's the one. Probably nothin' to it, but she's been tryin' to get somebody to take her out there."

"Well, she's had a rough time. If you give me a couple days off, I'll take her and see if there's anything to it."

"Oh, the judge won't mind. You just go ahead."

"I'll need to get a horse from the remuda to take her with me. Can't ride double."

"Oh, that's fine. Pick a gentle mare. I don't know how much ridin' she's done."

On second thought, Ty said, "You know, I don't think we ought to keep anything back from the judge. He has a way of finding out things. I'd rather him say no up front than to get back and find him in one of his mad spells."

"He's upstairs starin' at the docket. Go ahead and ask him. He won't care."

"Thanks, Heck, for telling me." Ty ascended the stairs, knocked on the judge's office door.

When he heard someone say, "Come in," he entered. He saw that the judge was sitting in his chair, but he had one foot without a sock or boot propped up on the desk. He was trimming his toenails with a pair of large tin snips, it looked like.

"You better be careful, Judge. You might cut your toe off."

"I'll take care of my own toes, thank you, Kincaid. What do you want?"

"I just heard that Miss Vernay's got a lead on her pa. I thought if it'd be all right with you, I'd take her out to the last place he was seen."

"What's your connection with that young woman? You got anything bad on your mind for her?"

Ty shook his head. "No, Judge, she did me a good turn before we came out here. I owe her something."

"All right, you can go. Get back as soon as you can. We got some fierce criminals roaming around. You ain't got time to romance any young women."

"I'll need a horse. Be all right if I take one of the spares?"

"Yeah, pick her out one. Take care of that young lady and behave yourself, or I'll put you where the dogs won't bite you."

Ty smiled. "I'll be careful, Judge. I know your reputation."

Raina looked up to see Ty coming in. He was dusty as if he had been out on a long ride.

"You look like you need a bath," she said.

"I sure do, but I hear you need some help looking for some man out to the north."

Raina straightened up. "Yes, I heard about a man named Eddie. One of the men in jail thinks he might be my pa, but he's not sure."

"Well, can you get off from work?"

"I'll have to. Why don't you go get cleaned up and I'll meet you?"

"You just wait here. I'll come by and pick you up. I'll have to get you a horse. You can ride, can't you?"

"Of course I can ride."

"All right." He smiled. "You better put some grub up, too. How far is this, you say?"

"Well, maybe forty miles. The man wasn't sure. I've got this map." She took the slip of paper out of her pocket and showed it to him.

"Yeah, that's a lot of territory to cover. We'll have to camp out one night. Maybe two. We'd better get enough grub off of Mrs. Mullins."

"She's not much for giving out grub, but I've saved some leftovers."

"I'll pick up some more stuff at the store. You better bring your blankets, too."

As soon as Ty left, she started thinking how she would tell Mrs. Mullins. Finally she decided there was no easy way, so she simply went and said, "Mrs. Mullins, I think I may have found my pa. I've got to be gone for maybe two days to find out."

"Well, I can't do without you that long." Mrs. Mullins was frowning and in a bad mood. "If you can't stay and do your job, I'll have to get somebody else."

For a moment Raina thought about not going, but then the stubbornness that played a part in her character emerged. "I've got to go, Mrs. Mullins. I'll get back as soon as I can."

"Never you mind. I've got a young woman who can do your work. Just have your room cleared out."

"All right. Thanks for the help you've given me."

"You're not very grateful."

"Come on now, Mrs. Mullins. If you hadn't had your pa around, but suddenly you might be able to find him, wouldn't you go?"

Emma Mullins was a hard woman. Running a boardinghouse for rough men did not bring out the gentleness in any female. She stared at Raina and said, "You can come back, but if anyone comes wantin' a job, I'm gonna put 'em to work. I'll take the best, her or you."

"I'll try my best to get back. I'm gonna have to sleep out. Can I borrow a couple of your blankets?"

"You be sure and bring 'em back, and make sure you wash 'em, too."

"Yes ma'am, I'll do that."

Quickly Raina pulled out some groceries that she had saved in case she did make the trip, put them in a meal sack, and got the two blankets off her bed. She packed a few of her warmer clothes and then looked around. "I'll have to come back for the rest of my things if Mrs. Mullins hires someone else." Quickly she exited the house and sat down in a home-built wooden chair.

Half an hour later, Ty came riding in, mounted on his buckskin and pulling a smaller horse. "Got you a good horse, Raina. Real gentle. Here, let me tie them blankets and that grub down."

"I don't know if I'll have a job when I get back."

Ty was busy folding the blankets. He tied them on with some rawhide thongs and then tied the grub on top of that. "Well, this is more important than a job."

"I don't know what I'll do, Ty."

"You'll find something." He looked at her and said, "You ready?"

"Yes, I am."

"I'm surprised you trust me."

Raina shook her head. She was feeling apprehensive. "I don't have any choice, Ty."

Ty came over and took her by the arm and led her over to the horse. "Here. I see you got that riding skirt on that you made on your way out here. That's good. Let's go." He helped her onto the mare, handed her the lines, and then he stopped long enough to say, "Raina, don't be afraid. I owe you, and I always pay my debt. Now, let's get as much daylight as we can between us and this town." He swung into the saddle, nodded, and then moved off into a slow walk.

As soon as they were out of town, he said, "Let's speed it up." He touched the buckskin and started out at a lope. He saw that Raina was a good rider and was keeping her seat well.

"Ty," Raina said, "I was feeling pretty bad, but I feel better now. Thank you for coming, for helping me."

"Why, it's nothing, Miss Raina. Let's go find that man and see if he's the one you're looking for."

"I—I really appreciate your help, Ty."

"Glad to do it, Raina, and if we don't find him on this trip, we'll go looking until we do. He's got to be somewhere, hasn't he?"

"Yes, but I've been discouraged, Ty."

"Natural you might be, but there's two of us looking now, and there's over a hundred federal marshals. I'll talk all of them into keeping their eyes open."

Ty's words encouraged Raina, and she felt a lift in her spirit. *I was wrong about Ty. He's a good man—just like I first thought he would be.*

CHAPTER 12

"How far do you think we've come, Ty?"

Turning sideways in the saddle, Ty looked back. "You getting tired?"

"I guess I've lost a little bit of my horsemanship doing nothing but washing dirty dishes and bedsheets. Back on the trail I thought I did pretty well."

"You did, but you lose it easy, too. Oh, I expect we've come around fifteen miles."

"How much farther is it to the river?"

"See that low-lying ridge over there? Just on the other side of that there's a canyon. There's a nice camping spot, too. I've stayed there once already. Can you last until then?"

Raina flashed him a smile. She was weary, but the more she had thought about it, the more she was grateful to Ty. She knew he was tired and had come in from a difficult hunt, although he made little of it. "I'm hungry," she said. "As soon as we get a place, we'll eat supper."

"That would go down right good."

The two rode steadily until the land began to lift. The ridge was not over seventy-five or a hundred feet high, but Ty's horse was tired, for he had come a long way. Ty said, "You know this is a tough horse. He's a stayer."

"He's not much to look at."

"Why, most horses and men aren't much to look at. Then you take ladies, they're the ones with the looks. Take you, for instance."

She suddenly laughed. "Never mind that. You're just along to shoot any outlaws that bother us."

"I doubt if we'll see anybody out here. I think I'll—" In a quick movement, he drew his gun from his side and extended it. The shot broke the silence of the badland.

"Did you hit anything?" she asked.

"Jackrabbit. We'll see if he's got enough meat on his bones to make it worth skinning him for."

They stopped fifty yards later, and he said, "This is a nice plump mama jackrabbit. I guess that makes her a doe rabbit. She'll make a good stew. There's the river along that line of trees. Come on." He stepped in the saddle again and led her down the hill, and when he came to the river, which was no more than twenty feet across, he said, "It doesn't look like much, but the water's good and clear. Spring fed, I think. Let's tie these horses out, and we'll make us a house for the night. I wish I had brought that tent I used to have."

"We'll make out."

"If it doesn't rain."

She followed him down, stepped off her horse, and tied the lines to a sapling. Ty came over and pulled their blankets and the food from behind the saddle and said, "I brought some hobbles. The grass isn't too bad here. They'll need to eat, too."

She watched as he put the hobbles on the front feet of the horses. They made no attempt to run away but bent over and began chomping at the grass, which was thin and a sort of brown color. Evidently they found something that they liked.

He said, "I brought some grain. We'll give 'em some first thing in the morning. Let them eat what they can here."

"I'll tell you what," Raina said, "if you'll build up a fire, I'll skin this rabbit. We'll make us a fresh rabbit stew."

"Well, I brought some meat, but it's not much. I'd like to have something fresh."

"You build that fire, and I'll show you how to cook jackrabbit."

As the sun was setting, Raina finished cooking the jackrabbit stew. She dipped out some of the meat into a deep dish and gave it to Ty. "Dinner's served, such as it is."

Ty had sat down and was poking at the fire, adding a branch from time to time. He took the dish she offered. "I bet I've had worse."

"So have I. Smells good. I wish I had some pepper."

"Oh, I got some in my saddlebag and some salt. Let me get it." He went to where his saddle was on the other side of the fire, rummaged through it, and came back. "Got several different things here. Got some spices. I like to try different things."

The two sat eating, and he said finally, "I'm glad you thought to bring that bread. It'd be hard to make biscuits out here in the open."

They finished eating and slowly drank the water from the river. "This is good, cold water," she said.

"See those mountains? I guess the stream that feeds this river comes from there."

When all the food was gone, he said, "I'll wash the dishes."

"No, I'll do it. You just sit back and relax. I know you've had a hard day."

"About usual." He watched her work for a while. "You ever miss your home?" he asked.

"You mean the saloon in La Tete. I guess I never really considered that home."

"But you lived there with your mother at one time, right?"

"I lost my mother. And my sister and I weren't very close. I've been all my life looking for somebody and don't even know if they exist. Hope I can find my pa."

He was quiet for a moment, then looked up and said, "Look at those stars. Aren't they pretty?"

"Yes, they are."

He turned to look at her. "You know, your pa might not want to be found."

"I know. But it's my only chance at a family."

"That's not so. You could marry and have a husband and some kids."

"I don't think about that much. Most married couples I've seen don't seem to care for each other."

Kincaid stretched his legs out and studied the sky thoughtfully. "I guess we're alike. I've been alone, in one way or another, all my life, just like you. You know, I saw an older couple once in San Antonio. They were walking down the street. Both of them had silver hair. Must have been in their sixties at least, and you know what? They were holding hands." He sighed and shook his head. "I've never forgotten that. I almost ran after them and asked, 'What's your secret? How do you keep love alive?' "

"Did you do it?"

"No. I wish I had. I've wondered about it ever since."

The two sat there talking for a time. He told her about the Jordans and their ranch. He planned for them to stop there before they continued on. They fell quiet and soon the weariness of the ride caught up with them.

Ty said, "Let's wrap up in these blankets. I'll keep the fire going. It's cold." He grinned. "You stay on that side now and don't bother me."

"Don't worry about that. You stay on your own side."

"Well, I think we'll get to the ranch tomorrow. That map shows a lot, but it's a big country."

"I think we'll find him, but what if we don't? I told Mrs. Mullins I'd be back in two days."

"I told Judge Parker the same thing, but if we get hot on the trail, we'll just follow it out. Okay?"

"All right. Good night." She spread the blankets on the ground and drew them up around her, fully dressed. She could hear the sound of his breathing as he lay down, and for a moment she thought, *What if he tries something?*

The thought troubled her, but she knew at once that she was safe with him.

Dawn came, and they both rose and cooked bacon and some old biscuits. They fried the biscuits in the bacon grease and again drank the river water.

After they finished eating, Ty said, "I guess we'd better get on the way. I'll saddle the horses and take the hobbles off. You pull everything together."

"All right, Ty."

The two made their preparations quickly, and in ten minutes they were loping out. Ty had fed the horses some of the grain, and they had a spirited attitude. "These horses like to run," Ty said. "That's good sometimes."

"You like horses, don't you?"

"Most of 'em. I had one—a pinto—she'd be good for two months just to get a chance to kick me." He laughed and cast a sly glance at her. "Like some females I've known."

"I'll bet you have."

They rode steadily until Ty said, "Somebody's coming."

Raina had been looking down at the ground, but now she lifted her gaze. Still a good distance away there were three riders. "Do you think they're outlaws?"

"Could be. There are plenty of 'em out here. We need to stop for a bit." He pulled his horse up.

Raina did the same. She was surprised to see him pull his rifle out.

He waited until they were in shouting distance, then hollered, "Turn around and go the other way!"

The leader of the band yelled, pulled out his gun, and shot. Ty at once lifted the rifle, took careful aim, and with one shot dropped the man's horse. He chambered another shell and began peppering the three.

"I think they're running," she said. She watched as the man, who now had no horse, got on behind the other. They then headed off in another direction. "Why did you do that?"

"You didn't see the man in back. He pulled his gun out as soon as he saw us. I don't trust anybody in this territory—not when they come at us with a gun."

Raina did not comment on that, but she was thinking what a dangerous life Ty had chosen for himself. She finally asked him about it. "There must be other jobs you could do that pay more and aren't quite so dangerous."

"I guess there are, but this is where I've landed, and this is where I'll stay for a while."

"You know, sometimes I wonder what it's like to have a family, a place. I never felt secure when I was growing up. We moved a lot, and my sister's husband was a cruel man. Made life miserable for me, and for lots of other people, too. I was always surprised somebody didn't shoot him."

"Why didn't you?"

"Why, I couldn't shoot anybody."

"No, I guess you couldn't. But if we run into him, maybe I can make a gentleman out of him."

"That's not likely. We won't be seeing them anymore."

By noon they started seeing cattle.

"Look at that brand."

"What brand, Ty?"

"There on that cow. See, it's a running J."

She saw that the brand was indeed a *J* with a tail on it that looked like a running river.

"You know that brand?"

"Yes, it's that family I told you about who came in not long ago. Remember, their name's Jordan? We'll stop here. You can meet them, and I'm sure they will help us with some more supplies. Maybe they even heard something about your pa."

They rode into the ranch, and as they approached the house, what appeared to be a man, his wife, and his daughter came out.

"Why, hello there, Mr. Kincaid," the man said. "Good to see you."

"Good to see you, Mr. Jordan. I'd like for you to meet a friend of mine. This is Miss Raina Vernay."

"Glad to know you, Miss Vernay. I'm Aaron, this is my wife, Lottie, and this is my daughter, Leoma."

"You didn't come out just to see the scenery, did you?" Leoma smiled. She was looking carefully at Raina. "You're not eloping, are you?"

"No, she'd have to be crazier than she is to take a galoot like me." Ty Kincaid grinned. "No, she's looking for her pa. As a matter of fact, we came out here together."

"What's his name?"

"His name is Ed Vernay."

"Don't know the name, but then, we've only been here a few weeks."

Lottie Jordan said, "We're just about to sit down and eat. Be glad to have you take a bite with us."

"Well, I'm in favor of that," Ty said.

"What about you, Miss Vernay?"

"That would be an imposition."

"No, it wouldn't," Leoma said. She smiled then at Ty and said, "Come on in. We'll see if your appetite is as good as the rest of your skills."

Thirty minutes later they were all seated around the table. The women had fixed steak, boiled potatoes, and some canned vegetables. There was also fresh-baked bread.

Ty said, "This is as good a baked bread as I've ever had, Mrs. Jordan. You're a fine cook."

"Why, of course she is. I wouldn't marry a sorry cook," Aaron said. He reached over and pinched his wife on the shoulder. "No, I would have married her if she couldn't cook a bit."

"You're looking for your father, Ed Vernay?" Leoma asked.

"Yes, I am, Miss Jordan. He left my family a long time ago. Wasn't entirely his fault. As a matter of fact, he tried to take me with him, but my mother wouldn't let me go."

"How long ago was that?"

"I was just a little girl."

Leoma seemed to sense Raina's discomfort with discussing her family, and she changed the subject. "How did you and Ty meet up?"

For a moment Raina was embarrassed, but then she began to tell a few of the details.

"You're not telling it right," Ty said. He was dipping into a dish of blackberry preserves and said, "I got sick, and she had to take care of me. Nearly died. We nearly froze, too, didn't we, Raina?"

"It was a hard time."

"Well, it's fortunate you met up with a good nurse," Leoma said.

"You can say that again," Ty said cheerfully.

The talk went on for some time. Aaron finally shook his head. "Well, as far as I can tell, there's nothing in that direction for the next hundred miles but some Basque sheepherders."

"What's Basque?" Ty asked.

"They are some kind of foreigners. I think they came from Spain a long time ago. We had some trouble with them back in Texas once."

"What sort of trouble?" Raina asked.

"Well, miss, you see, cattle and sheep don't go well together."

"Why not?"

"When the cattle eat grass, they leave some sticking up. The sheep will go right down past the dirt and eat the root, just about ruining the grazing ground, so we had some trouble over boundary lines. Well, it wasn't the most pleasant time in my life." He sighed and shook his head. "I hated to see those Basque herders."

"Are they violent men?"

"Not at all," Lottie said. "Most of them are very gentle, but of course that doesn't mean anything to people who are losing their land."

"Well, I guess we can go ask them if they've seen Raina's pa."

Aaron Jordan was still thinking about the situation. "I can't help you much in direction, but if you just head east of here, you'll probably run into them."

"Well, I guess we'll move on. That was a fine meal, ladies," Ty said, smiling at them.

"Yes, it was. I'll stay and help wash dishes," Raina said.

"No, there's no point in that. We have plenty of help around here," Lottie said.

Ty and Raina rode out shortly after that. She said, "They seem like nice people."

"Yeah, one of the boys is a little bit rambunctious. His name is

Ash. He's the oldest boy. They've got another one named Benny."

"Mr. Jordan seems to think that there'd be trouble with the sheepherders."

"Nearly always is. He was right about one thing. Sheep can tear up rangeland. You need a lot of acreage to carry sheep."

"Why do they raise sheep instead of cattle?"

"More money in it, I hear. You get the wool until the sheep get old, and then you sell the meat."

The two fell silent after a while, and the silence was broken only by a few observations by Kincaid. Finally he said, "Look."

Raina turned and said, "What is it?"

"It's a herd of sheep. See how white they look."

"They just run wild out here?"

"No, there'll be some sheepherders, and they'll have some dogs."

"They use dogs to herd the sheep?"

"They sure do. Smart dogs, too. These folks just seem to know how to get the best out of 'em."

They slowed down when Ty saw a man coming toward them on foot. He had a long staff in his hand with a crook on the end. "Looks like a welcoming committee," Ty said. He greeted the man and said, "Hello, neighbor."

"Hello to you." The man had a large-brimmed hat that shaded his face, but he was obviously a white man. He walked slower and finally came to a full stop. He was staring at Raina, and finally she got a complete shock when he said, "I'll bet your name is Raina, ain't it, miss?"

Raina's eyes flew open, and she covered her mouth to keep the exclamation. "Is that you, Pa?"

"It ain't nobody else. Get down off that horse and let me see." He waited until she had come up to stand before him, and he said, "Well, ain't you a pretty one now. I always knew you would be though. How'd you find me way out here?"

"Well, I got tired of living without seeing you," she said, "so I heard that you were here in this country."

"Is this your husband here?"

"Oh no. It's a long story. This is Ty Kincaid. He got us here all right. It was a pretty hard trip."

"Well, I tell you what." He came forward and stuck his hand out, and when Ty took it he felt the steely grip. Eddie, as he was called, was a strong man in his midfifties. "Appreciate you takin' care of my girl."

"Well, wasn't exactly like that," Ty said. "I got sick, and she had to take care of me."

"Is that so? But you both made it out here."

"Yes, we did, but I wouldn't want to go through it again. Would you, Raina?"

"It wasn't so bad."

"Well, come on. I want to introduce you to the hands. The cook has killed a sheep. You like mutton?"

"I don't think I've ever eaten any," Raina said.

"Well, our cook is a good man. His name is Yosu. Very religious fellow. Come along now."

They moved toward the camp leading the horses, and when they got there, several of the sheepherders came to watch them.

"This is Benat," Pa said. "Benat is the strongest man we've got. He's my right hand. Benat, this is my daughter, Raina, and this here is Ty Kincaid."

Benat did not speak. His muscles swelled his shirt out, and when he smiled there was a gentleness about him.

"This here's Danelle. He's little but he's tough. This is Mikel. He's one-quarter Chocktaw and a fast runner. And this is our cook, Yosu. Yosu, what do you say to these people?"

Yosu grinned. He was slowly turning the whole carcass of a sheep over a fire pit. "Are you Jesus people?"

"I'm afraid I'm not. Are you?" Raina asked.

"Yes. Born again. What about you, young man—you in the kingdom of God?"

Ty obviously felt embarrassed at the suddenness of the question, but Pa laughed. "He asks that of everyone. Now, let's eat. That sheep ought to be good enough."

Yosu at once began cutting slabs of meat off and putting them in tin plates. He also had some kind of stew and bread baked in an oven.

"This is good," Ty said. "You're a good cook, Yosu."

"Not as good as the bread that came down from heaven and fed Moses and the children of Israel."

"I read about that," Ty said. "My grandfather told me about it. Bread falling from heaven. That's a good way to get it."

"Yes, and the Lord Jesus is now our bread," Yosu replied. "He said, 'I am the bread from heaven.' You'll have to find that out one day."

The visit lasted quite awhile. Ty finally said, "We'd better get back."

"Not me," Raina said. "I'm going to stay out here. My pa says I can stay with him. He has a house built over the hill there. We can get to know each other now."

"Why, that's fine." Ty nodded with enthusiasm. "You'll find she's a good woman, Eddie."

"Yes, I can tell you I appreciate your looking out for her all the way on that long trip out here. Will you be coming back?"

"Oh, sure. I'm one of Judge Parker's marshals, so I'll be in and out. Do you ever go into town?"

"Once in a while to buy things. Supplies, you know." He looked over to where Raina sat. "It's good for you to be here, Raina. I have missed you all these years." He grinned. "It sure is something, an old ugly codger like me havin' a beautiful daughter like you."

"She is that," Ty said.

Raina blushed at their praise.

When Ty finished getting ready to go, he came back to stand before Raina and said, "Well, we did it, didn't we? You like the idea of staying here?"

"Yes, for a while."

"I'll be coming back to check on you. Anytime somebody goes to town, you go with 'em. I might be gone, but I'll try to keep in touch."

"I'll need to go soon to get the rest of my things. Would you mind packing them up for me? There isn't much. Oh, and please tell Mrs. Mullins what has happened. I'll go by to see her when I make it in."

"I'll take care of it." He put his hand out.

She clasped it in hers as she stared into his eyes. "Thank you for bringing me, Ty."

"No problem." Kincaid cleared his throat as if to break the spell. He then stepped into his saddle, waved at the group, and kicked the stallion into a fast lope.

"That is one good man," Pa said. "You were lucky to find him. You going to marry with him maybe?"

She said quietly, "I don't think so, Pa."

"Well, there'll be plenty of men wanting to marry a beautiful girl like you. Now, let's go to the house. I've got a room that you'll like, and you can fix it up however you want. . . ."

"Well, you're back again, Ty." Aaron Jordan, along with his wife, came out of their home.

Kincaid stepped off his buckskin and took off his hat. "Howdy, Aaron. Yeah, I'm back."

"Did you find the young woman's father?"

"You know, we did. It's really amazing. He was the only white man there. The rest of them were the Basques."

"The young woman. She didn't come with you?"

"No, she wanted to stay and enjoy her dad. I guess I would, too, if I hadn't had a dad all my life."

"Hope we don't have trouble with them."

Ty looked up suddenly. "Why would you?"

"Well, you know how it is. You've worked with cattle. You know what sheep can do."

"They're a long way from here though, Aaron. I doubt if your paths will ever cross."

"As long as they keep to their ground, I'll keep to mine. But there's been lots of wars fought with the woolies against the cattle."

"Yes, we saw some good land ruined by sheep," Lottie said. "You look tired. Come on in and spend the night."

"Well, I really shouldn't. Judge Parker let me go for two days."

Leoma had joined them as Ty spoke. "You can catch another criminal. We probably got some working here. Come on in. I want to hear some more about this marshaling business." She stepped forward and took Ty's arm. "Come on in. You can watch me make a stew."

"Nothing better than watching a good-looking woman make stew."

The two went inside, and Leoma began pulling ingredients together for a stew. "I've got everything here I need to make you something good. Why don't you tell me about yourself—all that's fit for me to know."

"You sound like you think I've got a lot to hide."

"All men have a lot to hide."

Ty grinned and asked, "You speaking from personal experience?"

"Pretty much. What's the worst thing you ever did?"

"Oh, I guess it was kissing Martha Fleming when she didn't want me to, but then, I always thought she really liked me."

"Nobody is that pure, Ty."

"No, I guess not. How long before that stew is ready?"

"I think your heart is in your stomach, Ty Kincaid. I've seen you eat, remember?"

"Man has to know his strengths." Ty grinned.

"Oh you, go on into the dining room, and I'll bring the food in a minute."

Ty went into the large room and took a seat at the oak table. While he waited, his mind wandered back to Eddie Vernay's land. Of course he could not see Eddie, the sheep, or the herders, but he thought about Raina and wondered how she would make out with her new life.

CHAPTER 13

After Ty ate what Leoma prepared for him, the Jordans persuaded Ty to spend the night with them. "We've got plenty of room here." Aaron Jordan shrugged. "Have your own bed in the bunkhouse. You'd be in the middle of the night getting back to Fort Smith. Just make yourself at home."

Ty was actually happy to stay. It was much better than riding all night or sleeping on the ground. And there were worse things than spending time with Leoma Jordan.

She led him to the parlor. "Let's sit down before the fire and get warm. It's getting colder out there."

"Sounds good to me."

They made their way to the large living area, and she stirred up the fire and put more wood on. The sparks rose upward like myriads of tiny worlds of their own.

When she sat down, he asked, "Are you happy here in this place, Leoma?"

"I hope to be. We needed to find a new life. We cut all of our ties at the old one." She looked over at him. The flickering of the fire on the walls made grotesque shadows and reflections around her. "You think the outlaws will be a problem?"

"They're always a danger. They're wild men, not just naughty but killers. You must be very careful, Leoma, about going out alone. Always carry a gun and take one of the men with you."

"You make it sound so bad."

"Well, it is bad. This is outlaw territory full of killers."

"You think there might be trouble with the sheepherders?"

"It might be troublesome, but I think Ed Vernay is a sensible man. The funny thing is, he's not really interested in sheep much. He's got a plan."

"What sort of a plan?"

"Well, he wants to preach the Gospel. Of course he's not an ordained minister, but he likes to talk to people about the Lord."

"Did he talk with you, Ty?"

"Sure did. Put it right up to me. And he's got a cook who's even more pointed."

The two sat there for a long time, and finally Leoma said, "This is a nice room. It's an old house, I think."

"Yes, it is." Ty watched the fire, and the sparks continued to rise with ebullience. "You never know what's happened in a room like this."

"What do you mean, what's happened? People lived here."

He smiled at her. "I guess I've got too much imagination."

"Have you? What do you think about this room?"

"Well, Leoma, just think about what might have happened right here where we're sitting. A man and a woman might have come in through different doorways, and their eyes could have met, and both of them knew right then that they were destined to love each other and spend all their lives together. They could have decided to raise their children here."

"You *do* have an imagination."

"Well, it could have happened. Or maybe something bad happened."

"Like what?"

"Well, maybe a murder took place here."

"A murder? What an awful thought!"

"Well, murders do take place. On the other hand, maybe a man or a woman found God right in this very room."

"Have you ever found God?"

"No, I guess I'm just a runner. Trying to get away from God takes some of my time."

"Are you an atheist?"

"No, of course not! Do you take me for a fool? Let's go outside. I'm getting too warm in here."

They both rose, went outside, and stood for a while on the porch. "I always liked the night." He looked over at the trees and said, "Look at those trees, Leoma. They look like soldiers in a line, kind of in disorganized ranks. Kind of like a regiment at ease."

"Do you have thoughts like this a lot?"

"I had one friend who told me I had too much imagination. But look at those tall trees there shouldering the moon out of its way before it's gone."

Suddenly both of them looked up, for a star had increased its light, streaked across the darkness, and then disappeared.

"Did you make a wish?" Ty asked.

"Yes."

"What was it?"

She laughed at him then and touched his arm. "I'm not telling. It'll never come true if you tell."

"All right. You keep it. Look at that moon, just a crescent of silver. Argent is what some people call it."

"Argent means silver?"

"Yes, it does."

"How do you know that?"

"Some of my aimless reading, I guess."

They stood on the porch, and she said, "Let's walk a bit."

They walked around the yard, and there were the usual night sounds, a coyote howling mournfully, the cry of some sort of bird.

She stopped and said, "You're a curious man. What do you think about men and women?"

"Well, I don't know much about women. I'm no expert."

"But what do you think?"

"Well, I think when a man and a woman really love each other, it's wonderful. I've seen it a few times. As a matter of fact, I read a poem once. It was so sad I never could get it out of my mind."

"What is it?"

"I don't know the name of it. Don't even remember who wrote it now."

"You remember any of it?"

"Yes. It goes like this:

"So we go no more a-roving
So late into the night,
Though the heart be still as lovely,
And the moon be still as bright.

157

"For the sword outwears its sheath,
And the soul wears out the breast,
And the heart must pause to breathe,
And love itself have rest.

"Though the night was made for loving,
And the day returns too soon,
Yet we'll go no more a-roving
By the light of the moon."

"What does it mean?"

"It made me sad the first time I read it. I thought about it a lot. It seems to say we'll grow old and die."

"But everybody knows that."

"I guess they do." He went silent.

The two walked along the fence that kept the pasture for the rest of the horses. Some of them were stirring now. One of them came over and stuck his head over the fence.

Leoma reached out and stroked it. "This is a good horse."

"You love horses?"

"Yes, I do."

"So do I. Something we have in common."

They made the circle of the house and came back, and he said, "I guess I need to get to bed. You must be tired, too."

Suddenly she turned to face him. "I think that woman Raina might be in love with you."

"No, not really. We're good friends."

Leoma shook her head. She was a woman of firm convictions, and he could see it in her face. He had told the truth. A breeze ruffled the edges of her hair, and a smile made its small break along her lips. Ty watched the slight changes of her face, the quickening, the loosening, the small expressions coming and going.

Suddenly he reached out, and the old hungers that he usually kept under firm control seemed to intensify. He saw a change go over her face as he pulled her closer. Her lips were heavier, and a warmth began to illuminate her eyes. He kissed her then. Her lips made a softly pursed line, and he felt the sweetness and the humor in the embrace and in her kiss.

When he lifted his head, her face was as purely expressive at that moment as he had ever seen it, graphically registering the light and the shadows of her feelings. She was, he suddenly realized, a woman who was lonely and could not understand why. She seemed to have everything. She wasn't smiling then, but the thought of a smile was a hint at the corners of her mouth and in the tilt of her head.

"You did that very well. You've had lots of practice."

"Not really, Leoma. I had one woman that I thought loved me—but she didn't."

"I'm sorry."

"Well, it was a long time ago."

Suddenly she said, "There's a dance in Fort Smith the day after tomorrow."

"You save me a dance."

"I'll do that. Be sure you come to claim it."

Ty was getting ready for the dance. He was sitting in a straight chair.

Larry Dolby, who claimed to be a barber, was cutting his hair.

"Be sure you make me pretty, Larry."

"Don't ask impossible stuff," Dolby said. He laughed. "I just cut a hunk out that's gonna look like you been hit with a stick."

"Just do the best you can."

"Well, it's free anyhow. You're going to that dance, are you?"

"Sure am," Ty answered. "Haven't been to a dance in a long time. Are you going?"

"No. I'm pretty down on women right now. I got jilted."

"Well, I did, too. But it was a long time ago."

A few of the other marshals gathered around, and Heck Thomas shook his head. "Next time let me cut your hair, Ty. Larry just thinks he's a barber. I believe he really worked for an undertaker."

"I didn't say whose hair I cut," Larry said indignantly.

"You mean you've never cut a live man's hair?" Ty's eyes flew open. "Why didn't you tell me that?"

"You didn't ask."

"Well, I'm going to the dance."

"Here. Try some of this." Heck handed him a bottle and grinned. "It smells good. Straight from France."

"I don't think I want any perfume," Ty said.

"This ain't perfume. It's lotion. All the men wear it."

"Well, I'm going to the dance."

Heck frowned. "You don't look very dressed up."

"This is the best I've got."

Leaving the marshals' quarters, Ty moved on to where he could hear the music playing. He made his way through the crowd that was growing and watched the dance. He saw Leoma. The music stopped, and a slower tune came. Ty moved quickly and said, "Leoma, you look good."

"You think so? This is just an old dress."

"Hello there, Kincaid."

The couple turned to see Judge Parker and his wife.

"Hello, Judge," Ty said. "This is Leoma Jordan. Her family bought the Manning ranch."

"Hello, Miss Jordan. It is nice to meet you. And this is my wife, Mary," Parker said. "She is the woman who keeps me safe. Well, she won't let me dance with any pretty women," Parker said and winked at Leoma.

"Why, Judge, I will so. You go right ahead."

"No, I'm claiming you, my dear. Let's go. By the way, how's the ranch going?"

"Very good. Very good indeed. We appreciate your interest."

"No trouble with the sheepherders?"

"No, not a bit."

"I met some of them, Judge," Ty said. "Real serious men. Good men, I think."

"Let's keep it that way."

"Good to meet you, Miss Jordan," Mrs. Parker said. Judge Parker led his wife onto the dance floor.

Ty turned to Leoma. "Now, how about a dance? I'm not very good."

She grinned. "I'm very good, so you just let me lead."

Ty laughed. "You women always want to lead. All right, that suits me."

They had two more dances, and then Leoma was chosen by several other men for dances.

Ty was getting refreshments when he heard a man cursing. He saw the man had a gun. He had left his own at home. When the man raised the gun, Ty could see he was totally drunk. "Leoma, get down!" Ty cried. He threw himself forward and pushed her to the floor, but at the same time he felt that someone had slapped him on the back, and he thought, *Who would be hitting me on the back?* Then he realized it was a bullet and not a hand that had struck the blow.

There were several marshals, and they grabbed the drunk and hustled him out of the room.

Aaron Jordan came over at once. "Are you all right, Leoma?"

"I am, but Ty took the bullet. Put himself right in the way of it between me and that drunk."

"Well, we are in your debt, Ty. We are indeed."

Judge Parker came over and said, "Well, they got him corralled. What about you?"

Ty grimaced. "Well, I got a bullet hole, but I'll live."

"We're going to get you to the doctor, and then you need to come home with us to recover," Aaron Jordan said. "We've got plenty of room and two good nurses, Leoma here and my wife."

"Why, there's no call for that. I'll be all right," Ty protested.

"No," Parker said. "You just go along with Mr. Jordan here. This will take more out of you than you now realize. Don't let him come back until he's fit, Mr. Jordan."

"I'll see to that. Now, come along. We're going to get you in a wagon."

Ty went protesting, but he was outvoted. As a matter of fact, he did feel somewhat weak, and the wound was becoming very painful. He knew the shock was wearing off. He felt himself slip into unconsciousness as the wagon hurried through the streets of Fort Smith.

Ty awoke confused, then realized he was in the Jordans' wagon and they were on their way to their home. He felt the bandages covering his wound and winced as he tried to sit up.

Leoma sat beside him and kept him from rising. "You need to stay put now. We don't want that wound to start bleeding again. How are you feeling?"

"All right, I guess. It's really not all that much. I've been shot before worse than this."

"Well, we'll get you home and put you to bed so you can rest."

"Sounds like I'm nothing but a burden."

"That other woman. She had to take care of you, too, when you were sick."

"Well, I like being taken care of. Haven't had much experience, but you just pamper me all you want."

Raina and her father got along fine. She discovered that the dream of his heart was to build a church somewhere in the territory.

"There's plenty of folks need the Lord," he said. "Maybe you can help me."

Raina had found that she had a real affection for her father.

After being there a couple of days, she knew she needed to go to town for her things. She told her pa, "I'm going to town to get my things and to get some supplies."

"Take your gun with you," her father said.

"I'll go along to be sure she's all right," Mikel said. Mikel was a nice-looking man somewhere in his early thirties. She questioned him a great deal as they rode along. She had hoped to find out more about him, but he said little about his own life.

"Look, there's the Jordan ranch," she said. "Let's stop there and see if they need anything from town."

"I may not be welcome. They don't like sheepherders."

"They may be a little bit nervous, but we'll just stop for a moment."

As they approached the porch of the house, she saw to her shock Ty Kincaid sitting in a rocker with an arm in a sling. Leoma Jordan sat beside him.

"Hello, Leoma." She stepped off her horse. "Ty, what happened to you?"

"Oh, a little accident. Hello, Mikel."

Raina looked at Leoma. "Do forgive my rudeness. This is Mikel. He works for my pa."

Mikel nodded at Ty and Leoma.

Raina then spoke plainly. "Now, tell me what happened to you, Ty Kincaid."

"He took a bullet for me," Leoma said, and she told of the incident at the dance. "Might've hit me in the heart." She smiled. "So I'm taking care of him." She laughed aloud then, and there was humor in her face. "Ty, it looks like you make a big thing of letting women take care of you."

"I like it that way. That's what women are for, to take care of us helpless men."

"I'm going into town. Can I bring you anything back, Leoma?"

"No, my father has gone there."

"Well, I'll stop back on the way and see how you're doing, Ty."

"How are you making it with your father?" he asked.

"Oh, I like him very much."

Leoma frowned. "I hope he's going to keep the woolies off of our ranch."

"I heard he brought all the sheepherders together and told them plainly to stay off Running J Ranch. I don't think you have anything to worry about. He's a strict man, and he'll work with you."

"That sounds good," Leoma said. "Come back in time for a meal."

"I'll probably be in a hurry, but thanks for the offer."

As they rode out, Raina said to Mikel, "That could have been serious. That bullet could have hit him in the head or in the heart."

"Not according to your father. He said everything happens according to a plan."

"Yes, I know. Do you believe that?"

"I don't know what I believe."

"I guess I don't either, but I'm not giving up hope."

PART THREE

CHAPTER 14

The main street of Fort Smith was practically empty. It was not a day for hangings, and the afternoon had fallen with the sun coming down in the west like a huge yellow ball. A mustard-colored dog ambled out of the Lucky Star Saloon, walked a few feet, and then plopped down and began to scratch his ears with a lazy motion.

"Look at that dog, Ty." Heck Thomas was sitting in his usual position with a straight-backed chair leaning back against the wall. There was no trouble, so there was no call for Heck's law-keeping abilities, and as usual when he had nothing else to do, he whittled on a piece of cedar. At his feet lay a pile of shavings as evidence that he had been at this task for quite a while.

"You look about as tired as I feel, Heck." Ty was sitting beside Heck, his hat pulled down over his eyes to keep out the rays of the dying sun. He had been back in Fort Smith for a couple of days after his recovery time with the Jordans. He was still on light duty as his shoulder was pretty stiff and could affect his shooting ability. "I wish I didn't have any more worries than that critter."

Heck grinned and shot a glance at Ty. "He does have an easy life, don't he? Just a bit of food, a place to sleep. Wish I had it that easy."

"No you don't, Heck. You'd go crazy with nothing to do."

"I reckon you're right, Ty. I tried it once. I had some money saved up, tried just being a bum, but I couldn't make it. I have to have my hand in something. As a matter of fact, I'm surprised we haven't had more action from these so-called outlaws."

Ty looked over at Heck with surprise. "Why do you call them 'so-called'?"

"Aw, the writers of them westerns that's comin' out like popcorn now, they always make the outlaws seem like heroes. You take all them stories about Wild Bill Hickok. He wasn't nothin' but a two-bit crook! They made him out to be a hero who kept the law, but he broke it. His favorite way was to sneak up behind somebody and shoot 'em in the back of the head. That's the kind of *hero* he was."

"Yeah, I tried to read one of those once. It didn't seem like it was very lifelike."

"Lifelike! There ain't nothin' lifelike about 'em. You take these fellows we've been chasin'. . . ."

"What fellows is that, Heck?" Ty asked lazily. His eyes scanned the streets, but there was no trouble, and if there had been, there was a sheriff to take care of the town trouble. The marshals all spent their time in Indian Territory.

"Why, you heard of Jesse James."

"Sure. Everybody's heard of the James boys."

"Yep. Frank and Jesse. They've written a dozen of them little novels about 'em, all makin' heroes out of 'em, and you know they even came here and served as marshals for a while."

This information caused Ty to open his eyes. "I didn't know that, Heck. Why did Judge Parker hire them?"

"They didn't have no reputation back then, but they could ride and they could shoot."

"Were they good marshals?"

"Not worth spit! They went out and broke the very laws they were supposed to enforce. One Indian wouldn't buy any of their rotgut whiskey, so Jesse just pulled his gun out and shot him right in the head. Killed him dead. They didn't last long. Judge Parker found out they were worthless and ran 'em off."

"Well, that's not the way the stories make them out. They call him the Robin Hood of the West. Robbing rich people and giving it to the poor."

"Huh! I'd say that's about as big a lie as you could tell." Heck grunted. He carefully peeled off another long sliver of the cedar, sniffed the stick he had left, and said, "Cedar smells better than anything, don't it?"

"Pretty good, I guess."

Heck peeled off several slivers, watching them curl and fall to his feet. He had a nice pile there, and he would gather them all up and put them in his bed to make it smell good. It was a peculiarity of the famous marshal, Heck Thomas, that few people knew about. "And then there's those Dalton brothers. You heard of them, I guess."

"Sure. They were bank robbers mostly, weren't they?"

"Yeah, there's Grat and Bob, his brother. They made most of the trouble. They were marshals for a while. You know it's a funny thing, they could have been great marshals. Grat was smart, and Bob was good with a gun. They did pretty well for a while here as marshals. Brought in some wanted men, but they didn't last either. Now they're out there stealin' and shootin' and killin'. We got orders to bring 'em in dead or alive."

"I guess they might be a little bit hard to take."

"I could take both of them with one hand." Heck suddenly grinned and turned to face Kincaid. "I sound like one of them boasters down at the saloon, don't I?"

"Well, you're not that."

The two sat silently, soaking up the last rays of the sun. Heck folded his knife and stuck it in his pocket. Then he carefully gathered up the shavings and put them into a small cotton sack he carried for that purpose. He leaned back in his chair and said, "You know, I've been watchin' you, Ty."

"I figured you would be. You keep an eye on all your marshals."

"Well, you know what? I don't think you're happy bein' a marshal."

Surprised by Heck's astute analysis of his mind-set, Ty Kincaid looked at the marshal and asked, "What makes you think that?"

"Well," Heck said slowly, "bein' a marshal ain't for everybody. It's a one-way street. We've lost fifty men, killed, and what have they got to show for it?"

"Nothing, I guess, except they were trying to do their job."

"Some were and some weren't. It's a sorry enough job, Ty. It's a wonder we're able to get any men a-workin' at it. The pay is practically nothing. It's dangerous. You can get killed just walkin' around in the Indian Territory."

"Well, I've got to admit I was glad to get the job. I was pretty low down and felt pretty useless. At least this way I feel like I'm doing a job that needs doing."

"Oh, I guess that's what some of the fellows do, but for others it's just a job. They get out there and get infected by all the criminals on every hand. The Indians cheatin' each other. Of course they got the Indian police to take care of 'em, but there's enough white gunmen out there to keep Judge Parker's court busy."

"Different kinds of men, I guess."

"That's what I'm tryin' to tell you, Ty." Heck Thomas was not a handsome man. He was hard and smart and knew how to handle men, and now he turned to face Ty and said, "You know, Kincaid, you're not fitted for this job. Oh, I know you can *do* it, but it ain't good for you. You need to find a better way to live."

Ty Kincaid did not speak, for he had been thinking exactly the same thing. Finally he sighed and said, "Well, I did what I had to do, Heck. I guess I'll stay at it for a while."

"I wish you wouldn't. You're too good a man to waste, but you're a good marshal. I need all that kind of man I can get."

Raina brought a piece of apple pie on a small cracked plate and set it down before her father. "There, Pa, see how you like that pie."

He looked down at the pie, and then he grinned. "Well, what a nice surprise."

"Taste it. See if it's any good."

He took the fork, cut off the end of the wedge, and stuck it in his mouth. He chewed thoughtfully, and then his eyes opened wide. "Why, this is as good a pie as I ever ate in my life."

"Oh, you eat anything. You throw it back in your mouth, and

you don't chew. I'm surprised you taste anything."

"That ain't so, daughter. Since you've been here cookin' for me, I must have gained five pounds."

Raina sat down and for a while just listened to her father as he talked about the sheep and the job.

Finally he turned and gave her an intent look. "I've been wondering about you, daughter."

"What about me?"

"Well, I've been wondering what you really want." Pa shrugged, ate the last bite of pie, and then swallowed it. "You want more than just chasin' around after a bunch of sheep."

"Well, if it's good enough for you, it's good enough for me."

Pa shook his head. "No, that ain't so. What do you really want if you could have anything you ask for?"

"Well, I'd like a place and a family. I guess every woman wants that. What do you want, Pa?"

"To serve God."

"Why, you're a Christian now."

"I know, but that ain't enough." He put the fork down, then picked the plate up and licked it until it was clean. "Now you don't have to wash it." He grinned at her. "Well, I tell you, daughter, what I really want to do. These poor Indians out here, they worship them heathen idols of theirs. Ain't got no more religion than a stick. They think they do, but they ain't. I want to start a church, a real church, that will hold up the Lord Jesus Christ as the Way for all men to follow."

"Do you think the Indians would come?"

Pa's eyes brightened, and he nodded vehemently. "Yeah, they would come. Where the Gospel is preached, they will come. So I want to start a church. Not a town church where you wear a white shirt and a fancy tie and a black suit. I want to start a church where these Indians, who don't have much anyhow, can have hope of a life after this one."

"I don't know if they would come to a church."

"Jesus said, 'If I be lifted up, I'll draw all men unto me,' " he said firmly. "The Indians would come, and some of these outlaws would come. Just down-and-outers, all of them losers."

Raina was quiet for a while, and then she leaned forward, picked up her father's hand, and held it as she prayed and asked the Lord to come into her heart. She looked up and felt a lightness in her heart. She told her father what she had just done.

He looked at her with surprise and then with a happy light. "Praise the Lord!" He hugged her for several minutes. "It's so good to have you here, daughter. I just want to see you have a good life."

"Well, God's given me a father. That's what I came here for. Now I want to give God whatever I can."

"Well, praise the Lord! We'll do it, daughter," he exclaimed. "We'll start this church, me and you. You do the singin', and I'll do the preachin'."

Raina knew that the Lord now dwelled in her heart. She had found her father, she had found a place, and now she was determined to serve God. "All right, Pa. We'll do it, you and me."

The five men sat around a rickety table in a filthy room. It was a room devoid of any woman's care. Dirty dishes were piled on a table close to a pump. The food had hardened in them, and the men's method was to scrape them off with a knife before they filled them up again. There had once been wallpaper in the room, but it was peeling off now and revealed the bare boards of the house.

The men themselves were as slovenly dressed as the room was adorned, except for one man. Johnny Taylor was only seventeen, but through some miracle he had developed a sense of pride in his appearance. His clothes were clean and fairly new, his hair was cut, and the men in his brother's band often called him Dandy Johnny.

Johnny was only of medium height. He had tow-colored hair, neatly trimmed, and pale blue eyes. He was by far the youngest man, for at the table was Grat Dalton and his brother, Bob, both hardened outlaws.

Mexican Jack had black hair and eyes and a mustache. Fritz Holder was the biggest man there, six-two. He had a scarred face, had lost most of his hair, and had a deadly look about him. The other man was Long Tom Slaughter, very tall with yellow hair. He was a killer to the core.

The men were cursing and playing poker, and Slaughter, who was the best poker player, had won most of their money.

"I think you're cheatin'," Grat Dalton said. He was short and tough, lantern jawed with hazel eyes.

He glared across at Slaughter, who merely laughed at him, saying, "It's all skill, Grat."

"No it ain't. It's just luck."

"All skill." Slaughter grinned. "Well, let's play another hand."

Johnny threw down his cards. He had lost all of his money, and he said, "I'm bored out of my skull. We need to get out of here and do something."

"We can't do nothin' until Garth comes back." Grat Dalton grunted. He spoke of Johnny's brother, the leader of the band, who was tall, strong, and fast with a gun. He had pale hazel eyes and ruled his band of outlaws with a firm hand.

Johnny got up and walked around the room. He picked up a whiskey bottle, poured himself a tumbler half full, and drank it down. "Garth might not come back for another week or two. We need to be doin' something."

"We're not doin' anything until Garth gets back. He's the boss," Long Tom Slaughter said. "We'll wait on Garth."

Johnny shot him a hard look, but though he tried to appear tough like the rest of the outlaws, he had been kept from all sorts of danger by his brother. The bond between the two men was obvious. Garth was old enough to be a big brother, which he was. If Garth Taylor cared about anything, it was his brother, Johnny. He protected him, and well he did, for the other men would have beat him to a pulp for his dandy ways.

Johnny finally threw himself into a chair and said suddenly and abruptly, "Garth might not come back for a month. You know how he is, but I know how we can pick up some easy money."

Fritz Holder grinned. "Where are you proposin' we get all this easy money, Johnny?"

"Why, it's that ranch that new fellow started. The name is Jordan. He's got more cattle than he can even count. We can go down there, take some of them, and go sell 'em across the border to Lowell Gearson. He'll take all the stolen cattle he can get."

Bob Dalton laughed. "So you want us to become cattle rustlers."

"Sure," Johnny said eagerly. He sat up straight, and his eyes were gleaming. "We could just go down there and take a hundred of those cattle and sell 'em, and by the time Garth gets back we'll have plenty of money."

All of the outlaws shook their heads, and it was Mexican Jack who said, "You know Garth. He's just liable to shoot us if we left without him."

"He wouldn't shoot me." Johnny swaggered. "Especially if we make a lot of money. We'll give him part of it."

"Well," Fritz Holder said, "I'm bored like you are, but you know how your brother is. We'll have to wait until he gets back."

"Yeah, your idea sounds good." Bob Dalton nodded. "But Garth will have to say."

Suddenly Johnny's eyes blinked as an idea struck him. "Why, he's already said."

"What are you talkin' about?" Grat Dalton said. "Said what?"

"He told me the day he left that if he didn't come back in a week we could go get some of that cattle."

"He didn't say anything to me about it," Grat said.

"He was on his way out. We just got to talkin' about it. He said it would be the easiest money we ever got."

"Well, I didn't know Garth said that," Grat Dalton said. "He usually tells me what he's got planned."

"Why, he said it'd be so easy we could get as many cattle as we need."

"Well, there's bound to be somebody guardin' those steers," Mexican Jack said. "They're not just runnin' wild."

"Aw, they just got a couple of hands. They won't be no trouble," Johnny said.

The idea caught on, and Johnny kept it going. Finally Grat

Dalton, who was, more or less, the first lieutenant of Garth Taylor, said, "Well, all right. If Garth says it's okay, we'll do it."

"I don't know," his brother, Bob, said, scratching his chin. "We'd better wait for Garth."

But in the end, Johnny convinced them, and they all agreed. They were bored and broke except for Long Tom Slaughter, who had won their money.

When they rode out, Johnny was excited. He said once to Bob, "Now I'm going to show my brother what I can do."

The grass close to the home ranch had been pretty well eaten down by the grazing steers, and only Harry Littleton and Nelly Fox were keeping them. It was really too big a herd for two men, and they were scattered pretty wildly. Many of them were gathered down by the small stream, drinking their fill. Both men looked up when they saw Ash driving his horse at a fast run as he loved to do.

"He's going to kill that horse," Nelly said.

"Well, he's killed others," Harry said. Harry was a small man with tow hair and blue eyes. He wasn't at all a hardened man, but he was good with cattle.

Ash pulled his horse up, and the two men saw that it was lathered. "You're going to ruin that horse."

"It's my horse, not yours," Ash said. "I come out to tell you to try to keep these steers close together, Pa said."

Nelly Fox lifted his head. His hearing was acute. Some said he could hear a cricket chirp a mile away. "Sounds like horses coming."

Ash looked over in the direction that Harry was pointing. "Strangers, ain't they."

Nelly said, "They may be coming to get the cattle. Paul said there would be cattle thieves around here."

"Okay. Scatter out here. If you see 'em take any cattle, shoot 'em down."

"Wait a minute. We're not supposed to shoot people unless they actually steal something," Harry said.

"You do what I tell you. If they give us any trouble, I'll kill the first one."

The outlaws had made the trip taking care their horses were not exhausted. Suddenly Grat said, "There's the cattle."

"There's a bunch of 'em," Johnny said excitedly. "I don't see nobody guardin' 'em. Spread out. We'll take about a hundred of 'em. Doesn't look like there's going to be any trouble."

The band spread out, but when they got close enough, suddenly they heard a yell, and a shot rang out.

"Watch out," Grat yelled. "There's three men guardin' 'em!"

The outlaws pulled their guns and began shooting. It was too far for any accurate shooting, and all they succeeded in doing was frightening the cattle so they started milling around while some ran away.

"Let's get out of here," Grat yelled. "We don't know how many there are."

"No," Johnny said. "There's only two or three of 'em." He rode forward, but before his horse could cover ten yards, one of the shots hit him.

Johnny heard somebody yell out, "You got him, Ash!"

Grat said, "Are you hurt bad, Johnny?"

"They shot me," Johnny said, surprised as he looked down at his bloody chest. "I didn't think they'd shoot me."

"We've got to get him back so we can take care of him," Slaughter said. He shook his head and said, "Garth's liable to shoot all of us for getting his kid brother shot."

Garth Taylor did not look the part of an outlaw. He was a handsome man with light hair and strange hazel-colored eyes. He had come out of the house, and when he saw Johnny being held in the saddle by a man on each side, he cursed and said, "Where have you been?"

Grat said, "Johnny told us you said it'd be all right to steal the cattle."

Even as he spoke, Johnny slumped, and Long Tom Slaughter grabbed him. "Get him into the house."

They carried the wounded man into the house, put him in a bed, and stripped his shirt off. When Garth saw the wound, he knew there was no hope. He glared around. "I ought to kill all of you."

"Wait a minute, Garth. Johnny told us you said it'd be all right," Bob said.

"You know I wouldn't have told you to do a thing like that." He leaned over and saw that the blood was bubbling from the wound in Johnny's chest. He had lost too much blood. Garth knew there was no hope.

Suddenly Johnny opened his eyes. He whispered, "I just wanted to be like you, Garth—tough like you." He did not speak anymore.

Garth was stricken. He looked down at the dead body of his brother and asked harshly, "Who shot him?"

Grat said, "Somebody named Ash. I reckon he's one of the owners of the ranch. And they captured Fritz."

Garth stood up and looked down. He gritted his teeth and said, "It's not gonna be safe for anybody who works for that ranch. What do they call it?"

"The Running J."

Mexican Jack said, "We are gonna hunt down that fella that shot Johnny. Ash is as good as dead already."

Garth straightened up and turned his eye away from his brother. "No, not just him. I'm gonna see him dead, but I'm gonna see the rest of them cowpunchers dead, too."

CHAPTER 15

Leoma Jordan bent over a bolt of material in Max's General Store. She had looked at every selection that existed but finally sighed and said, "Well, I guess I'll just have to make do with this."

Ty Kincaid entered the store. When he heard Leoma muttering to herself, he sauntered over. "So, you're talking to yourself."

"I suppose so, Ty. I guess the next step is the insane asylum."

"Oh, it's not that bad. That's a pretty piece of cloth there. You thinking about making me a shirt out of it?"

"Well, it would look better on you than it would me. It's not my color."

The two talked, and finally Ty asked her, "How long you been in town?"

"Oh, I've been here three days. I get so bored out on the ranch. Somebody had to come in and buy some supplies."

"Is all this yours?" He waved at the stack of groceries and supplies that she shoved to one part of the counter.

"Yes, it is."

"Well, I'll hang around and help you take it to your wagon."

"I'm ready to go now." She called Max Thornton over and said, "I want to take all this with me, Mr. Thornton."

"Sure thing, Miss Jordan. Let me add it up for you." After a few minutes he said, "That'll be twenty-seven dollars and fifty cents, Miss Leoma."

Leoma shook her head. "Things are sure high these days." She paid the bill, and Thornton put the material in cardboard boxes.

Ty carried them out and stacked them in the wagon. "Have you eaten?" he asked.

"Not much."

"Well, let me buy you a bowl of soup or something."

"That would be nice."

The two of them started down the street, but Leoma stopped abruptly. "Look," she said, "there's my father and my mother. What are they doing in town?"

"Looks like somebody ran into trouble," Ty said.

He saw that the men looked angry, and they pulled their horses up sharply.

Ty and Leoma went out to meet them. She asked, "What's wrong, Pa?"

"We had some trouble. Ty, a bunch of outlaws tried to run our cattle off."

"Any of our men hurt?" Leoma asked quickly.

"No, but we got two of them. That's one of them tied on the horse. You'll recognize him, Ty. He was one of the men you faced down at our ranch when we first arrived. The other one was able to ride off."

184

Ty walked down and pulled the head of the man on the horse up and looked at him. "Yeah, that's Fritz Holder."

Heck Thomas had approached and said, "Let me take a look." He pulled the head up and said, "Well, Holder, you got caught this time." He turned to Ty and Aaron. "He runs with Garth Taylor's bunch. What about the other one you saw, Mr. Jordan?"

"I wasn't there. You saw it, Ash. Tell him."

"There was a pretty big bunch of 'em and only three of us. When they started to run the cattle off, we opened up on 'em, and I guess they didn't know how many of us there was, so they took off runnin'. I hit one of 'em I think pretty bad, but they managed to get away with him."

Aaron said, "Can you arrest that bunch, Marshal?"

"Well, I don't know, Mr. Jordan. Can you identify any of them?"

"No, we couldn't see that well. It was dusty, and they was a pretty long way away," Ash said. "But I know one of them got hit that didn't fall to the ground."

"Well, you said this was part of a wild bunch, didn't you?"

"Yes, but those fellows move around, Mr. Jordan. They don't stay with one band long. When there's a big job going, they swap members, but I'll send a man out." He glanced at Ty and said, "Kincaid, you go out with Mr. Jordan. See what you can find."

"Sure will, Marshal."

"I might as well go back to the ranch with you, Pa," Leoma said. "I've got all the supplies."

"All right. We'll have to go slow. These horses are pretty tired."

Ty got his horse, tied him to the back of the wagon, and sat down on the seat to drive.

Leoma said, "I hate to hear about things like this. Men getting killed over cattle."

"Well, I've seen men killed over less than that, like a two-dollar bet on a poker game." Ty sighed. "That's the way men are. I think it's gonna be dark by the time we get in. I hope we don't run into that bunch."

"I don't see how you ever catch anybody in such a big space. The range is big," Leoma noted.

"Yes, it is. It's hard to catch 'em. They're pretty slick."

"Do you like being a marshal, Ty?"

"Not all that much."

"Why do you do it then?"

"I have to make a living some way, Leoma. I've done worse."

"I wish you could find a better way."

"So do I. I'd take it in a minute if I could find it."

By the time they reached the ranch, they were all tired. The sun had gone down, and the stars were coming out. "Look, there's just one star in the sky," Leoma said.

"Yes, that's Hesperus. People call it Venus. The evening star."

"It looks lonely up there."

He laughed and said, "I don't know if stars get lonely or not, but I know I do."

"Do you, Ty? You've never been married."

"No, haven't had that good fortune."

"Well, you will have."

"Maybe. Never know about things like that."

The two pulled up at the house, and Ty and the men unloaded the groceries. As Ty took the last bag in, Aaron came over to him and said, "Do you really think you can find something?"

"Well, tomorrow morning early I'd like one of the men that was there to take me out where the shooting took place. You never can tell. Might find some kind of clue that'd lead us to one of them, and then we could get the others."

When the supplies were in, Leoma said, "Come in. I'm sure Ma is fixing something to eat."

"Sounds pretty good." Ty followed Leoma into the parlor.

"We'll relax in here until the food is ready."

They sat for a while in silence until Leoma turned and said, "Why are you looking at me?"

Ty smiled. "I always like to look at good-looking women."

"Don't you try to get next to me, Ty. I know you men," she said playfully.

"Well, some men are pretty bad, but I was always good myself. When I was a kid I went to church every Sunday and helped old ladies cross the street."

"I'll just bet. You were a good-looking young man, and I'll bet women hid their daughters when you came around."

"No, nothing like that." He stretched and said, "I don't know where I'm going really, Leoma. Sometimes I feel like a man who's in the middle of a bridge and I've forgotten both ends of it. I'm just standing there looking down at a river not knowing which way to go."

"That's sad. Have you felt like that long?"

"Long enough. You know, Leoma, a woman should be better than a man."

"I don't know why you'd say that."

"Well, men are squirming around. They just fight and do most every ungodly thing that comes into their minds. Well, a woman should be better than that. Something a man could look up to."

"You've got high standards for women. Maybe women have them for men, too."

"I just don't know. I wonder sometimes if there's any sense to life, but I look around and I see God made everything that works, and there has to be more to it than just men and women wandering around."

They talked for a while, and he said, "You know, we're just like a married couple talking over things."

"I guess we are."

"Well, I'm looking forward to that supper."

"Could I go with you tomorrow?"

"No, it's liable to be dangerous, Leoma. I wouldn't want anything to happen to you."

When Lottie called everyone to supper, all the men came in, and everyone wanted to talk about the raid.

"It's those sheepherders, that's who it is," Ash said.

"I doubt that," Ty said.

Ash looked at Ty. "Why would you doubt it? They killed our cattle."

"Well, for one thing, they were all on horseback. Sheepherders don't have horses."

"How do they get around?" Leoma asked.

"They just walk. You know, one sheepherder can keep up with as many as two thousand sheep. Think how many riders it would take to do that," Ty said.

"I don't have any idea," Aaron said. "But that's the only enemy we've got around here. You've got some funny thoughts there, Ty," Aaron said.

"Yeah, I guess I do. Wish I could turn my head off and stop thinking sometimes."

"Well, you want the rest of us to go with you tomorrow morning?" Aaron asked.

"No, just somebody to tell me how to get there."

"I'll do that," Ash said.

"Okay. I want to leave early."

After the meal was over, Ty went out to the corral and leaned on the top rail. There were a few horses in, and they made snuffling noises. One of them came and stuck his head up to be fed.

"Got nothing for you, boy," Ty said. He stroked the horse's silky nose, but it snorted and walked away.

"Did you get enough to eat, Ty?"

Kincaid turned to see that Leoma had come to stand beside him. "It was a fine meal," he said.

"Do you think you'll find anything out there?"

"I'll be surprised. It sounds like a raid, but that could be anybody. There's a dozen outfits that would like to steal cattle like these fellows did. We don't know if they have anything to do with the sheep."

"What will you look for?"

"Oh, look for tracks, which way they'd go, how many were there. Some of the tracks will have particular appearances. I'd know them anywhere."

She put her arms over the top rail, and the silver moon put its lambent light upon her, lighting up her face. "If you find them, they'll fight, won't they?"

"Most outlaws do."

"You won't go by yourself surely."

"I don't know. It depends on how it falls out."

"I wish you wouldn't go, or I wish you'd promise me if you do find anything you'd come and get help."

"Well, I'll probably do that if they're with a big bunch."

She asked, "Have you seen Raina Vernay lately?"

"Yes, she was in town not long ago. Seems to be doing fine."

"It was strange how you met her."

"Well, it was something you wouldn't read in a book. There I was about to die. She didn't know hardly anything about me. Took care of me while I was sick, fed me, and then she made it possible for us to get out here. I owe her a lot."

"She's a beautiful woman, don't you think?"

He turned and said, "She looks very well. I admire her."

"Why?"

"Because she has grit," Ty said. He shook his head. "A lot of men wouldn't have the nerve to do what she did. She ran off and left everything she knew because she couldn't stand to do things that she didn't like. Not many men could do that."

"I suppose not. I hate it we have this trouble over the sheep."

"I think there's more to it than that. I've met Raina's pa. He's a good man. Starting a church out in the badlands for the Indians and outlaws, I guess."

"Well, I don't think he'll have many converts. The Indians have their own gods."

"That's what I told him, but he's bound and determined to do it."

The two stood talking, and finally she walked away, saying, "Good night, Ty."

"Good night, Leoma."

As he had expected, Ty found no evidence except a great many hoofprints. They could have been the hoofprints of the raiders' horses, but they could just as easily have been from a party crossing on the way to town.

He went back to Fort Smith and gave his report to the judge. "I couldn't find a thing, Judge. I guess if I had been there, I might have seen something."

Judge Parker shook his head. "Well, we've had more trouble. Mr. Jordan came in and said there have been more sheep on his range and more cattle killed. Eddie Vernay says the same thing. Some of his sheep have been killed. I don't understand it. Those sheep have been there for a long time and never gave anybody any trouble."

"The former owner, did he get along all right with the man that owned the ranch?"

"Fine. Eddie Vernay always kept his sheep on his own land. That's what I can't understand, why a man would change like that."

"You want me to go back and see what I can find out?"

"Well, we're going to have to have some kind of a hearing. Both men are complaining, Vernay that Jordan killed his sheep and Jordan that Vernay killed his cattle. Something's beyond this. It's gonna take a smart man to find it."

"Well, you better send somebody else. I never hired myself out as a smart man."

"We'll see how it turns out. I sure get tired of things like this. It's almost as bad as hanging people."

"You feel bad about that, Judge?"

Judge Isaac Parker gave Kincaid a disgusted look. "Of course I feel bad about it. You think I enjoy hangings?"

"No, I wouldn't think so. Why do you do it?"

"I was appointed to keep order in this Indian Territory. We're gonna do it, me and Heck and marshals like you."

"I haven't been much help yet."

"You just stay on the job. We've got to find out what's going on here, Ty."

Kincaid was silent for a time, and then he said, "Do you ever get the feeling that all that goes on here is wasted?"

"What does that mean? We catch killers, and most of the time we hang them. That's something."

"But isn't it true that no matter how many you hang, there's always a new crop you have to find and hang?"

"I can't think like that. It's my duty to do all I can to bring law and order to this territory, and I'm bound to do it."

"Judge, don't you ever get discouraged?"

"Of course I do, Kincaid, but a man can't quit because everything doesn't go right. I look at it like a sacred duty. I think God put me in this job, and I do the best I can. Can't you see that?"

Ty shrugged, and for a moment stood silently regarding the judge. He had immense admiration for Parker but not much faith in the processes of law. Finally he said, "I think you're an honorable man, Judge, and you do what you see as God's work. But it seems like an impossible task."

"Don't you think I've asked myself many times if I'm doing the right thing? No man can sit in my court handing out sentences of death without giving in to some doubts. I may have hanged some innocent men. The system isn't perfect, but it's all we have. Can you imagine what this territory would be like if we didn't do our jobs?"

"It would be bad," Ty admitted. "And I know your job is the hardest. None of us have to wonder about what we do—but I know you are a man of conscience, so you have to have had thoughts of what your life means."

Judge Isaac Parker whispered as if to himself, "I think a lot about that, Ty—more than people think."

CHAPTER 16

Raina looked up at her father and thought how wonderful it was that she had a family, at least a father who loved her. She thought of how he had asked her once, "What do you really want, daughter?" And she had replied, "A place and a family." She had asked him then what he wanted, and he had simply said, "To serve God and to start a church."

Raina brought her mare, Daisy, out past the porch, and she heard her father call out, "Where you going, daughter?"

"Oh, just going to visit the herders and see that no more sheep have been killed."

"Well, you be careful. There's some bad men around here."

"I'm always careful, Pa. You know that." She waved at him and then kicked Daisy in the side. The mare started up at once at a slow trot. She was a good horse, obedient to command, and Raina had become quite attached to her.

Thirty minutes later she drew up to Benat. She talked to him for a while and then asked, "Where's Mikel and Yosu?"

"They're over there to the west, but you be careful."

"Everybody warns me to be careful. I will be."

She rode away with no real goal in mind except simply getting out. For the next hour she rode aimlessly, seeing nothing but coyotes and far off to the left a group of buzzards circling. *Something died,* she thought and had no desire to see what it was.

She turned Daisy around, and as she did something caught her eye over to the right. "Whoa, Daisy." She fixed her eyes on where she thought she had seen the movement and saw another. "What could that be?" she muttered and rode in that direction at a slow walk.

Suddenly she stopped, for she saw that it was a man. He was on foot, but even as he walked, he stumbled and went down. *That man looks hurt,* she thought and immediately kicked Daisy into a gallop. She got to the man and saw that his face was sunburned and his lips were roughly burned also.

She stepped off Daisy, tied her to a bush, and went to him, carrying a canteen. *He's dressed oddly,* she thought, *not like a cowboy or a sheepherder at all.* His skin was so fair that he had burned terribly. She could see that he had blond hair. She could also see that he was practically dying. She removed the cap from the canteen, lifted his head, and put it to his lips.

At first he didn't move, but then he began eagerly gulping.

"Just a little bit at a time," she said and removed the canteen. His eyes opened, and she saw that they were an azure blue, a color she had rarely seen. She wanted to ask him questions about what he was doing out here without a horse or anything, but she knew he would not be able to answer. She sat beside him and from time to time propped him up.

Finally after half an hour and many short sips of water, he gasped, "Thanks, miss."

"What are you doing way out here without a horse?"

The man licked his lips and asked for another drink. When he got it, he sat up feebly. "Well, I was out just taking a ride, and I was robbed and set afoot by two men."

Instantly Raina noticed that he had an accent that she did not recognize. It wasn't Spanish—she would have known that. "You can't stay out here. You're already burned. If I help you, can you get on my horse?"

"I'll try."

"She's very gentle." She helped him up.

He staggered over, holding on to her, and got to where Daisy was. Raina had to put his foot in the stirrup and then shove him until he could throw the other leg over. She removed his foot, mounted behind him, and said, "Okay, Daisy, let's go home."

It took a long time for them to make the trip, but by giving him small sips of water, she found out more about him. "What's your name?" she asked.

"George Fairfax."

"You're not from around here, are you?"

"No, not at all. I'm a stranger in this part of the world."

"You've got an odd accent. Where are you from?"

"England. Could I have some more of that water?"

She pulled off her handkerchief, wet it down, and said, "Keep this on your face, but take a little water first."

It was all the man could do to stay in the saddle, and Raina was relieved when she saw the house in the distance. "We're almost home, Mr. Fairfax."

He nodded but did not speak.

As she rode up to the house, her father came out. "What have you found, daughter?"

"This man was out without a horse. He's been robbed."

"Well, I expect we'd better get him in the house. He looks like he's got sunstroke. What's your name, mister?"

"George Fairfax."

Pa helped the man down, and Fairfax clung to him and to Raina as they helped him up the steps, led him through the door, and got him to a bedroom. He plopped down on the bed and said in a cracked voice, "Thanks."

"How in the world did you get afoot in the desert?"

"Well, I wanted to see the country, so I bought a horse and rode through it."

"Well, that was a bad idea," Pa said. "You could have gotten killed. There are men who do that."

"Well, they took everything I had. What's your name, sir?"

"Eddie Vernay. This is my daughter, Raina."

Fairfax smiled with some difficulty. "Well, you two saved my life, so according to an old Irish folktale, I belong to you."

Raina thought that was odd. "It's not like that. We don't belong to each other. Are you hungry?"

"I think I am."

"Pa, you give him some small sips of this water. Nothing big. I'll go fix something light."

Pa stayed with him until Raina came back. She had a bowl and said, "Can you sit up to eat this?"

"Oh yes. I think so." Fairfax pushed himself up to a sitting position.

She sat down beside him and handed him the bowl. "Can you feed yourself?"

"Yes, I think I can. I haven't had anything to eat in two days now."

"Well, this is just some light chicken broth. You take in little bits, and later on you'll be able to take on something more steady."

He ate the bowl of broth, and she took it, saying, "That's enough now. Is there anybody we can get in touch with and tell them you're not dead?"

"No, I don't think so."

"You're kind of a miracle, Mr. Fairfax. You could have died out there. Been killed by outlaws or Indians or even got snake bit," Pa said.

"Yes sir, I see that now."

"Do you know the Lord, Mr. Fairfax?"

Fairfax smiled slowly and nodded slightly. "Yes, in a way."

Raina was intrigued by the man. He was tall and lanky, with a handsome face and fair hair, and she knew that when the skin peeled he would have a smooth complexion. She asked, "Why did you come here, Mr. Fairfax? Not many people come to the Indian Territory."

"Oh, I inherited some money, and I was pretty tired of England, so I traveled. I went to Africa for a while and then to Australia. While I was in Australia, I read about this place and I thought I might find some adventure here."

"Well, you did that." Pa laughed. "You nearly found too much."

"Could I have some more of that soup?"

She got him a little more. After he finished his second bowl, he fell asleep.

Raina looked at her dad. "It's strange, isn't it, that a man would strike out in a place like this by himself."

"I guess it's not much like England."

For two days Fairfax rested up, and finally he said, "I believe if you had a buggy of some sort, I could go to town and get myself pulled together."

"We've got a buggy. Raina, you drive him in, will you?"

"I will, Pa."

Raina saw that the Englishman moved much more easily, but his face was peeling, so she insisted he keep out of the sun and furnished him with a broad-brimmed hat that someone had left at the house.

"What do you need to do when we get to Fort Smith?"

"Well," Fairfax said, "my skin's tight, and it feels like it's going to fall off. But anyway I need to go to the bank and get some funds."

"You have an account there?"

"Yes, I had a rather large sum of money transferred to the bank there."

They arrived at Fort Smith and went at once to the bank.

Mr. Jenson, the banker, was surprised. "Why, Mr. Fairfax, I didn't expect to see you in this shape."

"I know. I look pretty bad. I got robbed and laid out in the desert. This lady found me, or I would have been dead."

"Well, here's the money. Of course you have a large balance here, as much as you need, but I wouldn't carry large sums if I were you. Not in Fort Smith."

"I believe you're right, sir. Come along, Miss Raina. I need to buy some decent clothes."

They left the bank, and Raina said, "Oh, there's one of the marshals. Ty, would you come here, please?"

Kincaid had been walking the other way, but hearing her call, he changed direction and hurried to her. He ran his eyes up and down the tall man with her.

She said, "This is George Fairfax. Mr. Fairfax, this is one of Judge Parker's marshals, Tyler Kincaid. A good friend of mine."

"You look the worse for wear, Mr. Fairfax."

"I really am. I would have been dead by this time if this young lady hadn't found me."

"What happened?" Ty listened as the man told about how he was robbed. "Can you describe the men who did it?"

"Well, not too well, but they took what I had and knocked me over the head and left me to die."

Ty said, "Well, there's any number of men that'll do that for you in this territory. Give me the description you got."

Ty listened as George gave very brief descriptions and shook his head. "There's not much chance of getting your horse and your money back."

"Well, that doesn't matter," Fairfax said. "I'll just be more careful how I hang on to things." He turned and said, "Miss Raina, would you have a meal with me after I get some decent clothes?"

"Yes, I'll even go shopping with you."

"I never had a lady pick out my clothes—except my mother when I was young."

"Come around and meet the judge when you get presentable," Ty said. "He'll want to hear about this."

"Yes, I'll do that."

For the next hour they picked what clothes Fairfax approved of, which weren't many. "I really will have to order some clothes from somewhere else."

"I don't think you can get anything better in this part of the country," Raina said.

"Well, let's get something to eat. Where's the best restaurant?"

Raina said, "The hotel's nice."

As the two walked along the street, she was aware that Fairfax attracted glances. He had bought an unusual hat, more like a derby than anything else, and with his height and sunburned face, she saw that he was the object of everyone's attention.

They had a good supper, and afterward she said, "You'd better find you a room and lie down."

"Well, I've got to find a barbershop first. I need a bath."

"You can get that at the hotel. They'll bring your hot water up, I'm sure."

"Miss Raina"—Fairfax turned and reached out, taking her hand and holding it with both of his—"I've never had to thank anybody for saving my life before, so I'm not very good at it, but I thank you."

"You're welcome, Mr. Fairfax."

"Oh please, just George if you don't mind."

"And I'm Raina."

"Beautiful name. Will I see you again?"

"Yes. I'll come by later and see how you're getting along."

"I'll look forward to that." Fairfax smiled.

Raina went to get a room in Mrs. Mullins's boardinghouse for the night. She was surprised as she could not stop thinking about the enigmatic Mr. George Fairfax.

CHAPTER 17

Judge Parker was on his way from his house to the courthouse when he met Fairfax and Ty Kincaid with him. They talked for a moment, and after Ty explained the predicament that Fairfax had gotten into, Parker stared at the Englishman. "What are you going to do here in this country?"

"You know, I have a law degree from Oxford. It's possible I might be able to use that here in this country."

"I should think so. A law degree from Oxford, that's better than what most of our lawyers have around here."

"I'd really like to know more about American court procedure."

"Well, come along to the hearing."

"I'll just do that."

Fairfax and Ty went in and found seats. It was crowded there, and as they waited for the judge to appear, Fairfax told Ty how Raina had saved his life.

"Well, we have something in common." Ty grinned. "She saved my life, too. You know, she could make a career out of saving fellows like us."

They sat talking quietly until finally the judge appeared. He was not wearing a robe but his usual black suit. He listened to Ed Vernay, and then he listened to Aaron Jordan. It was a long-drawn-out affair, with Jordan getting angry.

Finally the judge said, "There are no witnesses to this, so my ruling is that you, Mr. Jordan, will pay Mr. Vernay for the sheep that were killed, and you, Mr. Vernay, will pay Mr. Jordan for the cattle that were killed."

This was acceptable enough to Vernay. He said, "I know I'm innocent, Judge, but I'll obey your ruling."

"But it's not fair! I didn't kill any sheep," Aaron Jordan complained.

"That's my ruling, and you'll pay right now before you leave this courtroom." He waited until the men had put up the money and then said, "Now, there'll be no more of this nonsense."

Ty left the courtroom, but Fairfax remained behind as he wanted to see more of the court in action.

Ty met Raina, who said, "Fairfax is pretty well recovered. You know, he said he'd like to see a sheep operation."

"Why would he want to do that?"

"He told me he might want to become a sheepherder."

"Now there's a thought. I might resign from Judge Parker's marshals and become one myself."

"No, it'll be a little bit rough for your taste, I think. You can tell me about your misspent childhood, and George can tell me about England and Africa."

"You know, Judge, I think we need to send somebody to keep an eye on that situation out there about the sheep and the cattle."

"You may be right, Heck. All it takes is one more ambush of sheep on Jordan's ranch and he'll blow his top."

"We'd better see a man out. If they see a marshal hanging around, that might stop them."

"Who will you send?"

"Let's send Kincaid. He's familiar with the people there and with the lay of the land."

"One may not be enough."

"Well, I can send more if the war heats up."

Heck left and found Kincaid coming out of the general store. "The judge wants to send a man out to keep an eye on this trouble between the Jordans and Vernay."

"He thinks there'll be some more of this?"

"Those sheep didn't just wander onto Jordan's land. Sheep don't wander like that."

"Well, what then?"

"That's what we're sending you for."

"All right, Heck. I don't know what good I'll do, but I'll see what I can turn up."

Leoma rose from the porch where she had been sitting and stepped down to meet Ty as he got off his horse. "Come in for some lemonade. It's warm but it's wet."

Ty noticed she looked as beautiful as ever. "Sounds good to me." He followed her inside, and when she had sat down, he asked, "Where are all the men?"

"They're all out looking for a sheep under every bush. I think it's foolishness." She gave him a big glass of the lemonade and asked, "What are you doing now, Ty?"

He tasted the lemonade. "Well, the judge sent me out to see if we could find out what's causing the trouble."

"Well, we know that, don't we?"

"You mean Ed Vernay?"

"Yes, his are the only sheep around here."

"I don't know much about sheep, but I don't think they wander much. Vernay's sheep camp is miles from here."

"Well, how else could they get here?"

"They may have been driven, Leoma."

"By Vernay?"

"That's not likely. Something strange about this. From what I hear, Vernay never lets his sheep stray. He always keeps them on his own land."

She studied him carefully. "Are you going to talk to Pa?"

"Oh yes, and everybody else."

"Vernay, too?"

"Sure."

Leoma seemed troubled, and he asked what was bothering her. She said rather hesitantly, "You and Raina Vernay were pretty close at one time, weren't you?"

"At one time."

"I think you would be more likely to listen to her and to believe her."

"No, that's not so. Tell you what. I'll be roaming around, and if I see something that looks strange with either cattle or sheep, I'll look into it."

They talked for a while. He got up and said, "I'll be back to you and your family."

"Are you going to talk to Vernay now?"

"Well, I'm going to look over the ground where all the sheep were killed. Will you show me where you found the slaughtered cattle?"

"I'll take you."

He stood up and said, "I thought about all those cattle and sheep dying." He shook his head and said sadly, "I hate to see anything wasted."

"So do I," Leoma said.

Ty grinned and gave the young woman a wink. "Especially good-looking young women." He laughed at her expression.

She said, "Never mind that!"

"Just making talk."

"Yes, I notice you do that a lot."

"You're such an interesting lady, I can't help it."

Leoma gave him a quick smile then asked, "How many young women have you run after, Ty?"

"Oh, maybe three or four."

"What a liar."

"I expect I am. My life's been pretty dull."

"Mine, too, I guess. Nothing really exciting has ever happened to me. I wish it would."

Ty glanced at her and said, "Like what?"

"Oh, nothing like you have—lots of adventure."

"Most adventures are pretty hard. I can think of a few that I could have done without. But you'd better be happy you haven't had too many of them."

"Better to have an adventure that hurts than be bored to death."

Ty shook his head, not understanding her. "Haven't you had men who wanted you? I expect so."

"Most of them were boring."

"Marry a juggler. He can entertain you if that's what you need. Didn't you love any of the men who wanted you?"

"Not enough to spend the next forty years with them."

Ty laughed aloud. "Well, that's coming right out with it."

The two studied one another, and then Ty said, "Come along. You can tell me more about your love life."

CHAPTER 18

Raina was enjoying George Fairfax's company tremendously. He was the kind of man she had never met before, cultured, handsome, wealthy, and he had insisted that she take him out to look at the sheep.

"Why do you want to look at sheep, George?"

"Well, I just like to know things."

They rode for a time and finally dismounted by a small stream and let the horses drink. As they stood watching, she asked him about his home in England. "Did you ever see the queen?"

"As a matter of fact, I did."

"I've heard a lot about Victoria and her love for Prince Albert."

"Well, everybody's fascinated by that. She was only a young girl when she married him. Somebody asked her what she was going to do as a queen, and you know what she said?"

"No, what?"

"She said, 'I will be good.' "

"What a fine thing for a woman to say." She remained silent

for a minute, gathering courage to ask her next question. "Have you ever been in love?"

"Well, yes." Fairfax took off his hat and ran his hand over his blond hair. "I know something about love. I loved my wife greatly. Even though she's gone now, I still think about her every day."

"Do you, George?"

"I suppose I always will. I think when you have the right kind of marriage, husband and wife become one. Death may take one or the other, but there will be something still in you." He turned suddenly and took her hand. "You remind me of her in a way, Raina."

"Me? Like a member of the British aristocracy?"

"Yes, you do. You're honest like she was. Beautiful as she was." He suddenly raised her hand and kissed it.

For a moment Raina was unable to speak. Then she felt him release her hand.

"Tell me about this desire of your father's to bring God to the Indians."

"Not just the Indians, George. He wants to bring the Gospel to some of these outlaws."

"Well, that would indeed be a miracle. I'd like to go to your father's church."

"All right. There's a service starting soon. We can go now."

Ty had been spending a great deal of time out on the range, primarily looking over the slaughtered cattle. After looking around for a while, he decided to go to the sheep camp. When he arrived at Vernay's place, he saw Mikel working outside. "Hello, Mikel."

"Hello, Kincaid. What are you doing out here?"

"Just looking around. What about you?"

Mikel stared steadily at Kincaid. "You're not out here just for the ride."

Kincaid arched his back to relieve the tension, then shoved his hat back from his forehead. "I wanted to look over the ground, at least Judge Parker wanted me to. What do you make of it, Mikel?"

Mikel was silent. He was not a man to speak a lot, for that was part of his Indian blood. He studied Kincaid and said finally, "Sheep aren't likely to wander as far as they were. As long as they've got grass and water, they pretty well stay put."

"Well, maybe you can show me where they're supposed to wander from."

Mikel shrugged. "You'd better get the boss to agree with that."

"Sure. Where will I find him, Mikel?"

"In church." Mikel grinned at Ty's expression. "But maybe you're not a church man."

His words troubled Ty. "Well, I'm not, but I need to be."

"The boss has been trying to get a church started. Only Indians come to the meeting."

"How do I get there?"

Mikel turned to point. "He's using an empty barn about a mile from the house." He gave Ty directions.

Ty said, "Aren't you going, Mikel?"

"No. I gave up on God a long time ago." Then he seemed to think better of his words. "But I've been listening to the boss's preaching, and it's got me hooked. Maybe I'll get converted and become a preacher."

Ty laughed. "I'd like to see that. I'd come and hear you." He turned his horse and rode toward the "church."

As Ty rode up to the old, unpainted barn, he saw there were a great many horses and a few wagons outside. He dismounted and heard his name called.

Turning, he saw Raina, who walked over to him. "I'm so glad you came. Did you plan to sing in the choir?"

"No, but I'd like to hear a sermon."

Raina smiled.

Eddie Vernay approached, accompanied by Fairfax. The preacher said, "You're a long way from Judge Parker's court, Kincaid."

"For a fact I am. I came to hear a sermon."

"Well, I suspect you didn't come this far just to hear a sermon."

Ty saw that the older man was good at reading what was in a man's heart. "You're right. The judge wants me to keep a close eye on things."

"Have you found anything?" Vernay asked.

"Not much."

"Well, you will. I'm not much of a preacher, but come in if you like."

"I'll do that."

They all went inside, and Kincaid saw that it was a rough church indeed. The benches consisted of boards put across kegs for the most part. A few roughly hewn boards had been made into seats with straight backs. He grinned and thought, *Nobody's going to go to sleep while the preacher's at it. Nobody could sleep on a bench like that.*

Young Indian children were running around. The Indians had adopted the right side of the benches as their territory, and a group of white people sat on the left.

"Pretty good crowd," Vernay said. "I've got the cook killing a sheep, and we'll feed 'em good." He grinned and said, "They kind of like manna. I don't expect any to fall from heaven, but at least it'll give 'em a motive for coming."

"Good idea." Ty nodded.

"Well, let's get going here." Ed Vernay walked to a spot in front where there was no pulpit at all or even a platform. He looked out at the congregation and smiled. There was a kindly look on his face. He said, "We're going to sing some songs. My daughter, Raina, is a good singer. If you know 'em, just chime in. If you don't, just sit and listen till you learn it."

Raina was obviously startled. Her father had not told her this part of his plan, but she at once began to sing "Near the Cross."

Ty and several others joined in. He enjoyed singing and did so with gusto.

Raina led the congregation in two or three more of the old church songs before she took a seat between Ty and George.

Finally Vernay said, "Now it's time for a little preaching. I just want to remind you of one thing. There's nobody in this church this morning that's led a worse life than I did. I'm ashamed to tell you some of the things I've done." He continued to tell of some of the instances he was not proud of when he was a young man, and he said, "For a long time I felt that I was too bad a man for God to save, but then I was reading the Bible one day, and I read about the death of Jesus on the cross. Let me read you that part of the story." He opened the Bible and read about Jesus on the cross between the two thieves. After he read the story, he said, "It's kind of hard to think about this, but here was a man looking at a Savior who was bloody, whose face was marred, who had been beaten almost to death, but this thief said, 'Lord, remember me when you come into your kingdom.' The first time I read that," Vernay said, "I thought, well, Jesus won't have anything to do with him. But then I read the next line, and I'll tell you it knocked me out of the saddle. Some of you know it. When the thief said, 'Remember me when you come into your kingdom,' Jesus said, 'Today shalt thou be with me in paradise.' "

Vernay halted for a moment, and Kincaid could see tears forming in his eyes. He dashed them away and then continued.

"You know that thief couldn't do one thing to make himself attractive to God. He had been a thief, a criminal, probably a murderer. There was no time for him to go out and do anything good that would please God. He was just a poor, helpless, dying sinner, and I'll remember throughout all eternity, I think, how I felt when I read that Jesus welcomed him into His kingdom that very day. Something seemed to just turn over in my heart, and I realized I could be saved. It was something I'd never even thought of, so I made up my mind right then and there to do the same thing that the thief did. I just simply called on the Lord. I don't remember the words," Vernay said simply, "but I do remember telling God that I was a sinner, and I couldn't do anything about that. I don't know how long I prayed, but when the praying was over, I knew that I was a saved man. That thief has been with Jesus for two thousand years, just about, but his life with God began the day he died with Jesus. That's what I want for myself, and that's what every man and woman and young person here in this church needs. Just to be close to Jesus for all eternity."

Ty was intent on the sermon when he felt Raina touch his arm.

She said, "Does that mean anything to you, Ty?"

He turned to her, a struggle raging in him, and he said, "I guess I'm just about where your father was. I thought I was too bad a man." He said no more but just sat while the sermon ended.

When it was over, Ty, Raina, and Fairfax went at once to speak to Vernay.

George shook his hand. "It was a wonderful sermon, sir. You're a mighty preacher."

"I thank you, Mr. Fairfax."

George added, "If I can do anything to help you, I don't know what it would be. If it's money, I can help with that."

"Could always use money to build a better church, but even that's not necessary."

Ty stood by, and as he left, he saw that Raina had gone to stand beside her father and Fairfax, and he wondered what she thought about the man. He, however, was more troubled about his own condition. The sermon had affected him deeply, and all that day as he rode away and got out by himself, he could not get away from the words of the scripture. *"Today shalt thou be with me in paradise."*

For several days, Ty was very quiet. He couldn't quit thinking about his standing with God, and he couldn't get Ed Vernay's sermon out of his mind. He tried to put it aside but was mostly unsuccessful until he and Gale Young were sent to make an arrest.

Gale Young said, "What about this Jeb Cotton? What's he done?"

"Well, the story is he shot an Indian he claimed had stolen a cow from him. He's not known as a violent man, Gale, so it should be an easy arrest."

Gale was a talkative young man at times, and he began speaking of things he planned to do in his life.

Ty was happy Gale was doing most of the talking, because he was still a bit overwhelmed with the conviction he felt for the life he'd led.

"You know what I want to do most of all, Ty?"

"What's that, Gale?"

"I want to buy a small ranch. It doesn't have to be a big one. And I want to marry Ellen Franklin."

"Ellen Franklin? Who's she?"

"Oh, she's my childhood sweetheart. We both grew up in the same little town. Before I left there to come here, I asked her to marry me, and she said she would."

"Most women wouldn't like to be proposed to and then have the prospective bridegroom ride away."

"She didn't like it much. She begged me to stay. As a matter of fact, she even cried when I left."

"I'm surprised you left her, Gale."

"Well, I almost didn't, but I told her I'd just try this for a while, that in all probability it wouldn't last. I just want a small ranch and a wife. She's waitin' for me."

"What do you plan to do then?"

"Well, I've had about enough of being a marshal. I want to go home, marry Ellen, and have some children and raise them. Then when I get older, I'll be a grandpa and have the grandchildren all around my knees. I can tell them stories about what a great marshal I was and that I knew the great Ty Kincaid."

"That wouldn't impress 'em much."

"Well, we don't have anything, but Ellen says we ought to marry, even though we don't have any money."

Suddenly a strange thought crossed Kincaid's mind. "You know, if I had a feeling like that about a woman, I'd do something about it."

"What would you do, Ty?"

"I'd leave marshaling that very minute. I'd ride to her, and I'd get on my knees and beg her to marry me, and then I'd throw that marshal's badge as far away as I could."

Gale was surprised. "I thought you liked being a marshal."

"No, I don't."

"Well, I've got to save some money first."

"You'll never do it on this job."

"I know it." He was silent for a time and said, "Maybe Ellen's right."

"About what?"

"That we ought to marry even if we don't have any money."

"If you really love the woman, Gale, do it."

Gale turned and faced Ty Kincaid. "I think I will. This will be my last job."

"Good for you, Gale. You get back to that woman. Marry her and have those kids. Maybe I'll come and be a godfather to one of them."

"I'd like that a lot." Gale smiled.

Half an hour later the two rode into Jeb Cotton's place. They found him scalding a hog.

Ty said, "Be careful. He's not known to be a shooter, but you never can tell." The two stepped out of their saddles, and Ty said, "Hello, Cotton."

"Hello, Marshal. What you doin' out here?"

"I'm afraid I've got to take you in. You got to stand trial for shooting that Indian, Jeb."

Jeb was a tall, thin individual, almost gaunt. His eyes suddenly blazed with anger. "I was defending my property. That Indian had a gun, and he drew on me."

"Well, that's not the way we heard about it. There was a witness, you know."

"Some witness! He was another Indian. You going to believe him over a white man?"

Ty saw at once that this was not going to be as simple an arrest as he had thought, but he was still determined to do it easily. "Come on, Jeb. If you're innocent, Judge Parker will let you go. Let me have your gun."

Ty fully expected that Jeb would pull his gun from the holster at his side and hand it over. Instead Cotton drew the gun and fired off a shot. It caught Ty off guard when the bullet struck Gale in the chest and knocked him down. Jeb turned the pistol to shoot Ty, but Ty drew his pistol and put one shot into the man's heart. Ty knew Cotton was dead, so he went to Gale and saw that he had been hit bad. He pulled him up and saw that Gale's eyes were open, but he was breathing in a shallow fashion.

"Ty—"

"What is it, Gale?"

"You know what? I'll never—have Ellen—now." He breathed in short, quick puffs, and with his last gasp he said, "Ty, write

Ellen. Tell her—I loved her more than anything."

"I'll do that, Gale."

Gale's eyes fluttered, and he whispered, "Ty, don't die like this. Don't miss out on life." The light went out of Gale's eyes, and his body slumped.

Ty held him as a sense of utter frustration enveloped him. He hugged the man and shook his head. "You missed it all, Gale, and Ellen's missed it, too."

"Look, there comes Ty, and he's got two men tied down on horses." Heck Thomas stood with Judge Parker outside the courthouse.

"That wasn't supposed to be a hard job. I hope that's not Gale. He's a fine young man."

But when the two men approached Ty, he fell off his horse.

Parker said, "What happened, Ty?"

"I didn't expect any trouble, Judge. Jeb's not known to be a killer, but he drew and shot Gale before I could do anything. I got him, but it was too late. They're both dead now."

"What a shame," Heck said. "Gale's one of the finest young men I ever knew. He had a great life."

"Did you know he was going to marry a girl named Ellen?" Ty asked Heck.

"He did mention it one time."

"Well, he'll never do it now." There was bitterness in Ty's voice, and he said, "I promised him I'd write her a letter, but I don't know what I could say."

"No, there's not anything to say at a time like this."

Raina heard about what had happened from one of the marshals who had come by their home. She and her father immediately got ready and left to attend the funeral that would be held two days later.

When they arrived in Fort Smith and spoke to Heck and Ty, her father was asked to preach a sermon at the service. After the funeral, she tried to find Ty, who had stood on the outer ring of the crowd, but he was gone.

Raina was worried about Ty, so she went to the barracks and found him there. "I've been looking for you, Ty."

"I had to be by myself. I don't feel much like talking."

"Come along." It was nearly dusk now, and the town had gone quiet. "Let's go for a walk."

"All right. If you say so."

The two left the barracks, and for a time she simply walked beside him saying nothing.

Finally, when they were on the edge of the town, he looked over and saw that the sun was setting. "Look at that sun going down," he said quietly. Then he added bitterly, "But it will come up tomorrow. Not like Gale."

"I know it's terrible for you, Ty."

He turned to her and whispered, "He missed out on everything, Raina. He had a sweetheart named Ellen. He had decided to leave Fort Smith and go back and marry her, and now he never will."

Raina was shocked. She thought of Ty as one of the toughest men she knew, but she could see his broken will and the tears standing in his eyes. She suddenly reached out, put her arms around him, and said, "He was a Christian, Ty. He told me that. He won't have Ellen, but he'll be safe. He'll be with Jesus forever."

"I know, but it scares me. He wanted Ellen and kids and a family and a home. That's what I've always wanted."

"Have you, Ty?"

"Yes, and it's a lonely life, being without God."

"You don't have to be alone."

He looked at her with surprise, saying, "It's all I know, Raina."

"You've heard the Gospel. All you need is to find Jesus."

"I don't know how to do that. Wish I did."

"Talk to my pa. You trust him, don't you?"

"Sure, but—"

"Just do it." She hesitated then said, "I think it's easier to become a Christian than to be one from day to day."

"I don't understand that, Raina."

"Just think, a man can become a married man in five minutes— but I think it takes years to be a good husband, for most men at least. You can become a Christian in an instant, but sometimes it takes years to be a good one."

Kincaid blinked with surprise then whispered, "It sounds too easy."

"It's easy for us, but it was difficult for Jesus. He had to die to make a way for all of us to be saved."

Ty Kincaid said, "I'm just not sure that you're right about this, but I hope desperately that you are."

CHAPTER 19

Ty received word that Heck Thomas wanted to see him, so he went at once to the man's office. When he stepped inside, he asked, "You wanted to see me?"

"Yeah. Have you heard what's happened at the Jordan ranch?"

"No, I thought all was pretty well quiet out there."

"Well, Aaron Jordan came roarin' in about as mad as a man can get. He claims the sheepherders killed about twenty of his prime head of cattle."

"I was afraid of this. Did he have any proof?"

"No, not any, but he's on the rampage, Ty. I heard him tell Judge Parker if he don't send some marshals in, he'll take care of the trouble himself."

"Well, I don't imagine the judge liked that. What'd he say?"

"Said he would do his best, but he was short of men. Then the judge told me to ask you to look into it. I guess he knows, like everybody else, that you have good relationships with both sides. He said to go on a longtime scout. Find out what's goin' on." He stood up. He was not an impressive-looking man, this Heck

Thomas, but he had a mind like a razor. "You're a man who can find out things. This situation is bad, and it could get worse."

"I'll get right at it, Heck."

Ty left Thomas's office and immediately made preparations. He drew a packhorse and loaded it with all the supplies the animal could carry, then saddled his favorite horse. He was still preoccupied with his soul when he stepped into the saddle. More than that, he was more confused about this matter of God and his soul than he had told anybody.

He decided to go to the Jordan ranch first. When he arrived, Aaron Jordan was red in the face still with anger. "Come on. I'll show you those dead steers."

"All right, Aaron." Ty saw there was little reasoning with the man, and he went out and looked at the ground. "I don't see any tracks or sheepherders."

"Well, you're the tracker. You must have found something."

"The only thing I found was that one horseman has been through here, and his horse is missing a shoe on the right foreleg."

"Where does that get us?"

"Not very far, I don't guess. If we found a horse like that, we wouldn't have any proof that the man rode him here."

The two rode back to the ranch, and Aaron rode off still muttering threats.

Leoma came outside and asked Ty to come in the house.

"Don't have much time to stay, Leoma. Let's sit outside instead."

The two sat down on the porch, and he was quiet for so long, she said, "I know Gale Young's death hit you hard."

"Very hard. He was a fine young man, had his life before him. He was going to quit being a marshal and go back and marry his childhood sweetheart. A girl named Ellen."

"He told you that?"

"Yes, he did. And I told him it was a good idea. He got to talking on our way out to Cotton's place about what all he had missed in life." Ty turned and looked at her, his expression sad. He ran his hand over his abundant black hair. "He had it all planned out. He was going to marry her even if they had no money."

"They really loved each other then."

"Yes, you could tell that from talking to Gale."

She waited for him to go on, but he was silent for so long, she said, "It really bothers you, doesn't it?"

"Yes. You know why?"

"No. What is it, Ty?"

"It could happen to me. You know, one time I was going through the mountains, and I saw a deer. I got my rifle out to take a shot, but before I could get it out the deer just fell down."

"Somebody else shoot him?"

"No," Ty said. "That was the funny thing. I got to him and there wasn't a mark on him. He hadn't been hit by a bullet. I guess his heart just gave out, but he was dead, and the thing I thought of was this deer didn't know anything about this. When he woke up this morning, he thought he would have as much life as he ever had, but he didn't make it through the day." He shifted his weight in the chair and leaned over and stared down at the floor. "That's the way it was with Gale. It hit me hard."

"Death always does that."

"I guess so, but if a man's eighty years old you don't notice it so much, but he was just a young fellow. He had everything before him. He was even a Christian. He told me that."

"I'm glad to hear that."

"So am I. Well, I've got to go, Leoma."

"Come back after you've done some looking around."

"I'll do that."

For the next four days Kincaid looked over the ground. He stayed out away from the two men having the trouble, and at night he would build up a fire and read his Bible by the light of the flames. Most of the time he thought about Raina, but he couldn't forget Gale's death. He had written a letter to Ellen Franklin, which had been one of the hardest things he had ever done.

He spent a great deal of time trying to think how he could get right with God, and finally he went to the sheep camp. Raina was there, and he found he was a little bit restrained toward her.

It was Sunday, and he went to the church again. This time the sermon Vernay preached was on forgiveness. He read the scripture of the woman who was found in adultery and then brought to Jesus. Ty listened as Vernay read the story from the Bible: " 'The men who brought the woman asked Jesus, Moses in the law commanded us, that such should be stoned: but what sayest thou? But Jesus said nothing.' "

Ty had forgotten this part.

Vernay continued. "But Jesus simply knelt in the dust and began to write. The Bible says one at a time the men left."

I wonder what He wrote. Maybe the sins of those men, Kincaid thought.

Then Vernay read the most telling part. " 'Jesus said, Woman, where are those thine accusers? Hath no man condemned thee? She said, No man, Lord. And Jesus said unto her, Neither do I condemn thee: go, and sin no more.' "

The last words seemed to stick in Kincaid's mind, *"Go and sin no more."* Somehow he knew this was his problem. He had been a sinner all his life, that he well knew, but he had given little thought to changing. But now Jesus' order to "go and sin no more" was glued to his mind.

Raina knew she liked George Fairfax, and as he rode up and dismounted, she was pleased. "I'm glad to see you, George."

He smiled. "I'm delighted to see you, too."

"That's the way you English talk. No man ever told me he was delighted to see me before."

They talked for a time, and finally George heaved a sigh. "I've always been an impulsive man, and I need to tell you something, Raina."

"What is it, George?"

"Well, I've been thinking. I'm not getting any younger."

"None of us are." She smiled at him.

"And what I'd like to know is if you would entertain a proposal?"

"What sort of proposal?"

"I didn't think there was but one kind." Fairfax smiled. "A proposal of marriage."

Raina was caught off guard. She knew she liked Fairfax tremendously. He had qualities that no other man had ever shown to her. "Well, I'm not sure."

"I think I'm going to court you, and I believe we could be very happy."

"I've never thought of marriage for us."

"Well, think of it. We could do anything you like. I have plenty of money. We could buy us a ranch. We could live in the city. We could travel. You could go see England, Ireland, lots of things."

She stood waiting, and as she had expected, he put his arms around her and kissed her. It was a gentle kiss, and she liked that. She was surprised that she didn't draw back, for she usually held off from men. As he kissed her, she thought of Ty's kiss, and she knew she couldn't compare the two men. They were too different.

"I'll have to think about this," she said when he lifted his head. "There are other things in marriages."

"Yes. Some marriages. Well, you think about it." He kissed her again then left.

Raina's mind was in a whirl. Marriage to George Fairfax might be wonderful. She would certainly never want for anything. But was that enough? What about love? She thought about George's proposal, but somehow Ty kept intruding into her thoughts. She wasn't sure she even wanted to know what that meant.

Ty had spent several days riding around and finding mostly nothing. On the fourth day he was awakened in the middle of the night. It was a dark night with few stars in the skies and no moon except a tiny sliver. He suddenly heard the sound of sheep bleating. *Sheep don't move at night.* He got to his feet and picked up his gun. *Who would be moving sheep at this hour?*

"Who's out there?" he called, but several shots cut him off. One of them hit him in the chest. As he fell, Ty thought, *I'm going to die like Gale, not having done anything good in my life.* And then he knew nothing. . . .

PART FOUR

CHAPTER 20

The ebony darkness was almost palpable. At times a light appeared far in the darkness, but then it would fade away so he could sense it no more. He had been one acquainted with the night, and under the darkness of the blackest evenings there was always a faint flickering of stars or something that told him he was alive, but now he felt nothing except the slow passage of time.

From time to time a sound came to him—a faint voice from somewhere in the past. It seemed that he recognized the voice at times, but then it faded. He was aware that there was something out there, but his mind was buried so deep in unconsciousness he could not know it.

An acrid smell came to him, and for a moment he rose out of the depth of darkness that enveloped him. Underneath his body he felt the roughness of earth, but he could not recognize it.

Time meant nothing. He had no sense of its passage, and he could have been unconscious for as long as it took to build the pyramids, or it could have been only a few moments.

Finally he began to rise out of the darkness, and strange flashes of memory began to touch his mind. They were not fully developed, and he could not identify them. He was only faintly aware that they came from somewhere out of a past that he had left behind.

A figure and a face took shape in front of him. It was from his past, and he struggled to recognize it. Finally he remembered a scene in the woods, but he could not remember where it was. But there was a young boy there, and slowly as the features of the young man came together, he recognized Roy Gibbons, the best friend of his youth. It was an innocent face, youthful, unmarked by time, and yet he remembered it. It was very vivid. He saw himself and his friend as they crossed the field and came to a fence. Roy leaned his rifle against the fence and straddled it to go over, but as he did, he lost his balance and struck out. There was an explosion, and as clearly as he had seen anything, Ty recognized the crimson blood that spurted from his friend's throat. He cried out then as he must have cried out when he was watching this tragedy. "No, Roy!"

But then the terrible dream faded, and he suddenly knew that it was something he'd experienced as a young man. The darkness came again, and gratefully he lay back, glad not to see the awful scene of his friend dying.

Soon, however, another dream came. The face of a young woman took shape in the darkness and seemed to glow. She had an oval-shaped face. At first he did not recognize her, and then suddenly a name came to him. *Evelyn.* He tried to cry out to her, but she looked at him with a sadness that he could not identify. He lay there struggling, trying to shake the dream from his mind, for the young woman brought memories that he had tried to bury years ago. He remembered she had been his first love, the first young woman he had ever known, and then suddenly he saw the scene where she had come to him and said, "Ty, I'm going to have a baby."

The words seemed to be carved in some sort of glass or marble. *"Ty, I'm going to have a baby."* He remembered how he had been only seventeen and did not really love the girl.

He'd saddled his horse, without a word from anyone, and left the farm where he had been born without even leaving a note to his parents. He remembered fleeing over the country, trying to find a forgetfulness that would blot out the face of the young woman, but now as he lay there, suddenly, not for the first time, the queries came floating into his consciousness: *I wonder if she had a boy or a girl. I wonder if she ever found a man to be a father to the child. . .my child.* And he felt a sharp pang of keen regret.

Suddenly Ty felt a sharp sensation in his back. Something was poking at him, and he rolled over and made a harsh, croaking cry. He had the impression of several dark, hideous birds rising up, their wings flapping as their harsh cries etched into the silence of wherever he was. Finally he fell back into unconsciousness and felt a black hole closing in about him. He felt something seizing his legs, dragging him down, and he cried out in a desperate voice, "No, God! Don't let me die!"

And then came nothingness. No sounds. No smells. No touch. Just the blackness that devoured him.

Raina reached up and patted her mare's head. She took the bit well, and Raina smiled. "That's a good girl. Let's you and me go for a ride."

She stepped into the saddle and waved good-bye to her father, who was talking with one of the herdsmen. He waved back and smiled at her, and somehow the smile brought a good feeling of warm pleasure. She had found a father. Found one who was tied to her by blood and by the past, and somehow this meant that she was now a complete person.

It was a fine time of the morning, the part of the day that she loved best. The sun had risen and now was shedding warm beams over the land. She paused once and looked at the land that dropped below her, then lifted her eyes to where it rose to the hills over to the north. The sight of the Yellow River, as it wound its way across the plain and disappeared into the distance, gave her pleasure. The sun brought a sparkling to the water's surface, and she kept a fast pace until finally she reached a high ridge, the beginning of the Indian Territory.

She looked in both directions and saw not a single thing moving, leaned forward, and whispered, "Let's go, girl." The mare moved forward, and Raina rode slowly, enjoying the freshness and the fullness and the goodness of late morning. Finally she spotted a herd of sheep and lifted the mare to a slow gallop.

She pulled up, and Yosu, a small man with a dark complexion and white, shiny teeth, smiled at her. "Hello, miss," he said. "You're out early this morning."

"I brought you some food, Yosu. I baked yesterday. I remembered how you liked the cake, so I brought you part of it."

"Gracias." Yosu reached out eagerly and took the box that she handed him. He opened it at once, broke off a piece, then chewed and swallowed. His grin flashed again, and he said, "Very good. You're going to make some man a fine wife."

"Maybe." She liked Yosu, and they talked for some time, although she did not dismount. He looked up at her, and finally she smiled and said, "Are you still in love with Juanita?" Juanita was the Mexican daughter of one of the men who helped with the business of the camp.

She saw that Yosu said nothing, but finally he looked up and there was a sadness in his eyes as black as obsidian. "I have nothing to give her."

Yosu's answer shocked Raina, and she thought for a moment. It had not occurred to her that the economics of a sheepherder were not at all prosperous. "Well, you have yourself, Yosu."

Yosu's head went back, and he stared at her then shook his head almost violently. "No, a man needs something to bring to a woman." He hesitated, looked to the ground, and then lifted his eyes to her. "Have you ever loved a man, Miss Raina?"

The question troubled Raina, and she bit her lower lip, trying to think of a proper answer. She said, "No, I haven't—but I know Juanita likes you. My father trusts you. He's going to raise you up. He'll make it possible for you to marry."

"There's a man who lives in town that likes her. He has a house. A rich man." Rich might have meant anything, but his idea of riches would be a small frame house and a job.

Raina felt a twinge of sorrow. "Take a chance. Don't let her get away from you, Yosu. I know she likes you."

He suddenly smiled and said, "Maybe I will say so."

"You do that." Raina touched her heels to the sides of her horse and the mare shot off in a trotting gait. She kept her eyes on the plain before her, noting how it dipped into hollows and rose to slight ridges. The grass was green now, but one day would be gray and dead. It always came back though. The thought of resurrection gave her pleasure.

She was thinking, however, of what Yosu had asked her. *"Have you ever loved a man?"* The question troubled her, and she thought about Ty. Their meeting had been like nothing she had ever experienced before, and she had thought about it at length many times. As for Ty himself, there was some sort of connection between them that she did not understand. She knew he seemed to admire her, at least her looks, and their meeting and subsequent lives being twined together somehow troubled her.

Suddenly she thought of George Fairfax, the Englishman, who had dropped into her life. He had settled in Fort Smith for a time, but she was not sure how long he would be there. He admired her, too; she knew that as a woman always knows such things. She had seen warmth in his eyes when he looked at her, but only once had he commented, saying, "You have a beauty that I've never seen in a woman, Raina. It's not only outward—any man could see that—but it's inward." *What did he mean by that?* She pondered this question as she rode along for the next hour.

Buzzards circled up ahead. *It may be a sheep that's lost and dying,* she thought. She coaxed her mare into a gallop, and when she came over a rise, she looked down and saw the birds were descending. She called out, and with a flapping sound they all rose into the air. She was shocked to see a man lying on the ground facedown. As she drew close, she saw that his back was bloody. *He must be dead.*

She pulled up and dropped the reins. Her horse had been trained to stop and wait when the reins were left hanging. She walked over slowly, thinking it was a corpse, but when she got close she saw movement. Suddenly she recognized the side of his face and cried out, "Ty!"

She removed the canteen from the cantle of the saddle and went to him. He groaned as she turned him over, and the sunlight fell on the jagged gash on the side of his head, but she knew the wound in his back was from a bullet. She removed her neckerchief, soaked it with water, and then bathed his face. Carefully she rolled him over and saw that the bullet had struck him high in the back. She was grateful it seemingly had not hit a lung. His horse was gone, and he was lying there alone in the desert. *He's been shot, and somebody left him to die.* Looking around the scene, she saw a half-buried sharp rock, and it was bloody. *He must have hit his head on that rock.* She whispered, "Ty, can you hear me?"

He did not move, and she held the lip of the canteen to his mouth. At first it simply ran down his chin, but then he gulped thirstily, and his eyes fluttered but did not open.

"We've got to get you out of here, Ty. You'll have to help me." She lowered him carefully then moved over to her mare and led her to stand beside him. He was a big man, and she said, "Ty, you've got to help. Hang on to me and try to get up." At first she thought she could not move him, but then his eyes fluttered and opened. He did not seem to see her; his expression was empty. But when she kept encouraging, he heaved himself and nearly caused her to fall. She led him to the mare. "Lift up your foot. You've got to get into the saddle."

He groaned, and then his eyes opened and he focused on her. "Raina?" he whispered in a creaky voice.

"Yes, it's me. You've got to get on the horse. We've got to get you some help." She helped him guide his left foot into the stirrup, and she said, "Now, I'm going to push you, and you help all you can. Pull yourself into the saddle." At first she thought it was impossible. He was large, and she was not. But then he managed to rise up and throw his leg over the saddle, and then he swayed. Quickly she mounted behind him, and he was loose and disjointed as she reached her arms around him. She pulled him back to lean against her and said, "Come on, girl," then turned the mare around and headed back to where she had seen Yosu.

He saw her coming and came at once running, leaving the sheep. "What is it, señorita?"

"It's Ty. He's been shot. Take my horse and go to the house. Bring a wagon and blanket for a bed. Go as quick as you can. He needs help."

"*Si*. I will be back very soon."

She said, "Before you go, help me get him in the shade of that sapling." The two of them managed to lower Ty, and the shade blocked off most of the sun's rays.

Yosu slipped into the saddle and rode off at a fast gallop.

Raina did not watch him leave but turned her attention to Ty. His lips were baked and parched, and she moistened them with the water in her neckerchief from time to time and occasionally gave him a swallow.

The sun kept up in the sky, and she didn't know what to do for the wound in his back. Finally his shoulders moved, his head rolled, and his eyes came open. "Where am I, Raina?"

"You've been shot, Ty. What happened? Do you remember?"

His words were slow, and his lips were so parched he had to lick them. She gave him another swallow of water, and he said, "I caught somebody moving sheep, but before I could do anything about it, somebody knocked me down."

"You'll be all right. I sent Yosu to get a wagon. We'll take you to the camp. Dad's good with wounds, and we can send for a doctor."

He did not answer, and she saw that he was in a state of semiconsciousness. She wanted to question him but saw that he was not able to answer.

Finally he whispered, "Could I have some more water?"

"Yes. Just a few swallows. You can have all you want, but not all at once."

He swallowed three times, small, tentative swallows of the tepid water, and then looked at her. "That was good. How'd you find me?"

"I was just out visiting one of the sheepherders. I saw buzzards circling."

"I heard them. They would have got me if you hadn't come along."

"Are you in much pain?"

"Head hurts. My back. . ."

"You took a bullet in the back, but it was high up. I don't think it hit a lung or anything like that. You hit your head on a rock when you fell. The bullet will have to come out when we get you to a doctor."

He lay still, and for a time he didn't speak. Then he said, "You know, Raina, I had strange dreams while I was lying there all shot up and out of it." He looked up at her.

She saw sadness in him she had never seen before, even when she had found him in jail back when they had first met. "What sort of dreams?"

"About bad things that I've done."

"We all have things that we regret."

He began to speak and tell her about his best friend who had died.

"You didn't hurt him. It was an accident."

"I've never forgotten it, but the worst dream was about a young woman. Now—" He broke off and took a deep breath as he grimaced.

Raina knew that talking was taking a lot out of him, but she thought it was better he stay awake, so she encouraged him to go on. "What was her name?"

"Evelyn. She was the first girl I ever courted. No more than a girl really."

"Did you love her, Ty?"

"I thought I did, but I found out different."

"Found out how?"

He shut his eyes, and she saw a quiver go through his whole body. "She told me she was going to have a baby. It scared me. I wasn't ready for that. I ran away and left her, Raina. Been years ago, but I still remember her. I wonder what happened to her. If she had a boy or a girl, and if she found a man to take care of her and the child or gave the child to another family. I think about it almost every day. Never gotten away from it."

"Did you ever think about going back and looking for her?"

"By the time I reached the point I was ready to do that, it was too late. It was three years after I had left, and I knew whatever she had decided to do, it was done."

The wind began to whistle, blowing the loose, sandy soil across the plains. She looked up and saw far off a herd of pronghorn in their beautiful run, bounding into the air seemingly effortlessly. Then she looked back and said, "I'm sorry, Ty, but you can't live forever with a mistake you made."

"After I dreamed about Evelyn, I began thinking about what your pa said in his sermon. He said, 'God made every man and every woman for a purpose,' and that scares me."

"Why should it scare you, Ty?"

"Because I don't have any purpose, Raina. I'm just like a tumbleweed blowing wherever the wind takes it. I'm no good to anybody."

"Did you dream anything else?"

"No, but every time I'd come to, I'd think about God, and I was afraid I was going to die." He moved, turning his face away from the sun. "I've never been afraid of much of anything. Didn't have sense enough, I guess, but I was afraid of dying."

"I think most of us are when we think about it."

"I've been in some tight spots. Nearly died a couple times. You know that better than most. But this was different. It was like I was standing on a precipice. Below there was a horrible blackness. I was about to step off into it. I remembered a friend of mine who died at nineteen. When he died, he cried out, 'I never done anything. I never had a wife or a family. Now I never will.' That scared me, Raina."

Raina kept him talking even though his head nodded from time to time. Finally she saw Yosu coming with a wagon and one of the other sheepherders.

Yosu pulled the team up and said, "I came as quick as I could."

"Help me get him into the wagon."

"We have made a bed. I told your dad. He's going to try to get a doctor there, but if he can't, we'll take him to Fort Smith."

Carefully the two men picked up Ty with some struggle and put him into the wagon. She got on her horse, and the two men mounted the wagon.

She said, "Drive slow and avoid the worst of the ruts if you can, Yosu."

He nodded and said, "Get up!" and the team moved forward.

Leoma had learned about Ty's being shot from one of the hands. She immediately set out toward Vernay's place to see him. She had not traveled far when she looked up and saw George Fairfax coming toward her driving a buggy. She said at once, "Did you hear about Ty?"

George was wearing a fine suit as usual, but when he stopped, surprise washed across his face. "What about him?"

"He was shot."

"Shot? Is he all right?"

"I think he is now. He would have died, but Raina found him out lying on the plains. She and the sheepherders got him back to the camp, and her father evidently knows something about bullet wounds. He got the bullet out. They brought a doctor out to check on him, and he said it wasn't too serious. He was just dehydrated. However, he also said that Ty would have died if Raina hadn't found him. I'm going out to see him now."

"Let me take you."

"Well, that would be good. I'll tie my horse to the buggy and ride her back."

"Yes, certainly tie your horse to the buggy, but I will be happy to take you back home. You really shouldn't be riding around by yourself anyway."

"My father warned me about that, too, but I was too worried to wait on someone to ride along with me."

As they made their way toward the Vernay place, Leoma found herself interested in the Englishman. She said, "It must not be a very pleasant experience for you out here. I've always heard how beautiful England is. This is about as wild and woolly a place as you can find, George."

He was driving the team rather inexpertly and turned and gave her a quick smile. "Well, England is beautiful in a lot of ways. In the summer the grass is so green it almost hurts your eyes. You know, this land has a beauty of its own. It's stark, strange, and a little bit brutal. The other day I was out riding, and I saw a coyote pull down a young doe. She didn't have a chance. He tore her to pieces. That kind of reminds me what this land is like. It's cruel."

"Yes, it is."

"Do you like it here?"

"I haven't known much of any other kind of life."

He was silent, and finally he said, "You know, maybe sometime you could come and visit England. I could show you some beautiful things there."

She smiled and said, "We'd have to take a chaperone."

"Oh, you can always hire one of those," he said briefly. He smiled at her, and she saw goodness in his face that she didn't find in many men, and she finally said, "It was kind of you to ask me though. Your family might get upset, your dragging a wild woman home with you."

"I don't know. They've done nothing but nag me to get married for the last five years."

"Why do they want you to marry?"

"Oh, you know how it is."

"No, I don't."

"Well, the land is entailed. It goes to the oldest son of each family, so I need a son to pass the land on to."

She laughed. "Why don't you put an ad in the paper. Wanted: Young woman to bear son for titled Englishman."

"Oh, there'd be a line of them. There was one already. That's one reason why I left England. Every woman I met was after me, and I know it wasn't because of my good looks. It was because of the money and the title."

Leoma found this fascinating. "What about younger sons?"

"Well, I only have one younger brother. If I died, he'd be the earl. I've got him enrolled in Oxford. He's training to be an educator."

They talked steadily, and the trip seemed very short to Leoma. They pulled up in front of the sheep camp, and Raina came out to meet them along with her father. "We've come out to see how Ty's doing," Leoma said.

Eddie Vernay said, "Get down and come in. You're bound to be thirsty after that hot trip."

"How's Ty?" Leoma asked Raina as they headed toward the house.

"He's much better now. He was in pretty bad shape when I found him."

"A fortunate thing for him," George said, "that you were out there."

"I think it was the will of the Lord." Vernay smiled.

Raina said, "Let me take you in to see him. He's still in bed. He was dehydrated and just about dead from exposure." She entered the house and led them down a hall, where she opened a door. "Visitors, Ty."

They entered the room, and Ty looked up from the bed where he was sitting up with a pillow behind his back. "Well, hello. Good to see you."

"Good to see you, Ty. How do you feel?" Leoma asked.

"A lot better than I did awhile ago. If Raina there hadn't come across me, I'd be buzzard bait by now. How are you, George?"

"I'm fine. Just glad to see you're doing so well. I heard from Leoma that you got shot."

"The bullet took him real high in his shoulder up above the bone. Made a bad flesh wound," Raina said, "but Pa got the bullet out."

They talked for a while, but soon Leoma saw that Ty's eyes were drooping. "You're tired," she said. "We just wanted to find out how you are."

"Nice of you to come," Ty said.

The two left, and George looked to the west at the sun going down. George stared at it for a moment and said, "That looks like a big egg yolk going down."

Leoma laughed and said, "Well, you'll never be a poet. There should be a better way to describe a beautiful sunset like that than it looks like an egg yolk."

"What would you say?"

"Oh, I don't know. I'm not a poet either, George. I don't even read poetry much because I don't understand it."

"You know, I've tried to read some modern poetry, and it seems to me those fellows' worst fear is that someone will understand what they've written." He laughed and shook his head. "As a matter of fact, I've heard some politicians and preachers who did the same thing. They want to sound deep and profound, but if anybody understands them, that means they've been shallow."

The hooves of the team made a clopping sound as they plodded along, sending up a faint cloud of dust. George and Leoma said little for quite some time.

Leoma finally said, "What's it like to live in England?"

"Well, that depends."

"On what?"

"On whether you have money or not. If you have money, you can live in a fine house with fine furniture, have servants to wait on you, and be recognized by the aristocracy, or at least by the leaders in society."

"Well, not everyone lives like that, I'm sure."

"No, as a matter of fact there's that other side of England. Children working in mills when they are only ten years old, putting in twelve-hour days."

"That's frightful."

"The same thing's happening here in the United States in some of the woolen mills in New England and some of the big factories in New York and Chicago."

Leoma turned her head and studied George's profile. Instant charm and perfect diction were things that she had never encountered before, so she was interested in him. His comment on poetry caught at her attention, and she wondered what he was really like. He was of average height but looked taller because he was slender, and he moved with unusual grace. She guessed that he would make a fine dancer at the waltz and other dances at balls in England. She knew he was well educated in the classics, that he had a patrician face with a rather large, aquiline nose, and that his fair hair waved a trifle extravagantly. She found out that he had a quickness of intelligence, lines of wit and laughter around his mouth, and a hint of temper. At times, the space between his brows revealed his emotions. He had the face of a man of unusual charm, and more than that, one who had never had to suffer from any hard times. "What about you, George?"

"What do you mean, what about me?"

"What will you be doing? You won't stay in Fort Smith forever. It must seem pretty wild and woolly to you."

George's mouth twisted in a strange, sardonic manner, and he gave her a quick look and shook his head. "Well, I'll have to marry and produce an heir, a male heir."

Leoma suddenly laughed. "That's pretty much like a stud horse. I suppose you'll marry a duchess or someone like that."

"Oh, not necessarily. The upper class in England is pretty well bred down. Be much more likely to find a good sturdy woman who's not of the aristocracy."

A moment of humor came to Leoma then, and she turned and put her hand on his arm. "Well, how about me, George?"

Fairfax was obviously caught off guard by her direct question. The wind ruffled the edges of her hair, and a smile made a small break along her lips. Some private and ridiculous thought amused her, for he saw the effect of it dancing in her eyes.

"Do you think I might make a good wife for you?"

"Well, that's coming right out with it. I'll tell you what. I'll make me out a list of what the woman I marry will have to do to qualify. You know, beautiful, witty, strong-willed. . ."

"But what if she doesn't meet all your standards?"

Once again he smiled and said, "Well, I'll just cross that item off my list."

They talked nonstop practically until they got to her ranch, and she said, "Too dark to drive into Fort Smith. Come on in. We've got a spare bedroom. As a matter of fact, we've got three of them."

"Well, you don't have to ask anybody's permission?"

"Oh, it's about supper time. You can talk to my pa and my brothers about raising cattle."

"That'll be a one-sided conversation." George smiled. "I hardly know one end from another."

"You know horses though."

"We ride a lot in England. Ride to the hounds."

"What does that mean?"

"Oh, all the rich, titled people get together on horseback and wear funny-looking clothes as they chase a fox."

She stared at him. "I've heard about that. What do you do when you catch one? You don't eat him, do you?"

"Oh bless you, no, we don't eat them. If anybody's made an especially good ride, we give him the brush, that is, the tail."

"That's a funny way to spend an afternoon."

"Well, we English are funny people."

She said no more but was looking forward to his spending the night with them. She had not been entertained by a man so thoroughly in a long time. She knew most of it was the difference between the two of them, and she looked forward to finding out more about his requirements for a wife.

CHAPTER 21

Sit down, Garth. You're going to wear the floor out," Honey
Clagg said.

Garth Taylor had been pacing back and forth, running his
hand through his hair in a nervous mannerism. He was a man
who had to be in action of some sort or other most of the time,
and since the death of his brother, he had been even more nervous.
He turned quickly and faced Honey Clagg.

Honey was the biggest man in his gang. He had a neck as
wide as his jaw, and his muscles were spectacular. He had whipped
many men and kicked one to death, but Garth Taylor kept him on
for this very reason.

"Don't tell me what to do, Honey."

"We need to get out on a job. Everybody's gettin' sour just
sittin' around here. All we do is argue, and I'm gettin' tired
of it."

Garth stared at him. "I can't stop thinking about Johnny. He
was the only living relative I had that I know of, except for one

uncle somewhere back East who wouldn't claim me. He was a good kid."

Honey Clagg answered, "You might as well forget him. Let's go out and make some money."

"I'll decide when we leave," Garth said stiffly and continued his walking.

The rest of the gang was engaged at the other end of the room in a lackadaisical poker game. They were playing for penny ante stakes, and nobody really cared.

Honey said, "Those Daltons are gonna bust loose if we don't give 'em somethin' to do, Garth."

"We'll get along without 'em."

"They're pretty handy. All we'd have left is Mexican Jack and Long Tom, of course."

"That's all we need." He suddenly sat down in front of Clagg and said, "I've been waiting for the right time to get my revenge, but I can't get that cowman who killed my brother out of my mind. I can't let it pass."

"Well, what you need to do is just go shoot him and forget about it. Get it out of your system."

Garth sat with a dark look on his face. He was staring down at his strong hands, clasping them nervously together. He didn't speak for a long time. Finally Garth muttered, "I'd love nothing better, but I don't want to go to hang for it. I want to be free to enjoy my revenge. In fact, I'd give a big pile of money to any man who'd risk killing Ash Jordan for me." He got up and returned to his pacing.

Honey smiled. "In that case, I just might take care of that little chore myself." Clagg obviously took the statement as a challenge.

"Shouldn't be too hard to do," he said. "He's out riding the range, chasing those cattle half the time. Shouldn't be too hard to catch him off by himself."

Garth stopped his pacing again. "You'd have to bring somethin' in to prove to me that you shot and killed him."

Honey smiled again, but this time it looked like pure evil. "That won't be a problem either."

Leoma had always been partial to her younger brother, Benny. He was the youngest child and had a sunny disposition in contrast to Ash, who had a hair-trigger temper and could be hard to be around. "What are you going to do with yourself, Benny?"

Benny was five-ten, a well-built young man. He had a trace of the same auburn hair as she did, but his eyes were a warm brown. When he smiled, his whole face grew warm. Now he stared at her with a question in his face. "What do you mean, what am I going to do?"

"Well, are you gonna be a cowpuncher all your life?"

"Never thought about doing anything else."

"Why, you could be something if you wanted to. Why don't you become a doctor or something like that?"

"Not smart enough for that."

"Not all doctors are smart. Some of them are absolute terrors. I wouldn't want 'em doctoring on me."

"No, I guess I'll just stay on the ranch here."

The two were out leaning against the corral, watching Ash as he broke a buckskin. Ash was a fine rider, and he rode the big steed to a halt finally.

Benny called out, "That's good, Ash. He's gonna make a fine

mount." He turned then to Leoma and said, "Why'd you ask me what I was gonna do?"

"Well, you're getting old enough to make some kind of a career for yourself."

Benny smiled at her. "Maybe I could get me a fancy vest and some hair oil and become a gambler on a Mississippi riverboat."

"You're a terrible gambler. You'd go broke overnight."

"I guess you're right, sis." He turned and stared at her. "You've been goin' over to see Ty Kincaid a couple of times."

"I have. I like him."

Benny turned his head to one side. "You mean you like him like a woman likes a man?"

Leoma picked a sliver of wood off the top of the corral, held it up, looked at it, and then threw it away. "I might, but it's hard to tell."

"What's hard to tell, sis? Who's the right man for you?"

"A woman has to make that decision."

"Well, a man does, too."

"It's harder for women though."

Benny shrugged. "I think it'd be pretty easy."

Leoma turned and laughed at him. "You thought you were in love with Joanne Riggs when you were fifteen."

"I'm surprised you'd bring that up. I was just a kid. Anyway, you interested in marrying this Ty Kincaid?"

"I'm thinking about marriage. Not necessarily with him, but with somebody."

Ash called out, "Come and give me a hand with this critter, Benny."

Benny turned at once and left, as he always obeyed Ash's orders.

Leoma watched him go and then slowly walked up to the porch.

Her mother was sitting there in a rocking chair. She asked, "You went over to see Kincaid yesterday?"

"Yes, I did."

"How is he?"

"Oh, he's getting along fine. He's out of bed now. Walking around. Gonna have a scar on his head where he hit that rock."

The two talked about Ty, and Leoma suddenly turned and said, "Benny just asked me if I was interested in Ty."

"Well, you must be. You've gone over there two or three times."

"Well, a woman has to know a man."

"Just think about all the men you turned down. There was Arlie Hicks. He had money and wasn't bad looking. Why'd you turn him down?"

"He was boring."

"You want to marry a clown to perform for you?" She named off several other men back in their older home whom Leoma had refused. Finally she said, "Leoma, what about this George Fairfax? He's a fine-looking man. A little different from most of the men around here."

"He's altogether different from most of the men around here."

"You think he might be interested in you?"

Leoma was nervous. She got up and walked back and forth. "He'll marry an Englishwoman who has a pile of money." She turned toward the door. "I'm going in and set the table."

The supper had been good, but they had a fine cook. Everyone left the table except for Leoma and her father. He stared at her and said, "I'm going to hire some more men to guard the stock."

"Why don't you just let the marshal take care of it?"

"You know why," Pa said shortly. "He doesn't have enough marshals to handle the territory, much less ride herd on my cattle." He turned to her and studied her carefully. "What are you worried about? You've got everything you want."

"Nobody ever has everything they want, Pa."

"Well, I guess that's right enough."

"What do *you* want?" Leoma asked.

"I guess I want a big ranch. Make some money. See you and Benny and Ash grow up and make it in this world."

"That's pretty ambitious."

"Well, I suppose it is." He stirred in his chair and said, "I heard you went over to Vernay's sheep camp."

"Yes, I went to see if Ty Kincaid was all right."

Instantly, suspicion swept across her father's face. "You don't need that kind of man. You need a man with money."

"I've watched people with money. They're no happier than people without it. They're just more comfortable."

"That's crazy talk, girl. These marshals come and go. You know over fifty of them have been killed carrying out Judge Parker's orders."

She did not answer right away, but the thought took root in her mind. Finally she said, "Don't worry about it, Pa. I don't know what's in his heart, or what's in my own for that matter."

Judge Parker looked up, and his eyes opened wide. "Well, hello, Ty. Good to see you up and going."

Ty stood before the judge's desk. "Good to be up, sir."

Parker stared at his face. "That's a bad cut you've got there. You're going to have a scar."

"Well, a man needs a scar now and then to teach him what life is like."

"How's that bullet wound?"

"Oh, it's a little stiff. Didn't hit a bone, so it's all right. Anyway, I'm about ready to go back to work."

Parker leaned back in his chair. "What's bothering you, Ty?"

"Didn't say anything was."

"Well, I've got eyes, haven't I? Somethin's eatin' on ya."

Ty said, "Well, to tell the truth, when I was lying out there shot and dying, at least so I thought, I got scared."

"Scared of dying?"

"Not so much scared of dying," Ty said slowly, "but scared of what comes afterward."

"I didn't take you for a religious man."

"Well, I haven't been. Maybe that's my trouble."

Ty knew that Parker himself was a thoroughgoing Christian. He and his family attended church every Sunday. He never used the vile language he heard from many of the rougher men he had to deal with. "I guess I'm just a coward, sir."

"No, you're not a coward, Ty. A man's a fool not to be afraid of what happens after this life if he has any mind at all."

"You know, Judge, there are too many bad people in this place. I'm thinking of moving to Omaha."

The judge laughed then. "No bad people in Omaha, Ty?"

Kincaid stared back at the judge. "Some, but most of 'em don't kill each other."

"You start back on Wednesday. Until then you take it easy."

"Sure, Judge. See you Wednesday morning." Ty walked outside and sat down in a chair, tilting it back against the wall of the courthouse. His eyes were half shut as he watched men, women, and young people pass by. It was a habit he had, to watch people carefully, cautiously.

"Hello, Ty."

Kincaid looked up and saw Fairfax. "Sit down, George."

"You're looking pretty good except for that scar on your head. The doctor said you'd probably keep that."

"Won't hurt my manly beauty any."

"You know, I was talking with somebody once who wanted to know what I was going to do with my life."

"What did you tell 'em, George?"

"I told 'em back home everybody was jumping up and down with ambition trying to get me married off."

"Why didn't you marry somebody? There must be plenty of women in England who would want to find a rich man with a title."

"That's what I told them. But I hadn't found anybody yet who satisfied me."

"Why does everybody want you to get married?"

"Why, I have a title you know, and it's an entailed property."

"What does that mean?"

"It means the place can't be sold. A male heir will inherit it."

"I'm sure there are plenty of women looking for a rich husband. There's more to it than that, isn't there?"

"I always thought so."

The two men were quiet for a while; then abruptly George Fairfax turned and said, "I've been thinking about Raina Vernay."

The words caught at Ty's attention. He turned at once and said, "You courting her?"

"A little," he said casually.

"You think she'd fit in the English world?" Ty asked.

"She could if she tried." Fairfax stirred restlessly and got to his feet. "Or I might come and live here. It's a different world for me, but I could learn to like it."

"Look at that street," Ty said with a sweeping gesture. "It has people in it, good and bad, but so does London I expect. I don't know if a man can change his world."

George Fairfax was silent. "I could buy a ranch. Become a rancher."

"You don't know anything about cattle."

Fairfax smiled. "I could hire you to run it for me."

Ty laughed at that. "There are better men than I am at cattle. You'd better think this over, George. Marriage is for a long time."

"I'm doing that. It gives me a headache. I'm not used to deep thoughts. I'll see you later, Ty."

Kincaid watched as Fairfax moved down the street, taking in the fine clothes and wondering if he was serious about Raina Vernay. The thought troubled him, for he had felt a vested interest in Raina ever since the two had been thrown together in La Tete. He got up and began walking the streets of Fort Smith. As he thought about his future, he decided the best place for him to be was at church. Since he had a few days off, he saddled his horse and headed out to the Vernay place.

On Sunday, Ty entered the barn-church, which was fuller than the last time he had come, and saw Eddie Vernay. He walked up to him and shook his hand.

"Good to see you, Ty. You can get one of those good five-dollar seats."

"No, too close to you for my benefit."

"How have you been, Ty? How's that head wound?"

"Oh, I've had worse getting kicked by a stubborn mule."

"Come to hear the sermon? Well, I wish we had a better preacher."

"You're good enough for me." Ty smiled. He liked Eddie Vernay as much as he had liked any man. He envied him, for there was a stillness and a contentment in the older man's face that attracted him. It was the sort of thing he longed for, but he had not found it.

Vernay was staring at him. "You're troubled, Ty."

"Sure am."

"What's wrong?"

"Don't know, Eddie. Just don't feel right. I feel like I'm chasing my tail."

"That's what I did when God first got ahold of me. My sermon today on the prodigal son touches on that."

Ty Kincaid smiled slightly. "That sounds like it will fit me."

"That boy ran away from home, but he couldn't get away from himself."

"You been reading my mail, Eddie?"

"Not hard to tell when God's after a man. You sit there and listen to this sermon. It'll do you some good. Then you come and stay the night with us."

"All right. That would be fine."

He saw Raina near the front, but he slipped into a seat nearer the back. He wanted nothing to distract him from taking in every word.

The sermon was indeed about the prodigal son. Vernay had a way of bringing in other scriptures and other stories and personal references to his own life that moved Ty Kincaid greatly. He had heard of people speak of being under conviction, but he had never known what that meant.

Once he had asked Eddie Vernay what that signified, and he had shaken his head. "You'll be absolutely miserable."

"Well, what good does that do?"

"A man gets miserable enough, Ty, he'll do something about it. God's after you, and He's going to get you."

After the service, he went to the house and had dinner with Eddie and Raina. Later in the evening, he and Raina went outside and sat on the front porch. They were quiet, simply enjoying the cool evening breeze. Ty's mind kept going back over the sermon.

Raina finally asked, "What's the matter, Ty? You haven't said ten words."

Ty turned to her and said, "Well, something you probably won't know anything about. I want to serve God, and I don't know how."

Raina suddenly had the experience she heard her father speak of. A scripture came to her mind, and she quoted it for Ty. " 'I have set before thee an open door.' "

"A door set before me? I don't see anything like that."

"You have to wait on God, and He's ready now, Ty, but when

you get ready, that's when things will happen."

Her direct gaze made him nervous, and he said, "Maybe that's meant for you. George Fairfax seems to find you attractive. Maybe he's a door for you."

"Oh, he's a nice fellow."

"He'd make you a good husband. Give you an easier life."

"That's not what I'm looking for, Ty."

"That's what most women want. A good, steady husband with a comfortable income."

"There's more than that."

The two sat talking for a time.

Finally Raina stood. "Just look how the moon casts its lucent rays on the land." She sighed and turned to Ty. "I don't know how to find God's will sometimes, Ty. I wish there were an easier way, but I don't think there is. I remember a scripture where God says, 'Ye shall seek me, and find me, when ye shall search for me with all your heart.' I've never really done that."

"Neither have I. I'll bet your pa has though."

"Yes, he has, but I'm not as close to God as he is." She was silent for a time, then said, "I've just thought of a scripture about a man who sought God like that. Let's go in the house and I'll read it to you."

"I'd like to hear it."

They went into the house and sat down in the living area. Raina looked through the Bible and found what she sought. "Here it is. Daniel is one of the very few individuals in the Bible who seems to have been absolutely devoted to God. Most of the men and women have a black mark against them, even David, who was a man after God's own heart."

"Didn't know that was said about anyone in the Bible."

"This scripture is in the ninth chapter of the book of Daniel. It begins with verse three. The first two verses tell how Daniel wanted to know what the future held for his people, the Israelites. Verse three begins with Daniel setting out to find the answer:

" 'And I set my face unto the Lord God, to seek by prayer and supplications, with fasting, and sackcloth, and ashes.' "

"What does he mean, sackcloth?" Ty asked.

"In those days whenever people were in trouble or suffering, they put on garments made of sackcloth, the cheapest kind of material."

"Do we have to do that?"

"I don't think so." Raina shook her head. "It was a Jewish custom. The important thing is Daniel set out to find God's will, and he made it the most important thing in his life. Listen to what he did to find God. It begins with verse four:

" 'And I prayed unto the Lord my God, and made my confession, and said, O Lord, the great and dreadful God, keeping the covenant and mercy to them that love him, and to them that keep his commandments.' "

"Well, Raina, that lets me out," Ty said. "I haven't done any of that."

"Just listen to the next verse, Ty: 'We have sinned, and have committed iniquity, and have done wickedly, and have rebelled, even by departing from thy precepts and from thy judgments.' You see, Ty, Daniel did what we all have to do, confess to God that he was a sinner."

"But I thought Daniel was a godly man."

"So he was, but even the best of men and women have sinned

against God. Daniel was humble, and we all have to admit that we've sinned."

"Some worse than others, I'd think."

"Yes, all of us have sinned, but not all of us have sinned alike."

Ty said nothing for a moment, then added, "So even the best man or woman in the world has to confess his or her sin to God?"

"Exactly!"

"Well, I can see that."

"This prayer goes on for many verses, but I think this was not a 'one-time' prayer. I think Daniel may have prayed for many days or even weeks like this. Even Jesus prayed for forty days and nights at the beginning of His ministry."

"But Jesus never sinned, did He?"

"No, but God seeks us out so that we can know Him. That's what we need, Ty, to know the Lord."

"That's what I want, Raina, but I'm not a good man like Daniel. I may have to pray for months."

"Not necessarily, Ty. Sometimes God answers a sinner's prayer instantly. Remember the thief on the cross? He prayed one prayer, for Jesus to make him fit for heaven, and you remember that Jesus answered his prayer at once. He said, 'Today shalt thou be with me in paradise.' "

Ty bowed his head and was silent, and Raina wondered if she had disturbed him. Finally he looked up, and his eyes were bright. "I'm going to do it, Raina! I'm going to find Jesus if it takes me the rest of my life."

Tears gathered in Raina's eyes, and she took his hand and whispered, "That's exactly what you need, Ty. And Dad and I will be praying right with you."

CHAPTER 22

Ty arched himself into a sitting position, moving cautiously, and was pleased to find that though the movement was somewhat painful, it was less than it had been. Turning, he walked over to the chair by the window, sat down, and picked up a Bible.

The morning sun was casting golden bars on the worn carpet. As always, he was fascinated by the multitude of tiny motes that danced in the yellow light almost quicker than a man could see. He looked out and saw that the street was busy with people and wondered how he had been rescued from what could have been his death.

He put the Bible on his lap and moved his hand back and forth over the surface. *I've ignored this Bible for years,* he thought. *I should have known better, and I can't do that anymore.* The thought sobered him, and his lips tightened. This had happened often during his time of recovery, and he knew that his days of ignoring God and letting himself do anything he chose were over.

Slowly he opened the Bible to the page where he had placed

a red ribbon for a marker. He read slowly, beginning with the first verse from the ninth chapter of the book of Acts. *"And Saul, yet breathing out threatenings and slaughter against the disciples of the Lord, went unto the high priest, and desired of him letters to Damascus to the synagogues, that if he found any of this way, whether they were men or women, he might bring them bound unto Jerusalem."* The bluntness of the words and the cruelty that Paul had let come into his life were not new to Ty. He had heard this story before and had been affected by it.

He paused and looked out the window and was silent for a moment and absolutely still. Finally he muttered, "Lord, I need to know what to do with my life, but I'm helpless. You'll have to show me the way."

He continued reading the rest of Saul's story, and when he read the verses that spoke of Saul's being knocked to the earth and spoken to by Jesus Himself, his eyes fell on another verse. *"And he trembling and astonished said, Lord, what wilt thou have me to do?"* Again he paused and prayed, *That's what I need, Lord. I need You to speak to me and tell me what to do. You know I'm helpless. I don't know enough about You. I don't even know myself, but I ask You to guide me.* He ran his hand over the paper and slowly shook his head and whispered, "I wish God would just knock me flat like He did Saul and tell me what to do."

Nothing but silence and the sound of traffic on the street came to him. He heaved a sigh, got up, and plucked his gun belt from a peg driven into the wall. As he strapped it on, he paused abruptly, drew the gun, and stared at it. He was remembering something that Jesus said somewhere in the Bible. *"They that take the sword shall perish with the sword."* *I guess, Lord, if You let those that live by the gun perish by the gun, that about describes me.* The thought disturbed him. He slid the gun back into the holster, grabbed his hat from a peg, and left the room.

The sun was warm, and as he made his way toward the courthouse to pick up his duties, he greeted several men who spoke to him. He passed by two small boys playing marbles in the dirt of the street. The smaller one had a freckled face, and as Ty was passing by, the boy asked, "Are you a marshal?"

Ty paused and smiled. "Sure am."

"I'm gonna be a marshal when I get big."

Ty studied the boy and said, "You know, I played marbles when I was about your age. I was pretty good, too."

"Aw, I can beat you."

A notion took Ty. He knelt down, picked up a marble, shot, and sent it spinning toward the marbles in the circle. He missed and grinned. "I guess I've lost my touch."

The larger of the two boys asked, "Did you ever shoot anyone with that gun?"

"I don't like to think about that."

He walked away, but he heard the smaller boy say, "He ain't never shot no outlaws. He'd have said so if he had."

The scene troubled him as he continued his passage along the street. He thought back and realized that when he was the age of these boys he had been reading James Fenimore Cooper books glorifying Hawkeye. He realized that he had changed, and he muttered, "That seems like a thousand years ago, back when I was playing marbles. . . ." He reached headquarters and stepped up on the porch of the courthouse.

As usual, Heck Thomas was whittling on a cedar stick. He

looked up and studied Ty for a moment, then said, "Things are pretty quiet, Ty. Too quiet, I think. I get too itchy when it gets too quiet."

"Not me. I like it quiet." Ty smiled. "Is the judge in his office?"

Before he answered, Heck shaved another curling wisp-like piece of cedar and watched it fall on the mound at his feet. "Yep. There'll be a hangin' in two hours. He'll be at the window lookin' at it." He shaved two more slivers and shook his head. "I'd like to know what he thinks when he sees a man dangle that he's sentenced his own self."

Ty found no answer for that. "I guess I'll go see him." He entered the courtroom, took the stairs, and knocked on the judge's door.

When he heard, "Come in," he went in and found Judge Parker sitting at the desk with a Bible open before him. "Hello, Ty."

"Hello, Judge. Reckon I'd better go back to work."

"Are you sure?"

"Yes, I'm all right. Head's just a little scratched. The bullet wound doesn't amount to anything—but I'm pretty mixed up."

"Mixed up about what?"

Ty hesitated then said, "Well, I've been thinking about God a lot since that day, trying to figure it all out."

Parker ran his hand over his hair, and his lips tightened. "It's hard to be a marshal, and I guess it's hard to be a judge, too. It costs you something. You know, it cost Heck his family."

"How was that?"

"Well, he's the best man I have, but his wife didn't like his work. He was usually gone, and she was afraid he'd get killed, so she gave him his choice. She said, 'Either quit or I'm quitting you.'

Well, he's still here alone, so you can imagine what happened."

"Judge, I don't know what to do. I've been thinking about God ever since I nearly cashed in my chips out there in the territory."

The noise from the street floated in from the open window, and the judge walked over and looked down. "I hate the sight of that gallows."

"It bothers you to find men guilty knowing they're going to hang?"

"Of course it does. Why wouldn't it?"

"Well, maybe you need to quit, Judge."

"No, I'm doin' what God wants me to do, but it's hard."

Ty motioned at the Bible open on the judge's desk. "Do you think a man can find out what he ought to do with his life by reading that Bible?"

"Yes, I do. I think God speaks to us through His Word, but I'd hate to lose you, Ty."

"Plenty can do what I'm doin'."

"No, that's not right, but you do what you have to do. I always like to see a man get right with God."

"I'll take another day off, if that's all right. Read the Bible some more. I admire those fellows that God speaks to directly, like He did to Moses at the burning bush and to Saul on the road to Damascus."

"Doesn't usually happen like that. Usually takes two or three days, or sometimes months."

"Maybe another day will do me." Ty turned and left, and he passed Heck, who was coming up the stairs.

"You comin' back to work, Ty?"

"No, I'm going to take another day off." He shook his head. "Sure am in a messed-up situation, Heck."

Heck watched him go down the stairs, then mounted to the second floor and went in to see the judge. "You let him take some more time off?"

"Yep."

"He's pretty mixed up, Judge. You know, I got an idea he thinks God wants him to be a preacher."

"He tell you that?"

"No, he didn't tell me that, but a lot of fellows get confused like that. They want to do something to make God happy, and that seems to be what some of them do."

"Well, I don't know about that, but he's going to have to choose. I don't see how a man can be a marshal in Indian Territory and a preacher at the same time."

"Reckon you better tell him that, Judge."

"No man can really tell another what to do in a situation like he's in. Give him a few days. Maybe he'll find his way."

Ty had started over to the café to get a late breakfast when he ran into George Fairfax.

"Where you headed, Ty?"

"Going to get some breakfast."

"Well, let me buy for you. I'm hungry myself."

"Sounds good."

The two men made their way to the restaurant and went inside.

George said to the waiter, "Just bring us some of the best breakfast you can round up back there."

"Yes, sir. I'll do that. It'll be good, too."

George leaned back, and for a while they talked about unimportant things until the meal came.

Both men pitched in, and when they had finished their meal and were drinking their third cups of coffee, Ty fastened his gaze on Fairfax. "You look troubled, George."

"Yes, I guess I am."

"I don't see how you could have any problems. You're rich."

"That doesn't solve everything, you know," George said. He shifted in his chair and made an involuntary nervous gesture, pulling his hand across his face. "You know what? I've been having some strong feelings about Raina. In fact, I've asked her to marry me." At the look on Ty's face, George rushed on. "I should have told you sooner, Ty, but, well, this is sort of personal. Before you say anything, she hasn't given me an answer yet. You know her better than I do. Do you think she'd have me as a husband?"

He said simply, "I really don't know, George. All she can do is say no or yes."

"I know you're right." He drank the last of his coffee, put the cup down, and then stared at Kincaid. "I thought you and Raina were pretty close at one time."

"She pulled me out of a real hard time, and I guess that kind of thing never leaves a man. Maybe a woman neither." Kincaid turned the coffee cup around in a circular motion and stared down at the circles it left on the table.

"You have any thoughts about marriage, Ty?"

"I guess every man's got some thoughts about that."

"Well, what do you think?"

"I can't think about marriage now. To tell the truth, George, I don't know where I'm going, so I can't ask a woman to follow me."

"Why, you'll continue to be a marshal, won't you?"

"Not sure about that. I had some odd dreams when I was out there dying. One of them I haven't told anybody about. Maybe I could tell you. I keep thinking of it."

"What kind of a dream?"

"I dreamed I was in some place with a tall table in front of me and I was preaching. That's all I can remember. I don't even remember what I said, but I remember there were people there, and I was preaching to them." He laughed and shook his head. "Nothing further from my mind these last few years than preaching, and I couldn't ask a woman to go into that."

"I want Raina to go back to England with me."

"I don't think Raina would be interested in that. She just found her father and is enjoying being with him right now."

"I keep trying to wonder what would happen if I tried to take her back to England. She'd probably be out of place in my world back home."

"Maybe you could live here."

"No, I'm a misfit."

Ty studied George Fairfax and thought with a strong humor, *He's got some problem. Money and everything, and he's worried about whether he can find a wife or not.*

"I guess I'll head on down the way. Let me know what Raina answers."

"I wouldn't be cutting in on you, would I, Ty?"

"No, nothing like that. I wish you well, whatever happens." Ty did his best to put a lot of sincerity in his words, but he couldn't help but feel like he had lost something special.

George watched the tall man walk away and sat for a while staring down at the table.

Finally the waiter came and said, "Anything else, Mr. Fairfax?"

"No. Here you go." He put money on the table, including a large tip, and left the café. All morning he wandered around, not knowing what to do with himself, thinking mostly about what he'd said to Ty Kincaid. Finally he threw up his hands and muttered, "I might as well go find out."

He went to the livery stable and had the hostler saddle his buckskin. He mounted up and rode out of town at a fast gait. As he left town and headed toward the sheep camp, he was worried about his way. *She probably never thought of me as a man she might marry. Why should she?*

As he rode along, he studied the land and thought about how different it was from England. There he had been used to grass so green it hurt the eyes in the summer, but here it was summer and the grass was still not greened out. The hills were rough, and rocky buttes broke against the morning sky. It was tough, hard-edged territory, and he was well aware that some of the men and the Indians who inhabited this place were as rough as the land itself.

George finally arrived at the sheep camp early the next morning. He saw Eddie Vernay trimming the wool from a sheep. "Hello, Eddie."

"Hello, Mr. Fairfax."

"That looks like a lot of work."

269

"It ain't bad. It's when you have to do a hundred of them in a day that it gets tough. Everything gets bad when you have to do a lot of it. What can I do for you?"

"Is Raina here?"

"No, she's gone out to look at the sheep."

George Fairfax stood uncertainly.

Finally Vernay said, "You got somethin' on your mind, Mr. Fairfax?"

"Well, I do, but I'm not sure I need to say it."

"Let it be said. Can't be too bad."

Fairfax hesitated then blurted out, "You know, in my country if a man's serious about a woman, he goes to her father to ask if he can make an offer to his daughter."

Eddie Vernay threw the pile of wool on the ground, then tossed the shears down and let the sheep go. "What kind of an offer?"

"Well, I'm sorry I didn't do this the right way by coming to you first, but I asked Raina to marry me some time ago. She hasn't given me an answer yet."

Vernay took off his hat and scratched his head. "Well, I do wish you had come to me first. But I haven't really been a father to her for long, so I will leave it up to her. However, if you want my two cents' worth, I'm not sure it'd work."

"Why not? You don't like me?"

"No, it ain't that, but you know this ain't England, Mr. Fairfax."

"I know. I thought about that. But if she married me, we could go back to England. I've even got a castle there. It's not the biggest one, but she could have anything she wanted. Anyway, I came to see if I could get an answer from her. I think it's been long enough."

Eddie Vernay stared at the tall Englishman. "You're welcome to go find her."

"Which way do I go?"

"See them two peaks over there? I've got a herd of sheep there. You ride straight for it. When you see sheep, Raina will be close."

"Thank you, Mr. Vernay."

"Good luck, son."

As Fairfax rode away, he felt like a fool. "I could have said that a little bit better. I'm surprised he didn't run me off."

He kept the horse at a fast gait, and finally he saw the sheep. Five minutes later he saw Raina.

She was talking to one of the herders, and they both turned to see him. When he stopped the horse, she cried out, "Hello, George. Get down."

George dismounted, tied his horse to one of the saplings, and said, "What are you doing?"

"Trying to learn about sheep."

"There's a lot to learn, I suppose."

"Yes, there is. There's different kinds, and you have to know a lot to keep them from running away." The sheepherder was Mikel.

"You like sheep, Mikel?"

"No."

His brief answer amused Fairfax. "Well, why do you do it then?"

"A man has to do somethin'. Beats other things I've done."

"Come on, George. Let's go get in the shade. I've got some cool water over there, or it was when I left the house."

He walked over with her, and for the next thirty minutes they stood in the shade and Raina talked about sheep. As she spoke,

George tried to think of some way to say something.

Finally she asked him, "George, have you decided what you're going to do?"

"You mean about where I'm going to live?"

"Yes. You didn't seem too sure the last time we talked about it."

"Well, I've been thinking about one thing. I guess there are better ways to say this, but I've been thinking about you, Raina." He hesitated then said, "Have you thought any more about me as a man you might marry?"

She was staring at him strangely and said quietly, "Yes, I have, George."

When she said nothing more, George nervously said, "I don't know how to court an American woman. And I don't know enough about sheep to talk about that."

"Marriage is more than sheep, isn't it, George?"

"Well, of course it is, but I don't know how you feel about me."

"I'm interested in you. You're an interesting fellow." She did not seem disturbed by his talk of marriage, and he bent to catch a better view of her face. He was not sure what her expression meant, and he had a great dread of making a mistake with this girl.

For a moment he watched her; he saw no anger, and without saying anything else, he reached out and pulled her to him. He saw that she was smiling, and he kissed her. When he lifted his lips, he found that the kiss had disturbed him more than her. She had combed her hair so that it lay soft and neat against her head and there were lights dancing in her eyes.

He said, "I don't know what to think of you. You're not like any woman I ever met."

"I'm just a woman, George."

"You haven't answered my question."

"No, I haven't, but I can tell you this. It's going to take a little bit more courting than you've shown me so far. You've hardly been around since you asked me. I know you've been giving me time to decide, but I need to see you a bit more to really decide a thing as important as this."

"Can't you tell me what you think of me?"

"Well, George, I can tell you one thing," Raina said. "I don't feel about you like I would a man I want to spend the rest of my life with. At least not yet."

George was disappointed, but he determined to see this thing through, believing she could come to love him. "Well, tell me how to go about this."

"That's for you to find out. I'm not even sure I want to get married now to anybody, so you've got to change my mind about that."

"All right. I'll come courting. I guess that's what you mean."

"Yes. Can you play a guitar? I'll have you bring a guitar and sing love songs outside my window."

"I'm sorry about that. I've got no musical talent at all, but I can quote some poetry for you."

"Well, we can make do with that. Come along. I'll show you some more sheep."

CHAPTER 23

Ever since George had spoken to her again about getting married, Raina had been disturbed. She knew many women would jump at the chance to marry a man with his qualities. Not only was he wealthy and entertaining, but she could tell he was a good man, which was to her a most important factor.

The next morning, she got up, helped make breakfast for the herders, and then cleaned up the kitchen. Finally she went out on the porch of the small house and sat down on a chair that her father had built.

The sun was well up, and she could hear the plaintive cries of the sheep, a sound that had almost become second nature to the land where she now lived. She had come to the sheep ranch with prejudice about the woolly animals, but during the months she had been here, she had become aware of their helplessness and how they needed the almost constant watch care of the shepherds. They were foolish in a way, but somehow she found this made them more endearing.

From far off she heard the sound of a coyote, always a lonesome, plaintive cry to her. They were nocturnal creatures, and one was rarely seen or heard during the daylight hours. They also could be destructive, and the shepherds always had to be on constant guard so they would not lose their sheep to a pack of them.

She turned her eyes down toward the corral, where she watched one of the herders, Benat, a huge man, and by far the strongest of the shepherds, break in a horse. He was a good rider, and his heavy weight prevented the small mustang from throwing him off. She watched as the big man pulled himself into the saddle and the horse bucked, but Benat simply sat there until the animal quieted. He stepped off and led the animal away.

Raina got up and walked across the yard, noting that since she had come she had insisted on cleaning it up. The men had been careless with tin cans and papers and other trash that littered the place. Now it was clean, and one of the men was assigned each day to make sure it stayed that way. They had objected at first, but they had become accustomed to it.

She went inside, poured herself a cup of coffee from the pot that sat on the wood-burning stove, and then walked outside again. She could not understand her restlessness, but she knew it had something to do with trying to make up her mind about her future life. She was aware that there was some relationship between her and Ty, but then George had proposed marriage to her, and she found herself unable to think very clearly about it.

For a while she sipped the coffee, and as she was draining the cup, she saw a rider coming. When he came closer, she recognized Ty.

He rode in, dismounted, tied his horse up, and came over to the porch.

"Good morning, Ty. How about some coffee?"

"That sounds good."

"Have you eaten?"

"Just a little."

"I've got some biscuits left and some preserves. I can fry you up some bacon."

"Oh, don't bother. Just coffee will be fine."

Raina went inside and quickly returned with a steaming cup of coffee. She put the cup down on the table beside the chair Ty had sat in. As she took the chair beside his, she said, "How are you feeling?"

"Oh, I'm fine. I've been hurt worse. I came pretty close to cashing in, but now I'm getting better every day."

"Have you gone back to your job yet?"

"I'm actually on the job now. Judge Parker sent me out here to check on things. I think he just wanted to give me an easy assignment as I get back to work." He hesitated. "I guess he sees something in me that I can't hide."

Raina was curious. "What would that be, Ty?"

"I'm just restless. I don't know what to do with myself. And all those dreams I had when I was dying out on the plains, they keep coming back to me." He paused then said, "One of them I haven't told you about."

"What was it?"

Ty hesitated then shook his head. "It sounds meaningless to me. Most of my dreams are, but in this dream I found myself speaking to a group of people. It was like I was a preacher. They were listening and I was speaking. I don't remember a word I said, but that's what it was."

Raina leaned closer to him. "You think God might be leading you to become a preacher?"

"I don't know, Raina. That would have been the last thought in my mind, but now it keeps coming back, and I can even see the faces of the people I was speaking to."

Raina put her hand on his arm and felt the muscular structure. He was a strong man. She studied his face. She found herself wondering what it would be like to be married to a man like this. He had definitely established jaws, and his eyes were sharp and restless. He had high cheekbones and minute weather lines slanting out from his eyes across a smooth and bronzed skin.

"I don't know what to think," he murmured.

Raina instantly was filled with compassion for him. A strong man who did not know what was happening to him. "I'm sure if God wants you for something, He'll let you know what it is."

"Maybe so."

Raina was aware that trouble had painted its shadows on Ty's eyes and weighted silence on his tongue. It had touched his solid face with a brand of loneliness, and he was looking at her with some sort of question that she could not quite understand. She simply sat beside him, noting he was a limber man with gray eyes half hidden. There was a looseness about him, and all of his features were solid. But his expression held a dark preoccupation, and she knew he was in misery.

Finally the silence grew between them until it was almost palpable, and then Ty said, "Did George come out and speak to you?"

Raina was surprised. "Yes, he did. How did you know?"

"He told me he was probably going to do it, that in fact he

already had asked you to marry him, and he just wanted to see if you had an answer for him." He smiled slightly. "I think he was asking me for my permission."

"And what did you tell him?"

"I told him it was your decision."

"Well, he did ask for my answer."

"What did you say? You see him as a husband?"

"No—at least I don't think so."

He said, "It would be an easy life for you."

"I'm not looking for an easy life."

"I'm surprised."

"That I wouldn't marry George?"

"Most women would jump at the chance."

"Well, I'm not most women." She saw a strange expression on his face. "What are you thinking, Ty? I can't read you."

Ty shook his head slightly and then said evenly, "I love you, Raina. I have for a long time. I just couldn't understand it, but we couldn't ever marry."

"Why not, Ty?"

"Well, if this dream means anything, I may wind up being a preacher, but I'd never be a city preacher in a big church. I'd be like your pa. That's what I see about Jesus. He went to the poor and the outcasts. Maybe preaching here in the territory to the bad men and the Indians that are sullen and resentful wouldn't be a happy experience. I don't know much, but I do know that would be too much to ask of a woman."

In a sudden, desperate move, he reached out, took Raina in his arms, and kissed her. She could not speak, and there were tears in her eyes.

"I'm not asking you for anything, Raina, but a woman should know when a man loves her, and that's all I have to offer."

She started to speak, but he shook his head. "Don't say anything, Raina. Maybe God will tell you what to do, but He hasn't told me." He turned, went to his horse, mounted, and rode off quickly.

Raina went inside and found her father sitting at the table doing his book work. "Ty's just left."

"What did he come for?"

"I think he came to ask me to marry him, but he didn't."

Pa leaned back and studied her. "I don't know what to say, daughter. Do you love this man?"

"I'm confused, Pa," Raina said. She bit her lower lip and shook her head with confusion in her eyes. "George asked me to marry him—and now there's Ty, both good men. How am I going to choose between them?"

Pa studied her thoughtfully, and with wisdom in his eyes and certainty in his voice, he said, "You'd better let God make your decision, daughter."

She turned and left the house, knowing she was as uncertain as she had ever been in her life. As she got on her horse and rode out, she thought about nothing but the two men who had sought her as a wife.

Clark Simmons had been hired by Aaron Jordan to handle the excess of cattle that he had accumulated. He was not a good hand, but Jordan couldn't afford to be picky. What he didn't know was that Simmons had been hired by Honey Clagg to keep track of

Ash Jordan. His instructions had been, "I want you to isolate Ash Jordan for me. When he goes out sometime by himself, I want you to get word to me."

"How much is this worth to you, Clagg?"

"A hundred dollars."

"That'll do it. You gonna shoot him?"

"That's none of your business. You just get me word."

Simmons kept his ears opened, and it was late in the afternoon when Aaron Jordan told Ash, "You take the wagon tomorrow and go to town and get some supplies. Here's the list."

"I may stay over for a while."

"No, you come right back. I need you here."

"All right, Pa."

Simmons left at once. It was a hard ride to the outlaws' hideout, but he found it. He got Clagg off to one side and said, "Ash is going to leave to go to town tomorrow."

"Will he be alone?"

"I reckon so. He didn't say anything about takin' anybody. He's takin' a wagon in to get some supplies."

"All right. You did your job."

"How about that hundred dollars."

Clagg dug into his pocket and came out with it and said, "How will he get to town?"

"Same road he always takes. There won't be no witnesses."

"Okay. You forget about this. Just keep your mouth shut. . .if you know what's good for you."

Clagg's evil grin told Simmons all he needed to know to be sure he would never tell a soul about this.

As Ash crawled into the wagon, suddenly Benny came to say, "Reckon I'll come to town with you."

"What for? Pa wants you to stay here and work."

"Aw, all he thinks about is work." Benny climbed up and sat down. "I need a break every now and then."

The trip was boring for most of the time, but when they got to a pass between two hills, suddenly all that changed.

Benny saw a man step out into the open. "You need some help, mister?" he asked. From the look on the man's face, Benny felt a prickle of fear run down his back.

The man said, "Okay, Ash, you killed Johnny Taylor, Garth Taylor's brother, so that's it for you." Without warning he raised his rifle and got off a shot.

Benny was caught off guard, but when Ash slumped over, he pulled his pistol and emptied it. He saw that one of the shots grazed the gunman.

The man rode off, yelling, "We're going to wipe out your whole ranch!"

Benny turned and said, "Are you all right, Ash?"

But Ash had been hit in the chest, and blood stained his shirt.

Benny was so shook up, he didn't know what to do at first. But he quickly came to himself and put his brother in the back and whipped the horses up. "I'll get you to a doctor, Ash. I'll get you there as soon as I can."

The horses broke into a dead run, and dust traced his flight across the range. He feared that Ash was dying and thought of how his pa would take it. He was afraid that his father's answer would be to spill blood all over the territory until those responsible lay dead. . .or Aaron Jordan himself did.

Heck was in his office when Larry Dolby came in, saying with excitement, "Heck, it's some trouble I hear. You'd better come."

Heck was used to trouble coming, and he came up out of his chair and hurried outside. He saw the buggy pulling up and walked over quickly. "What's the matter, Benny?"

"It's Ash. He's been shot. We've got to get Dr. Stapleton."

"Let's take him down to his office. How'd it happen?"

"Let's get Ash there and then I'll tell you."

The doctor's office was only a few doors down. They brought Ash in.

Dr. Stapleton immediately began stripping Ash's clothes off. "He's got a pretty bad gunshot wound here. That bullet's got to come out," he said grimly.

"Is he gonna make it, Doc?" Benny asked, anxiety scoring his face.

"Can't say, but I'll do the best I can."

"How'd this happen, Benny?" Heck said. He listened as Benny told him the story of how they had been ambushed. Heck shook his head. "Had to be the sheepherders."

"No, it wasn't," Benny said. "I saw who it was, and it wasn't one of Vernay's men. In fact, he said something about shooting Ash because he had killed Johnny Taylor, Garth Taylor's brother."

"He must be one of Garth Taylor's band. Johnny must have been the one that Ash shot when that gang tried to run some of your cattle awhile back. You know, when they captured Holder."

"I bet you're right. I think he was gonna shoot me, too, because he threatened that they would be coming to get all of my family. But I got my gun out and emptied it at him. It was a long shot for a pistol, but I grazed him, I think. At least he turned and rode away."

Heck shook his head. "Your father will go after the sheepherders. He'll think it's them."

Ty had come in and was standing beside Heck. "It couldn't have been them. I was at their camp all morning."

"That won't stop Jordan, not if his son may be dead."

Benny said, "I know it's Taylor's gang."

Heck said stolidly, "Everybody knows Garth Taylor is a low-down outlaw."

Ty said, "We'd better get Garth and that bunch. It's the only thing to keep Aaron Jordan from killing every sheepherder in the territory."

"We'll have to get him word. He'll want to be with his boy."

"Now, what are we going to do about Garth's gang?" Ty asked.

"We're gonna have to go after 'em."

"He's got at least seven or eight men in that band of his," Ty said. "At least that's what I hear."

"Well," Heck said, "we've got me and Larry Dolby and you."

Ty said, "That's not enough to handle Garth's bunch."

Heck Thomas thought for a moment then said, "We've got to go after him. Maybe we can get a few more men."

Benny said at once, "I'm going, too."

"Well, that's four of us," Ty said.

"That's still not enough. I reckon Garth will know we're comin'," Heck said. "But it's maybe the best chance we'll have."

Ty was surprised to see Aaron Jordan ride in, his horse lathered, and step off at Dr. Stapleton's office. He came inside, and when the doctor turned, he said, "How's my boy?"

Stapleton nodded. "He's going to make it, Aaron."

"I'll kill every sheepherder in the country!"

"It wasn't the sheepherders that shot Ash," Ty said.

"How do you know that?"

"Benny was with him, and he heard the shooter claim to be part of Garth Taylor's band. They want revenge for Ash killing Johnny Taylor. We figure he was the other one shot when that gang came after some of your cattle awhile back. He also threatened the rest of your family, Aaron."

"How did you find out about Ash so quickly, Jordan?" Heck asked.

"I was actually coming to town as I forgot to tell Ash to get a couple of items we really needed. When I arrived, Larry Dolby told me what happened. Now that I know Ash is going to be all right, I've got to get back to the ranch. I don't know Garth, but I bet he's headed there."

"It sounds like the kind of thing Garth would do. He'll come in and kill everything at your ranch, kill off the cattle, and burn the house. And you're not going alone. Ty, Larry, and me are coming with you," Heck said. "Your boy Benny insists he's comin', too."

"We still need more men," Aaron said. "We've got two more hands at the house."

"That may make it enough," Heck said. "We'll go nail the whole bunch. I've been looking for an excuse to cut down on

Garth Taylor. He's caused enough trouble in this territory."

Garth stood staring at Clagg and listening as the big man told him what he had done.

"So you shot Ash Jordan, but you're not positive he's dead?" Garth stared at Clagg, cursed, and then said, "I should have just done it myself. You've let everyone know someone's after Ash. They'll eventually figure out it's me."

Clagg was taken aback. "Sorry, Garth, but I didn't know his brother would be with him."

Garth's thirst for revenge was still burning, and he said, "We're going to Jordan's ranch as soon as we can get ready. We've got to move now since they know someone is after them. We're going to burn the ranch to the ground and kill as many cattle as we can. Get the men together."

Long Tom Slaughter said, "Maybe we better hold off on this. It'll bring every marshal from Parker's court down on us. We don't want that."

"We're going—and that means all of you. We're going to wipe out the Running J!"

CHAPTER 24

Heck, Ty, Aaron Jordan, Dolby, and Benny rode out of town. The five of them swung toward the north and soon arrived in the Aspen Hills.

Ty cast a glance at Heck and saw his hardness. He was as tough a man as Ty had ever seen, and he knew that Judge Parker trusted him completely.

He turned his glance toward Larry Dolby. He was a good enough marshal, but Ty wished they had half a dozen more with them. As for Benny, he was too young for this but had insisted on coming. Even his father had not been able to dissuade him.

They rode steadily until the sun was half down in the sky. The summer grass made a great yellow-green carpet all the way into the distance that lay before them, and heat gathered as they angled toward the height of the Aspen Hills. They passed through Little Bear Creek, followed it into a trail, and passed the first line of timber.

As they passed the pines, Heck shook his head. "I wish we

had half a dozen marshals with us."

"We'll do all right," Ty said.

"I don't know. I tell myself that every time I go out to take a man, but this is different. Garth's a tough enough man. Tough as I'd ever want to meet, and he's got the Daltons with him. I don't know how many more."

"More than we've got, I expect," Ty said. He was leaning sideways in the saddle, a peculiar way of riding, but it was one he always followed. "I still think we should have waited until we got some more men."

"That wouldn't do," Aaron said. "According to what that shooter said, they'll be comin' to burn our ranch out. We've got to be there to stop 'em."

No one spoke to that, and finally they crossed a creek and followed a parallel trail. The trees made a close stand, free of underbrush, and the five men were sweating freely. Ty saw Heck's face drenched in perspiration, and he wiped his own face. "It's going to be a tough thing, but if we get there first, we'll be all right."

They rode steadily, and finally they came to the high points of the hills where the ranch was located. The sun burned dark red and was sinking as they rode in.

They were met by Lottie and Leoma, who walked out of the house. "What is it?" Lottie asked.

"We've got to get you women out of here," Heck said. "Garth Taylor's comin' with his bunch to raid the ranch."

Leoma stared at her father then said, "I'll take Ma into town."

As Leoma and Lottie stepped inside the house to get ready to leave, Aaron said, "I can go get Mingan and Nelly Fox. That'll make seven of us."

"Better make it quick, Aaron," Ty said instantly. "They're going to be here soon enough."

"I'll get them here quick if I have to break this horse down!" He wheeled his horse around and sped off toward the low-lying hills where Mingan and Nelly were working with the herd.

Leoma came out of the house, accompanied by her mother. Lottie was pale, but she had a steely look on her face.

Leoma looked at the men and said, "We're leaving now. Send us word about what happens as soon as you can."

"We'll do that," Ty said. "Don't linger anywhere." He suddenly remembered that Leoma and Lottie had no idea that Ash had been shot. In a sparse voice, he said, "Sorry to have to tell you this, but Ash was shot earlier today."

"Is he all right?" Lottie asked quickly, fear now in her eyes.

Heck said, "Dr. Stapleton says he's gonna make it. Would be a good thing if you'd go on now, ladies."

Heck waited until the two women got into the buggy, then said, "Ty, you go get in that barn over there. Take your rifle with you. When they ride in, we'll wait until they're all inside and you knock Garth out of the saddle. That'll be the sign for the rest of us to start shootin'."

"You gonna kill him without warning?" Benny said with surprise.

"You don't warn rattlesnakes, Benny. They warn you. We know well and good," Heck said, "what they'll be comin' for."

Benny swallowed hard then nodded. "Where do you want me, Marshal?"

"Go into the house and poke your rifle out the window. You'll have cover there. Larry, you join him in the house. They'll be after that first thing. When the shootin' starts, get as many as you can."

"Where will you be, Heck?" Ty asked.

"I'm gonna get over behind that feeding station. Remember, there's gonna be more of them than there are of us. All of them are wanted men. Any of them that live through this will be tried and hanged. Keep a sharp lookout. As soon as we see them comin', we'll go to our places. Be sure you've got plenty of ammunition."

Ty asked, "You mean what you said about knocking them out of the saddle?"

"This is war, Ty. You know that. Those men are all killers. This bunch has been raisin' trouble in the territory long enough!"

The men were all fairly jumpy and everybody was looking into the direction where they expected the outlaws to come. Mingan and Nelly Fox returned with Aaron, and Heck nodded. "That'll give us some more firepower." He then assigned them to places close by.

Half an hour later, Benny said, "I see some dust out there."

"Where?" Heck demanded.

"Right over there to the east."

"You've got good eyes there, boy. Everybody get to their places. Remember, Ty, let 'em all get in the yard. Knock Garth out of the saddle if you can. The rest of us will open up as soon as we hear your shot."

Garth raised his hand and stopped the men. He looked over and saw that there were seven of them. "We ride in, and anybody gives us any trouble, shoot 'em down."

"There's women in there," Long Tom Slaughter said. "At least they're usually there. That's Jordan's wife and his daughter."

"Well, don't shoot them if you can help it, but everybody else goes. You all ready?" A murmur of assent came to him, and he said, "We go in hard and fast. We take everybody out, fire the house, then run off as many of the cattle as we can."

"You sure you want to do this, Garth?" Long Tom Slaughter said. "It'll stir the marshals up. They'll be after us heavy."

"We'll be out of this country by the time they hear about it. Let's go." He spurred his stallion forward, and the horse broke into a hard run. He glanced to see that all the men were with him, and they swept into the yard. "I don't see anybody," Mexican Jack said. "Why ain't they here?"

Even as they spoke, a rifle shot broke the silence, and Garth Taylor fell off his horse. Even before he hit the ground, other shots were raking the yard. Garth Taylor knew he was done for. He just hoped his men exacted revenge on the Jordans before he died.

"They're all hid," Slaughter hollered. "We can't take this."

"Let's get out of here!" Grat Dalton yelled. "We ain't got a chance!"

They all tried to calm their horses, but some men came into the open. The outlaws emptied their guns.

Mexican Jack emptied his Colt and saw one of the men drop. "I got him!" he yelled, but then a bullet struck him in the heart, and Garth could tell he was dead when he hit the ground.

"Let's get out of here, Bob!" Grat Dalton yelled. "We ain't got a chance!" The two of them fled, but the Dalton brothers left Mexican Jack dead and Clagg, Slaughter, and Garth bleeding their lives out in the dust.

Raina was in town with her father. She had been struggling to figure out the decision she knew she would have to make. Which man? The aristocratic English lord or the hard-bitten marshal? Both men were strong, but she knew that was not enough.

Judge Parker stopped beside her and her father and said, "Some word came in that Tom Rawlings just rode in from a shootout at the Jordan ranch. Let him tell us." He hollered, "Tom, come over here."

A short, well-built man came over, his face drenched with sweat. "Yes, Judge."

"You saw the thing?"

"I was just riding by and heard gunfire. I didn't know what was going on, so I come to get help. Before I left I could see it was quite a slaughter. All of the outlaws went down except two. I didn't know who it was, but they got away."

"Were any of my men hurt?" Parker said.

"I saw one of them go down. I think he's dead. At least he looked like it. I didn't take time to stay around. The two outlaws left were comin' toward me."

"Do you know which one of my men it was?"

"I think it was Kincaid."

At those words, Raina knew that she had lost something that she would mourn for the rest of her life. She turned and walked away, her face frozen and immobile, and she could not speak. Her heart was clutched in an icy grasp.

George came rushing up to say, "I just heard what happened."

"Did you hear that Ty got killed?"

George stared at her. "No, I didn't hear that."

"I might as well tell you, George. I can't marry you."

George studied her face and said, "It's Ty you love."

"I didn't know it before, but it is."

"I'm sorry. Will you be all right?"

"No, I don't think I'll ever be all right."

"Well, I'll be around if I can do anything."

Two hours later, Raina was in the general store. She had wept over Ty and knew she would never cease to regret his death.

She heard a man call, "Here comes the group from the Jordan place."

She walked outside, expecting to see a body draped over a horse. Instead she saw Ty Kincaid, and Raina suddenly did not breathe. Tears began to flow, and she ran out crying, "Ty—Ty!"

Ty had stepped out of the saddle, and when she struck him running full speed, he reached out and held her. "What is it, Raina?"

"I heard you were dead!"

"No, I just stumbled and fell. None of us got hit."

She held on to him, her face against his chest. He smelled of dust and sweat, but she was crying so hard she did not even care.

"What is it, Raina?"

"When I heard you were dead, Ty, it was like the sun went out."

Ty stared at her then said, "I had to stay alive—long enough to do whatever it is that God wants me to do."

She came to him, and as he held her, she suddenly knew what

she wanted. She waited for Ty to speak, to tell her that he loved her, but he only held her tightly.

Thirty yards away, George Fairfax was watching the scene. Leoma Jordan came up, and he turned to look at her. "Well, I asked her about marrying me."

"What did she say?"

"Nothing much, but it would have been no. She loves Kincaid."

"You know what you need, George? You need a cause."

"What kind of a cause?" he said.

"Me." Leoma smiled. "I'll be your cause. You can come courting me."

George suddenly smiled. He liked this girl. She had a vividness and a life about her that he had rarely seen. "I've got a broken heart," he said, but he was smiling.

"I'll fix it," Leoma said. "Come along. We'll talk about how I like to be courted."

"Well, I need something," George said. "Maybe it's you."

"We'll find out about that, won't we?"

CHAPTER 25

Word of the demise of Garth Taylor's bunch of outlaws spread like wildfire through the territory. People talked about nothing else, and most of the decent men of Fort Smith, and the ranchers who were scattered throughout the Indian lands, were glad, for Garth Taylor was a man who could do great harm.

The only fly in the ointment was the escape of the Dalton brothers, but the word was out that they had fled to the east and would not be any problem for Judge Parker or for his marshals.

Heck Thomas sat in the early afternoon sunlight. As usual he had taken station in his cane-bottom chair and tilted it back against the face of the courthouse and the jail. The sun was warm, but Heck could take hot weather. It was the cold weather that troubled him. Now, as usual, he was whittling on a piece of cedar and looking down at the pile of curled shavings, wondering why he had such an impulse to do this. Of course he saved all the shavings and made cushions out of them that made his room smell better, but it seemed like a foolish thing for a grown man and the head of more than a hundred marshals to do.

The people of the town, men and women, youngsters and adolescents, all paraded by, and many of them stopped to congratulate Heck on his action against Garth Taylor's bunch. Heck was aware that he had not done this single-handedly, but he was the one who got the congratulations.

The town drunk, Pete Barton, came down the sidewalk. Heck had learned to gauge Pete's condition by the way he walked. Now he stood straight and kept in the middle of the sidewalk, so he wasn't drunk yet. His drunken progress was a weaving back and forth, sometimes falling down, running into people, mumbling to himself, but Pete showed none of these signs yet.

He stopped in front of Heck and said, "Well, Marshal, it looks like you got yourself a reputation."

"I've had a reputation, Pete, for a long time. I'm not sure I need any more." He studied Pete, who was wearing leftover clothes that he had evidently found. Nothing matched and nothing fit. The hat he had on was far too small and was perched on top of his head like a cap on a small boy. "Where are you headed, Pete?" Heck asked.

Pete took his hat off, scratched his thatch of graying hair, and thought for a moment. Finally he said, "Well, Marshal, I'm going to get drunk, and do I dread it!"

It was an enigmatic answer, and Heck thought for a moment that he had misheard him, but finally he saw that Pete was totally serious. "If you dread it, why do you do it?"

"I don't know why I do it. You know, once, Marshal, I was a respected lawyer back East."

"I've heard that."

"Made lots of money, married a good woman, and had three children. Had everything going for me."

"Well, what happened?"

"I never had a drink until one day at a celebration someone gave me a glass of whiskey. I drank it, and that was the last of my sobriety."

"I can't understand that. If you saw it was ruining you, why did you do it?"

"Can't tell you that. Someone asked me how I lost my honor, and I got me a stock answer. You like to hear it, Marshal?"

"Let her rip, Pete."

"Well, you don't lose your honor in one bad moment."

"What does that mean?"

"I didn't wake up one morning and say, 'I've been a good man, a good husband, a good father, but I've decided I'm going to become a worthless, drunken bum and throw everything away.' It didn't happen like that."

"How did it happen then?"

"Well, it come on slow. I took one little drink, and the next day I took another one. Just them two drinks, but by that time I guess I was a drunk even though I still went on with my work and did my job. But it was like little mice coming in taking away cheese. They didn't take the whole chunk of cheese; they just took a little nibble at it. So whiskey nibbled at me, and I woke up one day and looked around and saw that I had become a drunk, my wife and kids had left me, I didn't have any money, and I wasn't welcome anyplace in the town where I'd practiced. I'd lost my license. So I came out here."

"Is it any better here?"

"It is in one way, Marshal. Nobody cares if you're drunk here."

Heck Thomas felt a sudden sympathy for Pete Barton. He had watched him for years, and the man lived in total misery, and he could not understand why a man would do a thing like that.

"Well, I guess you've gotten enough good advice, so I won't give you any."

"Wouldn't do any good, Marshal." He looked around and said, "What do you think is going to happen to Fort Smith?"

"What do you mean?"

"Well, I mean towns change. Some of them become big cities. Some of them just dry up and blow away."

"You know, I've thought about that, Pete. Right now this is a wild place with Indians and outlaws and Judge Parker hangin' those he can get convicted. But it'll calm down sooner or later. I was at Dodge City when it was at its height. They had a man killed every morning before breakfast, but now it's just a nice little town, not very big, nothing much going on. That'll happen to Fort Smith one of these days."

"Well, you'll be out of a job."

"No, not really. There'll still be crooks and outlaws. They'll need men like me."

"I'm ruined, Marshal. I hope you don't ever fall like I did. Well, I'll be going now."

Heck watched as Pete Barton walked off. He thought about Judge Parker, and suddenly the question came to his mind. *What'll happen to Judge Parker when he can't serve as a judge anymore?* He heard rumors already that there were people in Washington concerned with the severity and the strictness with which Parker ran his court and that there were moves under way to replace him.

Heck got up, stretched, and shook the thought out of his mind. He knew that if Parker left, he would be fired, too. *I wonder if I could go back to Emily. She never has married again, and the kids are grown up. Maybe we could make something out of it.*

He was interrupted when Dave Ennis, the banker at the Cattleman's Bank, stopped in front of him. "That was a good job, Marshal." Ennis beamed. He reached out and shook Heck's hand. "Good to be rid of that bunch of snakes."

"Well, it is. I've been after them for a long time, Dave, but there's plenty more where they came from."

"Well, you'll get them all." Ennis nodded.

"I don't think so. There'll always be bad men."

"Just takes a little time, don't it?"

"Takes time and men willing to die to make the peace. I don't like to think about the young fellows that I've lost. Over fifty of them dead and buried in a cemetery out there."

"Well, this bunch you won't have to hang 'em. They're already dead except for the Dalton brothers."

"I'd just as soon we'd taken them alive and put 'em through the court. The Daltons are gone, but someone will take their place."

"The whole territory is proud of you."

"I didn't do it by myself, you know."

"No, I hear you had some good help. Maybe things are looking up."

"Maybe so, but not this week. Still got work to do."

Ennis moved on, and Heck grew tired of hearing people comment on his ability as a lawman when he knew well that it was not his achievement alone. Heck took a small feed sack out of his pocket, filled it with the cedar shavings, folded his knife, and went inside. He mounted the stairs and went right to Judge Parker's office. He knocked on the door, and when Judge Parker said, "Come in," he opened it.

He found the judge sitting at his desk, staring out into space. "What is it, Heck?"

"I'm tired of sitting out there being told how wonderful I am."

Parker did not laugh often, but he found this amusing. "I don't suppose many men find out they're wonderful when they're as young as you. I wish I could."

"Oh, Judge, everybody knows you're a great man."

"No, they don't."

Heck looked down at his hand and said, "I've shook more hands than a politician running for office."

Parker shook his head. "Soak it up."

"Never was one to do a lot of that."

"Just wait," Parker said. "The first time some more bad men shoot a citizen up, those same folks that have been shaking your hand will be yelling at you to get off your duff and do your job."

"That what they tell you?"

"No, they're afraid of me, but I think most of them would like to bawl me out. But that wouldn't be smart, so they pretty well keep quiet."

"Well, they don't mind tellin' me when things go wrong."

"You did do a good job."

"I guess. At least you didn't have to fool around with a trial, Judge."

"I'm sorry the Daltons got away. They deserved the rope."

"I heard they left the territory."

"Yes, I heard that, too." Judge Parker rubbed his chin and

shook his head. "Good riddance, but they'll not change. That kind never does."

"Well, I think I'll be headin' out. Got a few chores to do. See you later, Judge."

Heck left the judge's office. As he stepped out into the street, he saw Aaron Jordan and his wife. "Hello, Aaron. Mrs. Jordan. How is Ash doing?"

She answered for the pair. "Good morning, Marshal. We just came from seeing him. The doctor says he can come home with us tomorrow. We are so thankful."

"You're looking fine, Mrs. Jordan."

"Thank you." She smiled. "I feel better."

"So do I." Aaron Jordan beamed. "I feel like a new man with those outlaws on the run. We owe you a lot, Marshal."

"Just doing my job."

Aaron said, "I can sleep better at night now that Garth Taylor and his bunch are dead."

Heck Thomas was a plainspoken man, often rough in his speech. He stared at Aaron Jordan and said, "You were ready to go after Ed Vernay with your gun, Mr. Jordan. How do you feel about that now?"

The blunt words seemed to strike against Jordan, and he said, "Well, I was wrong about him, Marshal."

"Yes, you were. Real wrong. About as wrong as a man can be. Have you told him you were wrong?"

"No, he hasn't, Marshal," Lottie Jordan spoke up. "My husband isn't very good at admitting he's wrong."

"It's about time he learns how then. I'd hate to have seen you dangling on the judge's gallows for shooting a man who hadn't done you any harm."

Aaron Jordan dropped his head and stared at his feet. He gnawed on his lower lip; then he raised his head and nodded. "You're both right. I'll go see Ed and tell him I was wrong."

"It'll do you good." Lottie smiled. "You're a good man, Aaron, not nearly as bad as you used to be."

"Great Scot," Jordan said. "That's the nicest thing you ever said about me."

Heck suddenly found that amusing. "You go make it right. Ed Vernay is a good man, and you two can be good neighbors for a long time."

"Well, I'll take my medicine. We'll go by his place soon, Lottie," Jordan said. "You may have to help me apologize."

The two left, and Heck watched them go. He found it amusing that Jordan was ready to change his mind when he had been so adamantly sure that Ed Vernay had been his enemy. He would, no doubt, have shot him if he could, but now he had found out differently. Heck knew there would be no danger of that.

He turned and moved on down the street, thinking of the next outlaws he would have to run down.

CHAPTER 26

Raina and her father had made a trip into town and were in the general store. Pa went at once to look at some farm equipment that he had heard about, and Raina wandered through the store. The odors of coffee, pickles, and fresh meat filled the store. She wandered around alone.

Her father joined her soon and said, "You know, I've been thinking. You need to buy some new clothes. There's a dress over there I seen when we came in."

"I don't need a new dress."

He grinned, took her by the arm, and led her over to where a dress was laid out on a table. "That would suit you."

Raina reached out and stroked the material. "It is fine," she said. "Too fine for me."

"Daughter, nothing's too fine for you. I want to buy it for you."

"I don't have anywhere to wear fancy clothes to."

"Well, we'll find a place. Why don't you go try it on?"

Raina stroked the material again, trying to make up her mind, when suddenly Aaron and Lottie Jordan entered. She braced herself, for Jordan had been outspoken in his rage against her father. She saw that he was wearing a gun as most men did, and this troubled her.

Aaron stopped and said, "I want to talk to you, Vernay."

"Well, you're talking." Pa was staring and keeping his eyes fixed on Aaron Jordan.

"I got something to say all right, and it's mighty hard for me." Aaron shrugged, moved his feet around, and twisted his neck.

Suddenly his wife said, "Go on, Aaron, say what you need to say."

"Well, all right, Lottie." Aaron swallowed hard and said, "I want to tell you that I've been wrong about you, Ed. I acted like an idiot, and I'm sorry. I hope you'll overlook it."

At once Pa smiled. "Of course, Aaron. Since we're going to be neighbors, let's be good ones."

Lottie went over to stand beside Raina. "Are you thinking of buying this dress?" she said while the men continued to talk.

"Pa wants me to have it, but it's too fancy for me."

"Oh, I don't think so. A woman needs fancy clothes once in a while." She hesitated and then said, "I hear you had a bad time during the raid."

"I did. I really did."

"Was it when you heard that Ty was killed?"

"Yes, it was a hard time for me."

Lottie hesitated then said, "You two were pretty close, weren't you?"

"Very close. We went through some hard times together. You know, I think that makes a bond that's not easily broken."

"I think that's right. I hear it's true of soldiers who go through battle together. They never forget it. Well, what are you going to do about Ty?"

Raina stared at Mrs. Jordan. "I don't think I'll do anything."

The men joined them then, effectively ending their conversation.

Aaron said, "I heard about this barbed wire that some stockmen use."

"Yeah, I've heard about that. We don't need that, Aaron. You know how to handle cattle and keep 'em in place, and sheep don't wander all that much."

"Well, we'll work on it. You ready to go, Lottie?"

"Yes, I am."

The two left, and Raina turned to her father and said, "Let's buy our supplies and go home."

"Well, why don't you just go for a walk. I'll take care of the supplies. I've got the list you gave me."

"No, I'll help."

The two went through the store, and Max Thornton put their purchases into boxes and helped load them up. They were about to get into the wagon when Raina heard her name called.

She turned to see Ty, who came up and stood before them. He removed his hat and said, "It's good to see you. Come down for supplies?"

"Yes, and I wanted to see you."

"Well, here I stand."

"I want you to come out for the service Sunday."

"I'll sure do that. I was planning to anyway if I wasn't out on assignment."

"Come to the house early. We'll have a meal cooked after the service," Raina said. "You can come and join us."

"I've never turned a good meal down yet, Raina."

They said their good-byes.

Raina looked back and saw him standing there, and there was something pitiful about him, for he was a confused man.

"You know, Pa, we've talked about God chasing a man. I never was comfortable with that. I thought we had to chase after God."

"I think it works both ways. He chases us first, and when we find out about it, we set out to catch Him. I think God found Ty out there on the prairie when he was dying, but Ty's not sure yet. But we'll just keep praying that he will be."

Leoma Jordan stopped abruptly. She had come into town with her parents but had separated from them when they went after the needed supplies. She had other plans and headed out to find George Fairfax.

She was walking down her third street when she saw George headed toward her. He was not looking up but seemed to be in deep thought.

"Hello, George," Leoma said. She saw him look up, and there was an uncertainty about him that she was not accustomed to.

"Good to see you, Leoma," he said.

"I'm just going down to get a cup of tea. You Englishmen like tea. Come and go with me."

"I'll be glad to. I'm tired of my own company."

The two walked down the boardwalk until they got to the restaurant. They went in and soon were drinking their tea.

"You seem troubled, George."

"I guess all of us have some worries."

"It's not like you to let it show like that. What's the matter?"

Fairfax took a sip of the tea, put it down, and then picked the cup back up and turned it around nervously between his hands. He seemed reluctant to speak, but finally he said, "Well, I got some news from home."

"It must be bad news if it troubles you like this."

"It is. My brother died. He was younger than I am."

"Oh, I'm sorry to hear that, George. Were you close?"

"Not as close as we could have been."

"Will you go to the funeral?"

"No, it takes too long. He's already been buried."

"Will you go back to England now and take over?"

"I don't know. I've never been so confused. What my family wants me to do is to marry and produce more male heirs."

Leoma did not really understand this system, but she felt compassion for the man. "I'm sorry, George. I wish I could help."

"Well, I wish somebody could. I don't want to marry a woman I don't love. You made a joke once," he said, "about our getting married. Or was it a joke?"

Leoma remembered the remark. It had been made as part of a joke, but she saw he was serious. "You need to marry an Englishwoman who is used to nobility and things like that."

Fairfax kept his eyes fixed on Leoma. Suddenly he said, "I don't want to marry a woman just to be sure a legal requirement is met. Were you serious about marriage when we talked?"

"George, I'm serious now, but I'd hate for you to make a mistake. Don't you see if you made a mistake, the woman you would marry would have made a mistake, too?"

"I guess I can see that. I've made my share of mistakes. Marriage is for a lifetime."

Leoma hesitated then said, "I have an idea. Why don't you come back to the ranch with me? It's quiet out there. We can take long rides. Have long talks. You can think about your future."

Fairfax straightened up, and some of the heaviness lifted from his face. "Yes, I'd be glad to do that. When shall we go?"

"I'm ready now. We can follow my parents. They should be finished getting what they needed." Leoma took his arm and led him toward the store.

Ty entered and came to stand before Heck Thomas. "Mason said you wanted me."

"Got a job for you. Doesn't amount to much. Somebody's got to go out and arrest Chester Swan."

"Who's he?"

"Oh, he's sort of a small rancher, got a few cattle, raises some grain. But he's had a feud over land boundaries with a half-breed named Charlie Ten Deer. They never have gotten along. I got word that Swan took a shot at Ten Deer."

"You want me to arrest him?"

"Well, I don't know, Ty. The man's never been in trouble. He's kind of sullen, but he's a good man. Don't really arrest him, but I need for him to think you might. Just bring him in."

"So, it's sort of an arrest then?"

"Yes. His hot temper might give you some trouble. I can scare some sense into him, I'm pretty sure."

"I'll go right away, Heck." Ty picked up some supplies, went to his horse, and saddled him. As he rode out, his mind was on his own troubles. He looked up at the sky and saw the clouds like huge bunches of cotton slowly drifting across an azure sky and tried to pray, but the words wouldn't come. "I wonder if everybody has as much trouble trying to pray as I do," he muttered. Then he continued his journey. He rode for an hour and then came into an Indian trading post. He found White Eagle, who ran the trading post. They had become friends over the last few months.

"Hello, Ty." White Eagle was coppery-skinned and trimmed down so that there was not an ounce of fat on him. "What are you out for today?"

"Oh, got a little job to do."

"Are you married yet?"

The two had a joke about marriage. Both were single, and they all but made a bet about which one of them would marry first.

"No, not yet. How about you?"

"No, but I can give you some advice."

"What's that, White Eagle?"

"Don't marry a woman that's taller than you are."

"Well, that's not likely. Is that the only advice to the lovelorn you can give?" He liked the Indian very much. "I got to go pick up Chester Swan."

"Well, he's a grumpy cuss. Got a good Indian wife though. Two kids. What'd he do?"

"Nothing much. He's having a fuss over some boundary with Ten Deer."

"Well, he's always having a fuss with somebody. You be careful."

"I'll do that. Pick up some more advice for the lovelorn."

Ty left the trading post and rode for another hour. He had

been watching the clouds roll, and from time to time he saw a band of pronghorn and once a dark-colored wolf that was unlike anything he had ever seen. The wolf had a rabbit between his jaws, and he took one look at Ty and wheeled and ran away. "I don't want your dinner," Ty said.

For some reason at that moment he thought about Gale Young's death, and the thought grieved him as it always did. *I'd give anything if I could have saved Gale. His life was all planned out. He never got to do any of it. Could happen to me.* The thought sobered him, and by the time he reached Swan's property, he was depressed.

He rode up, and Swan got to his feet and came out of the house. His wife was with him, holding on to his arm. Ty heard her say, "Don't go out there. You're drunk."

Then Ty saw that she had two small children hanging on to her skirt, but Swan shook her off. "Leave me alone, Dawn."

"Leave that gun here."

It was then that Ty noticed that Swan had a rifle in his hand.

"I've got to keep this gun. That stealin' Ten Deer might creep up and shoot me."

"He's not going to shoot you."

"What do you want, Marshal?"

Ty stepped out of the saddle and said, "I just came to talk a little bit, Swan."

"I ain't talkin' to no marshal. Get off my land."

Then something happened that caught Ty completely off guard. Swan, without a word of warning, lifted the rifle and fired. The bullet knocked his hat off, and he pulled his gun quickly and aimed it right in the middle of Swan's chest. He didn't fire, for he saw Swan pull the trigger, but the rifle wouldn't fire.

"Please don't kill him!" The woman got in front of Swan, standing between him and Ty. The children were hanging on to her, and both of them were big-eyed with fear.

Ty holstered his gun and came up with disgust. He reached out and took the rifle from Swan. "You're a sorry excuse for a man, Chester Swan," he said with disgust. "I could have killed you."

Swan sobered up when he saw that Ty had his gun, and he knew he had come close to being shot.

"I'm going to tell you what I'm going to do with you, Chester. Heck Thomas sent me out here to bring you in, but you've got a good wife here, and people say you are a good man when you're not drunk. You sober up and you go in by yourself. The judge will like that. It'll show you've got a little sense. You tell the judge you were wrong to pull a gun on Ten Deer. Don't tell him about trying to shoot me. Tell him you'll make it right with Ten Deer, and he'll give you a chance to do it. It's the only way out for you, Chester. Otherwise you're going to go down."

"Listen to him," Dawn begged.

Swan dropped his head as he was still swaying. "Okay, Marshal, I'll do as you say."

"Do it then," Ty said. "You make sure of it, Mrs. Swan."

"Yes," Dawn said. "He will do it. I promise you."

Ty got into his saddle and rode away. He was headed back to town, but something came to him, and he headed toward the sheep camp. He suddenly stopped his horse, removed his hat, and began to pray. *Lord, I don't know how to pray. I'm not eloquent. Never was. I'm asking You to do something to me. Tell me what to do.*

He got off his horse and walked slowly, continually asking

God to help him. When the night came, he still had no peace.

By the time morning came, he had stayed up most of the night begging God to help him. And as the sun came up over the eastern hills, he knew suddenly what to do.

He stepped into the saddle and spurred the horse forward. When he got to the sheep camp, he saw Raina hanging clothes on a line.

She saw him and came at once to where he was. "What are you doing out here, Ty?"

"Came on a job, but that's not my news." He took her by the arms and said, "I've been praying all night, and I've given my heart to the Lord."

Raina was excited. Her eyes glowed, and she said, "I'm so glad, Ty. What are you going to do now?"

"I also heard from the Lord about what He wants me to do, and I'm sure now that God wants me to be a preacher."

"My dad and I both thought that would be your decision."

"But what I came to tell you is, Raina, that I love you." He pulled her close and kissed her, and for the moment they were the only two people on the planet. When he lifted his head, he saw the joy in her face and knew he had done the right thing. "The only thing is, we can't marry for a long time."

"Why not, Ty?"

"I've got to save money. I've got to go get some training somewhere. Either go to some preacher who will help me or go to some Bible school. Either one would take money."

She reached up, pulled his head down, and kissed him again. "I love you, Ty, and God has brought you this far. He'll take us the rest of the way."

CHAPTER 27

Judge Isaac Parker sat back in his chair and studied the man in front of him. "Well, Ty, I think I saw this coming. I just wish I had a hundred more like you." He smiled and shook his head. "Are you absolutely sure about this?"

"Yes, Judge, it's got to be." Ty took the badge off his vest pocket and handed it to Judge Parker. "I appreciate you giving me the work, but I've got to move on."

Parker studied the badge in the palm of his hand. "Well, I hate to lose a good man, but I think you're making the right choice. What are you going to do specifically?"

"I'm planning to be a preacher." Ty grinned. "Judge, you have no idea how ignorant I am about so many things. I've got to learn the Bible. I've got to learn how to work with people. I've got to change my whole way of life. So I think I've got to go get some training at a college somewhere."

"Good for you, Ty," Parker said. "I wish all my marshals ended up with lives like you're after, but they won't. Are you going to

312

marry that young woman?"

"No, Judge, at least not right away. Not until I have something to offer her."

"Well, you probably got as much to offer her as I had to offer my wife."

"I doubt that, Judge. You had a good education, and you knew where you were going. I'm setting to sea in a sieve it seems like."

"Don't be an idiot, Kincaid. That young woman loves you. She'll be right with you every step of the way."

"Well, good-bye, Judge. I'll let you know how this story turns out."

"Be sure and do that. My wife and I have grown interested in your life. We'll be praying for you."

"Good-bye, Judge." Ty left the office, went at once to the stable, got his horse, and rode out of Fort Smith.

All the way out to the sheep camp, he was thinking about what would happen to him. He had always had very little planning in his life, but now he had a whole new world of decisions to make, and it troubled him. He knew he was embarking on a voyage that held mystery and wonder, and more than once he prayed, *Well, God, You've got to help me with this. I can't do it by myself....*

"Well, I did it, Raina."

Raina had seen Ty coming. She took him inside the small house. "What have you done?"

"Handed my badge in to the judge. He was real nice about it. I know he hates to lose a man, but he said some nice things."

"Well, you had to do it," Raina said. "Now what?"

"Well, that's the problem," Ty said. He sat at the kitchen table drinking a cup of black, bitter coffee. He sipped it and said, "Kind of funny to be drinking hot coffee on a hot day like this."

"Tell me what you're going to do."

"Well, I'm out of work."

"You'll find something. What are you going to do next?"

"Why, Raina, I'm studying new ways to tell you how I love you."

She laughed suddenly, reached over, and took his hand in both of hers. "Good. I like that. I want you to tell me every day that we're married that you love me. Will you do that?"

"Sure I will."

"I'm going to have it put in the marriage vows when Pa marries us."

"Well, to tell the truth, getting married is kind of a problem."

"Don't you have the money for a wedding license?" She smiled.

"Well, it's not that, but as much as I love you, Raina, I can't ask you to lead the kind of life that I'm gonna probably have. You know how it is. Preachers never get rich that I know of. Sometimes they're the poorest men in town, and I keep thinking that you could have married George and had everything."

"No, I wouldn't. I wouldn't have had you." She smiled and squeezed his hand.

"We'll wait on marrying until I can get enough money to go to school and learn how to be a preacher."

"I'm disappointed."

"Well, so am I. I'd like to get married right now, but that wouldn't be right for me to put you in that kind of a situation."

She rose from her chair, came over, and stood behind him. She reached around, pulled his head back, and kissed him. "Maybe

God will do a miracle."

He reached up and put his hands on her arms and said, "That's about what it's gonna take. A miracle!"

Raina's pa had been watching her very carefully. "What's wrong with you, Raina?"

"Nothing, Pa."

"Well, you don't look happy. You're gonna be a bride, ain't you?"

"No, not anytime soon."

Vernay blinked with surprise. "What's stopping you? Both of you want to get married."

"Well, Ty says he's got to get ready to be a minister, and it's going to take time and money. We've got the time but no money."

"What does he want to do with money?"

"He wants to go to school and at least learn the fundamentals of Bible study. He thinks that's the key to being a good preacher and knowing the Bible."

Pa did not speak for some time, but then he said, "Well, you go get that young man. I've got something that's been jolting around in my head."

"What is it, Pa?"

"I need to tell both of you together."

"All right. I'll get him."

It was that evening before Ty and Raina sat down with Eddie. He smiled at them, saying, "Well, I didn't get to keep you long, daughter, but you got a good man."

"Not as good as she deserves, Eddie, but I promise you she'll never know meanness from me."

"I know that, but I've got to tell you two something. Ty, Raina already told me about your plan to be a preacher. I think that's great, and I know what you mean. I just started out preaching and no tellin' how many ways I blundered, so I kept asking God, 'How can I serve You?' I'm not getting any younger, you know."

"Why, you're as strong as two men, Pa," Raina said.

"We all have our time, and I want to use it the best I can. But I can only have so many years left, and this church is on my heart, so I made a decision. I'm going to keep on with the sheep business now that I made up with Aaron. There won't be no shooting each other, but I've decided what to do with the money."

"You mean earnings off the sheep?" Raina asked.

"It's going really well. So what I'm going to do is this. I'll stay here and preach at the church and try to build it up, and then when the new preacher comes, he can take over."

Ty spoke. "You got a preacher in mind, Eddie?"

"More than that. I know him. It's you, Ty. I'm gonna pay your expenses to go to school, and in a couple of years you come back. I'll be even weaker than I am now, I guess, but you'll be the pastor. Maybe I can be your helper."

"I couldn't take your money," Ty said.

"That's pride," Eddie said.

Raina said, "It certainly is. I made a hard decision about who to marry, and now you've got to make one." When Ty hesitated, she said, "It's your pride, Ty."

"I guess it is."

Raina faced him squarely. "Well, I've got pride, too, but I'm ready to be the wife of a preacher. We'll honeymoon at the school you go to. We both will have a lot to learn."

"You'll take me up on my offer then?" Eddie asked.

Raina laughed and said, "Yes, he does."

"You're getting mighty bossy! Have I got this to put up with for a lifetime, Raina?"

"We both have a lot to learn," she said.

The sanctuary was full of people for the wedding at the Baptist church in Fort Smith.

George and Leoma were in the front row, and they watched as Raina came down the aisle dressed in white. As Ed Vernay stood to perform the ceremony, Leoma turned and whispered, "Well, George, was your heart broken when you lost your prospective bride?"

He turned and smiled at her. They had spent a great deal of time together for the past month. "Well, just sort of bent out of shape, I'd say."

She squeezed his arm. "I can fix that," she said.

They sat listening and were aware of the shining countenances of both Raina and Ty. Ed Vernay was a rough-hewn preacher, but as he tied the knot, he practically shouted, "I now pronounce you man and wife. Now kiss the bride, son!"

Eddie Vernay had been at the session along with Judge Parker to see the newly married couple off on their honeymoon.

Now Ty and Raina waved as the figures receded and the train

317

pulled out of Fort Smith. Raina turned to Ty and said, "Are you afraid of what lies before us?"

"Maybe a little. I guess that's what men are afraid of, something that they don't know. I don't have any idea of how to be a pastor."

"I do. You love your sheep."

He laughed and pulled her forward and kissed her.

The conductor was passing, and he stopped and grinned. "You got your kissing permit in order?"

"The ink's still wet on the marriage license," Ty said.

They left the conductor and went to their seats. Raina said, "Well, we're man and wife now. Feel any different?"

"I feel happier than I've ever been."

A tall man was sitting across the aisle and said, "You two just get hitched?"

Ty grinned. "Yep. Just got married."

"Well, I'm your man if you need advice. I've worn out three wives. I know all about it."

"Well, I've got my plan already made to keep this one happy."

"What's that, son?"

"I'm gonna give her everything she wants, when she wants it. The Bible says in one place that when a couple gets married the new bridegroom stays at home for a year."

"What does he do all that time, brother?"

"He makes his wife happy."

"Why, you won't last six months with a plan like that."

"Yes, we'll last," Raina said. She reached up and placed her hand on Ty's cheek. "We're in this thing for the long run."

The whistle broke the silence, and Ty felt as if he and his new bride were moving out of one life and into another.

ABOUT THE AUTHOR

Award-winning, bestselling author Gilbert Morris is well known for penning numerous Christian novels for adults and children since 1984 with 6.5 million books in print. He is probably best known for the forty-book House of Winslow series, and his *Edge of Honor* was a 2001 Christy Award winner. He lives with his wife in Gulf Shores, Alabama.

Other books by Gilbert Morris. . .